DEAD IN THE WATER

A GRIM DAYS MYSTERY

J. KENT HOLLOWAY

CHARADE
MEDIA

Dead in the Water (A Grim Days Mystery, Book 2)

2nd Edition

ISBN: 979-8-9876847-2-6

Copyright © 2020 by J. Kent Holloway

Cover Art by M. Wayne Miller

Published by Charade Media, LLC

CHAPTER
ONE

SUMMER HAVEN PIER
SUMMER HAVEN, FLORIDA
SATURDAY, 9:35 PM

Summer Haven Police Chief Becca Cole stood on the periphery of the town-wide celebration, watching the festivities with the detached interest of a seasoned cop. A virtual 'who's who' of the town's elite, as well as businessmen, lawyers, and politicians from all over the state now mingled together in the muggy summer evening decked out in formal wear of all shapes and sizes. The sound of wine glasses clinking over the live Calypso band playing on stage at the end of the marina distracted her as she took in the incessant schmoozing of those sober enough to stand up straight.

"Can you believe this turn out?" someone off to her left asked.

She turned to see an awkward little man, dressed in a rumpled suit, a poorly tied bow tie, and an old pair of Converse sneakers. His disheveled mop of ginger hair and pale freckled

1

skin almost made her ignore the patches of green that had begun to mottle Elliot Newman's face.

His stench, which had only begun to manifest in the last few days, was another story entirely.

"Couldn't bother to have your suit pressed for this shindig?" she asked, ignoring his decomposing body, and giving him a nod of greeting. Besides, he wasn't yet aware of the recent changes to his own body, but Silas had thought it best to let him discover it for himself.

He shrugged. "Eh," he said. "Figure it didn't really matter what I looked like. I'm dead, remember?"

The former archaeologist from the city of Saint Augustine was, she knew, exaggerating. But only a smidge. In fact, he *had* been dead. For a total of three days, in fact. Until, that is, the man calling himself Silas Mot came along. Then Elliot was inexplicably very much alive and Becca's world had been sent careening topsy-turvy ever sense.

Still, despite his recent inexplicable 'skin condition', as Silas put it, the little guy needed to give the whole *dead* bit a rest. It was wearing thin.

"You look pretty good for a dead guy," she exaggerated. "Most dead people don't get the chance to hang with the living elite like this."

He laughed. It reeked of frustration and self-pity. "Lucky me." He turned to look her in the face. "Do you know he's actually taken to referring to me as his 'minion' now? His minion!"

She chuckled at this despite herself. It sounded like something Silas would say.

"He is the 'Supreme Lord of Death', after all," she said, using the nickname Elliot himself had taken to calling him. "I guess you couldn't call him something as ominous as that if he didn't take a minion or two here and there."

"And then there's this." Elliot waved his hand out toward

the town celebration, oblivious to her joke. "A celebration of the discovery of the sunken pirate ship *The Lord's Vengeance*, just a few miles offshore. That was *my* discovery. I should be up there hobnobbing with the snooty backers and politicians. I should be the one drinking champagne with Ilene Nebbles-Fielding as she throws money at me for the excavation and salvage operation."

Her eyes continued scanning the crowd. She was only half-listening. She'd heard it all before anyway. Right now, she was more interested in the security for the event. Granted, she had about six of her officers, including Commander Jeremy Tanner, strategically located throughout the party for this duty, and technically, she was an invited guest meant to mingle with the rest. But she was a cop...the gold gleam of her badge and crisp blue uniform said as much. She wouldn't feel right about leaving her officers to work while she danced the night away to the rhythmic beat of Robbie Jenkins and the Calypso Crew.

"...of course, all Silas is interested in is his precious 'Hand of Cain'." Elliot was still blabbering on. As normal, the more he ranted, the more of a struggle it was to listen. "And bloody Baron Tombstone. Geez! The guy can't shut up about how he's orchestrating the Enclave to usurp his throne. Just because I discovered *The Lord's Vengeance* around the time the Hand started doing its mojo, he's been freakin' out about..."

"Elliot!" Becca shouted. "Enough."

The little guy's lips tightened as he looked up at her with big, brown puppy dog eyes.

"Sorry," she said. "I didn't mean to snap. I know Silas hasn't been playing fair with you—holding you emotionally hostage and threatening to send you back to the grave unless you help him find the Hand." She looked him square in the eye. "But it *is* important. People are dying because of that thing. And I'm worried that a lot more will die if we don't find it.

That's a heck of a lot more important than some old boat that's been buried at sea for four hundred years."

He held up a finger, as if he was about to respond, when the band's rendition of *Run Joe* stopped and Mrs. Ilene Nebbles-Fielding trotted up the steps to the stage, clapping joyously at the band, and moved over to the microphone. For a woman of about seventy, she was awfully spry for her age. Larger than life. And one of the biggest power players Summer Haven had ever seen—along with her younger sister, Gertrude.

"Thank you, Robbie," Ilene said, still clapping along with the crowd's applause. "Give it up for Robbie Jenkins and the Calypso Crew, ladies and gentlemen!"

The crowd erupted with even louder praise for the band that had been specially flown out here from Trinidad. Ilene waited a few beats before raising her hands in the air and the cacophony instantly ceased.

"Now don't worry," the old woman in the brightly sequined gown laughed. "The party's far from over and the band will be back up here before you know it. But right now, I wanted to take a few minutes to formally fill you in on what's happening with the excavation of *The Lord's Vengeance*."

All eyes were fixed on Ilene. No one dared even utter a whisper. Even the wait staff had ceased serving their food and beverages as the old woman spoke. That was the power she commanded in this town. In the whole state really.

Her deceased husband, Gerald Fielding, had been one of the most popular state senators Florida had ever known. He, and by association, Ilene, had been revered in the hallowed congressional halls in Tallahassee, as well as in Washington. Buildings, streets, and even land developments bore the name Fielding in honor of the dynamic couple, and the respect was most evident on the attentive ears of every person attending the party tonight.

Becca glanced over at Elliot. Even he had finally shut up to give the woman her due respect.

"As Chairman of the Summer Haven Historical Society, I've worked tirelessly on this project," Ilene continued to a smattering of applause. "Everyone within the society has put in one hundred and twenty percent. The discovery of such an extraordinary relic as this legendary pirate ship is just too important. And after months of backroom meetings, corralling the appropriate support from Tallahassee, and finally filing for the proper legal documents, I am proud to say that we have been given permission to proceed with the excavation on our own terms!"

The crowd exploded once more in a round of applause.

Ilene Nebbles-Fielding continued once the clapping had died down. "But I have some even more exciting news for our sleepy little beach town," she said. "While getting our state sponsored approval to excavate the ship, I've been in contact with executives from the World of Wonder television network. After a few weeks of negotiations, we've finally struck a deal to bring Lance Avery and his *Mysterious Expedition* crew to document the whole process in a way only Lance's wit and creativity could."

The party-goers went wild at the news. *Mysterious Expedition*, a reality documentary show following the adventurous exploits of the handsome Lance Avery and his team as they searched the world for some of the strangest archaeological finds known to man, had recently become a huge sensation nationwide—ever since their alleged discovery of a lost chamber in King Tut's tomb after experts had announced there were none left to find. The fact that the show was going to be filming right here in Summer Haven was huge news and would put their sleepy little beach town on the map.

Becca wasn't so sure that was a good thing. The majority of

the town's citizens strived to keep it as sleepy as possible. They worked tirelessly to discourage the usual tourism that most beach towns on the east coast of Florida vied for. She couldn't imagine many of the town's elders being very happy about the new publicity this deal was going to bring. But she was talking about Ilene Nebbles-Fielding here, a juggernaut of clout that could wrestle even the staunchest of critics to the ground with a withering glare.

"So, without further ado, allow me to introduce everyone to the world famous and breathtakingly gorgeous TV show host, Lance Avery!" Ilene announced as she turned to look off stage while clapping enthusiastically.

A moment later, a tall man, nearly six-foot-three in height, with a thick mane of flowing sandy blond hair and a chiseled square jaw dipped out from the crowd, and jogged up the platform to stand next to Ilene Nebbles-Fielding. He beamed at the crowd, dazzling them with his perfectly white teeth under his trademark five o'clock shadow. He wore his usual safari khakis and trademark Afghani scarf loosely tied around his neck. He waved to the crowd, which sent them into even more hysterics. He was like a rock star to a swooning horde of hormonal teenage girls.

"Thank you," Lance said, laughing rakishly with the crowd. "Thank you everyone."

The throng's applause didn't let up, which only helped to propel the celebrity on.

A sudden chill washed down Becca's spine. She stiffened and looked at Elliot.

"Wait a minute," she whispered to him. "You're here."

He blinked at her as if her observation was the dumbest thing he'd heard since rising from the dead.

"I mean, you're Silas' minion."

His eyes narrowed at her, but she ignored his irritation.

"So, if you're here," she continued, "Silas wouldn't be too far off." Becca's eyes swept the crowd. She had a very bad feeling. Since the living embodiment of the Grim Reaper had come to Summer Haven, he had done his very best to turn the town up onto its ears...more out of mischievous boredom than anything else. "Question is, where is he and what is he up to?"

Elliot shrugged. "No idea. He just suggested we come to what he kept calling 'the party of the year'."

Oh crap. That doesn't sound good at all.

She'd discussed the party with Silas earlier that week and had vehemently discouraged his attendance. They'd both agreed that he needed to keep a much lower profile than he had in the past. After helping to solve the Andrea Alvarez case a little over a year earlier, he'd become something of a local celebrity himself...albeit in a more infamous sense than anything else. And during the handful of death investigations he'd assisted with since that first case, he'd rubbed a lot of people the wrong way with his oftentimes child-like awkwardness in social situations and tendency toward chaos. He'd quickly become a favorite subject among the gossip-mongers of the blue-haired brigade that called Summer Haven home. His attendance in a setting like *The Lord's Vengeance* Preservation Celebration would undoubtedly ruffle quite a few feathers.

"...I can't wait to get started on this exciting endeavor," Lance was saying when Becca returned her attention to the stage. "The legends surrounding *The Lord's Vengeance* and its rather intriguing captain—supposedly a zombified slave from a pirate king's plantation, by the way—is perfect for our show and I know..."

"It's going to be fantastic!" someone shouted from near the stage. Becca's blood ran cold. She recognized the voice with its unusual blend of British and Middle Eastern accent. "I can't tell you how excited we are to have you documenting this circus act!"

Amid the exasperated gasps, another man emerged from the crowd. He, too, was tall. And lanky, wearing a perfectly tailored all-black suit, which surprised Becca a little as he'd taken to wearing more colorful, tropical clothing in recent months—he said death colors were so morbid. His jet-black hair, slicked back and immaculately manicured, glistened in the overheard paper lanterns that illuminated the party. If possible, his smile was even brighter than the TV show host's. And his neatly groomed Errol Flynn mustache and goatee framed his aristocratically handsome features like a work of art in the Louvre.

His name was Silas Mot. The Grim Reaper in the flesh, though only she and Elliot knew the truth about his origins.

He dashed up onto stage before anyone could stop him, swung his arms around the shoulders of both Ilene and Lance Avery, and beamed at the crowd with a twinkle in his eyes.

Oh, I'm gonna kill him, Becca Cole thought as she started making her way toward the stage with her hand twitching at the gun strapped in her holster. *I'm so going to kill him for this.*

CHAPTER
TWO

Ilene Nebbles-Fielding and Lance Avery could only gawk at the golden-tanned man who'd commandeered the night's festivities. The party-goers stood aghast. Cardboard fans swinging up and down in a futile attempt to cool a few of the older women in the crowd suddenly stopped their fluttering. And Silas Mot's grin stretched unnaturally wide across his face.

"Ah, my adoring fans!" he said, snagging the microphone from the TV show host's hands, and strolling to the very edge of the stage. "It's a pleasure to see you all tonight."

Becca inched up to the stage. "Get down from there now," she hissed, pointing vehemently at the ground.

"Ladies and gentlemen, the lovely chief of our illustrious police department, Rebecca Cole!" He gestured down at her before offering her a round of applause. A few onlookers, uncertain of whether respect for the chief should outweigh their mortification at the strange man's intrusion, clapped half-heartedly. "She's an amazing woman," Silas continued. "A brilliant detective. Trust me, you all are beyond fortunate to have her lead your stalwart law enforcement agency."

"Silas!" Becca whisper-shouted. "I'm serious. Stop it."

But the man ignored her, turning back to Lance Avery and the late senator's widow. "And you two!" He strolled over to them, gave Ilene a big bear hug before gripping Lance's hand in a energetic handshake. "What can I say about you? After all this time, that vile pirate Baron Tombstone's ship has finally been discovered, and you two are going to televise it for all the world to see. How brilliantly mortal of you!"

"Young man," Ilene said, her cheeks flushed. "This is not the time to..."

"I mean, never mind the whispered rumors about the pirate captain himself or the superstitions about voodoo curses and whatnot," he continued, unaffected by her protests. "Screw 'em, you say! Why should we concern ourselves with riling up the gods of death? Why be worried about unleashing a mad immortal on the world by wrapping the excavation up in a star-studded extravaganza with a nice blood-red bow on top?"

"They're just stories, dude," Lance said with a derisive shrug. "No one really believes that stuff about Tombstone being possessed by a voodoo loa."

"Not just a loa, Mr. Avery. One of the *Ghede*!" Silas said into the microphone. "A clan of loa spirits that watch over the dead, according to Vodou theology. Quinn Bennett was merely a vessel for something dark and evil. Something mad and immortal with a hatred of humanity. And you're going to muck about with his ship for the whole world to see?" He laughed, spinning around with a flourish. "That's just bloody brilliant!"

Becca watched the whole thing, paralyzed with shock and rage. They had agreed that Silas would start keeping a low profile around town—especially when it came to their investigation into whoever was in possession of a mystical artifact known as the Hand of Cain, a device capable of giving the power over life and death to anyone who wields it.

This was *not* keeping a low profile.

Finally recovering her senses, Becca trotted up the stairs to the stage, and approached Silas.

"Mr. Mot, I believe you might have had a little too much to drink," she said, hoping her announcement would be a good cover for his antics.

"Nonsense, Chief Cole," he said, then leaned in toward Ilene and whispered, "Do you have it? Is it you?"

The old woman gasped, placing a hand over her heart as she did so.

"Young man, I have no idea what you are referring to," she huffed, then looked at Becca. "Chief Cole, I insist you arrest this man for loitering or vagabondery. Something! He's not welcome here."

"Sounds like you're evading the question to me," Silas retorted. "A sign of guilt maybe?"

"Look, buddy," Lance Avery said, placing a hand on Silas' chest and gently shoving him away. "I think you need to leave now. You're obviously drunk."

To be honest, Becca wasn't sure Silas' ectoplasmic body could even become inebriated. It had never been discussed. Granted, since coming to the Land of the Living, he'd grown enamored with a special libation a bartender had created for him that he called 'Death on a Beach', but he'd never seemed drunk while consuming it. Tonight, he really did appear intoxicated.

At the moment though, his blood alcohol level was the least of the chief's problems. The moment the TV show host's hand pressed against Silas' chest, his brows curved upward with rage-filled eyes.

"How dare you," Silas growled. He raised a single finger in the air and began to level it at Lance's face.

"No...no. Don't do it." Becca shot forward, grabbing Silas' arm and bringing it down toward his side. She knew what could happen when an angry Silas Mot threw his finger gun around at people that irked him, and it wouldn't have been a pretty site if the celebrity dropped dead on stage in front of hundreds of witnesses. "Silas, come on," she whispered in his ear. "I don't know what's going on, but you've got to stop. Before you blow your cover and this investigation."

Silas glared at her for a split second, glanced at her hand holding his hand at bay, then looked back at her with a gleam in his eyes. He gave her a hidden wink and cracked the slightest of smiles behind his angry face.

Ah, crap. This is a game he's playing. He's stirring the pot to see what shakes to the surface.

"Unhand me, woman!" He tore his arm away from her grip and turned back to Lance. "And never touch me again, you buffoon. I'll see you buried six feet under if you do."

With that, he made his way off the stage, making a show of stumbling and swaying as he did so. He was playing the drunken troublemaker up to the crowd, before disappearing past them and into the night.

Becca offered an apologetic bow to Mrs. Nebbles-Fielding and Lance, then muttered an embarrassed apology to the crowd. Everyone in town knew of her relationship with Silas Mot. Many hadn't approved of her use of a civilian to help solve a string of strange, inexplicable deaths that had begun to plague the community. Others had no idea why the strange man was even still in town.

There was going to be hell to pay on Monday when she returned to her office. Though she couldn't pick his face out from the crowd, she could already envision the mayor's wrathful, sweat-covered glare, and she shuddered.

"Sorry, everyone," she repeated before looking at Ilene Nebbles-Fielding again. "I really am sorry. Please, continue with the festivities."

With that, she scurried off the stage in search of her troublesome partner. She had a few choice words of her own to give him.

THREE

GILDED GRILL DINER
SUMMER HAVEN, FLORIDA
MONDAY, 11:57 AM

Becca Cole sat down in her favorite booth in the back of the Gilded Grill and perused the menu. She hadn't eaten a crumb since lunch the day before, and her stomach roiled in her gut with bestial growls that refused to be ignored.

"You gonna get your usual today, Chief?" Alice Carpenter, the perennial waitress of the restaurant asked from behind the counter across the room.

As usual, the place was packed with lunch-goers, most on break from the town's administration building. No one paid the loud waitress any mind. It was, after all, her customary way of doing business.

Becca shook her head. "Not sure yet, Alice. Give me a minute, will you?"

The blue-haired waitress nodded, before resuming her work, wiping down the counter with a wet cloth.

Becca's eyes scanned the menu, but her mind found it difficult to focus. She was still dwelling on the events of Saturday night and the mortification she'd endured by the antics of Silas Mot. After the party, she'd been unable to find him or Elliot Newman. They'd been suspiciously AWOL ever since. But the whole town was talking about the strange man with angry whispers of how he'd almost ruined the most star-studded event the town had seen in twenty-five years.

The discovery of *The Lord's Vengeance* at the bottom of the ocean represented a lot of things for a great many people in Summer Haven. For the historical society, the importance was obvious. But it also meant an increase in revenue to the town itself in the form of renewed tourism—something not appealing to most of the town's citizens, but certainly to its businesses. It also meant more work for the local marine salvage operation that stood to earn quite a bit of money on the deal, and a general increase in jobs in the area. That old derelict pirate ship was one of the most important things to happen to the town since its incorporation in 1974.

And Silas Mot had almost blown the whole thing with his drunken escapade.

Not many people in the town had taken a liking to him as it was. They saw him as odd. Unconventional. And harbored a grating personality that threw old fashioned southern etiquette to the wind. Becca, however, had figured out a while back the real issue behind everyone's distrust and dislike for the man. She believed that somehow, down deep within their very souls, they could sense his true nature. Somehow, everyone who came in contact with him just knew, instinctively, what he was. That he was Death incarnate. The Reaper of the Grave.

Becca looked up from her menu. "On second thought, Alice...sure, give me my usual."

The old waitress smiled knowingly, scribbled a few things down on her pad, and placed the order in the spinning order rack.

Becca slid the menu back in its spot between the wall and the napkin dispenser and sighed. She was supposed to be having lunch with her 'sort of' boyfriend, Dr. Brad Harris, but he'd cancelled last minute when an emergency appendectomy walked into the clinic in which he worked. The sad thing was, she wasn't sure whether she was disappointed or not in the cancellation. Although Brad was breathtakingly handsome, not to mention brilliant, he was, as Silas put it, dull as a rubber mallet. There had never really been a spark there, but in a town the size of Summer Haven, the choice for viable dating candidates were slim to none.

"Is anyone sitting here?" someone said, interrupting her train of thought.

She looked up to see Lance Avery's chiseled, but stubbly face smiling down at her. He had a cup of coffee in his hand, and he motioned to the booth seat across from her.

She returned the smile, but shrugged. "I'm afraid I won't be very good company right now," she said.

He slid into the booth anyway. "Oh, I can't ever imagine a scenario where that would be possible," he said with a laugh. "A woman as beautiful as you could dim the sun."

Becca rolled her eyes, but couldn't help smiling at the cheesy line. The TV show host might be awfully sure of himself, but he certainly had good reason to be. He was pretty much the picture of charm and charisma wrapped up in a rugged body of a demigod. Then again, so was Silas Mot and she'd had no trouble at all resisting him. Of course, knowing who and what he was might have helped her resolve in that area.

"That's rather kind of you to say," she said, looking up as Alice traipsed over with her glass of Coca Cola. She nodded at the waitress, who returned to the counter to wait at the kitchen window. "You're not going to order anything?"

Lance shook his head. "Already ate." He smiled as she sipped from her straw. "So, you're the chief of police in this town, eh?"

She nodded, her eyes sweeping the diner, mindful of the patrons and their proclivity toward gossip. If too many people saw her sitting here with the television celebrity, it wouldn't take long before her lunch became the talk of the town. Then again, with any luck, perhaps it would overshadow her association with Silas Mot.

"How did that happen?" Lance asked, placing his elbows on the table and resting his chin in his hands.

"How did I become the police chief, you mean?"

He nodded.

"Grew up here. My dad was the chief before me," she answered, not quite sure what business it was of his. But it was a matter of public record, so she didn't mind telling him. "I worked as a homicide detective in Jacksonville a few years. Then, my dad passed away and the town elders asked me to come here and replace him."

"Interesting," he said, nodding enthusiastically, although she was pretty sure he hadn't heard a word she'd just said. "Interesting." Alice reappeared at the table holding her plate of grilled cheese sandwich and fries. Lance waited until she'd set the food down and walked away before continuing. "So, I was wondering..."

Becca took a bite of her sandwich and looked up at him.

"I have a few things I'd like to discuss with you, so I thought I might take you to a proper dinner," he said with an iceberg melting smile. "Can I pick you up around seven?"

She stopped mid-chew, her eyes widening. Had he just assumed she would say yes? Was the man that sure of himself?

He leaned back in the booth, resting an arm on the back of the seat, and giving her his most rakish look. Becca resumed chewing her sandwich, holding up her finger as she did so. While awkward, she was thankful she'd just taken a bite before he'd asked her the question. It allowed some time to ponder her answer.

Oh, it wasn't a matter of whether she would say yes or no. The TV show host was far too cocky for her taste and since she'd never watched a single episode—didn't even have cable for crying out loud—she wasn't as enamored with him as others in the town might be. No, the real issue here was how best to turn the jerk down. She was tempted to throw her glass of Coke into his face and storm off, but that would leave an unnecessary mess for Alice to have to clean up. Plus, it might be seen as bad PR for the town, not to mention just a bad example for her to set among the residents.

Becca envisioned the summons she would receive to Ilene's office if she chose to embarrass Summer Haven, and risk the continued partnership with *Mysterious Expedition* and the World of Wonders Television Network. It wouldn't be a pretty sight.

She swallowed the creamy golden bite of melted cheese and bread, and shrugged. "I'm really flattered," she began. Lance's jaw dropped as she spoke. "But I'm going to have to pass."

"Oh." He paused. His eyes swiveled in his head as if he was truly astonished with what she'd just said. Then, they lit up and his smile returned. "Oh, my! I didn't even think! You must be involved with someone."

She shook her head. "Nope, not really." She thought of Brad. Hoped it wouldn't get back to him that she'd denied his existence. But it was just too much fun to mess with this guy's ego. She took another bite from her sandwich.

"But...I mean..." Poor guy didn't know what to say to that. "Are you...are you a lesbian or something?"

Becca rolled her eyes. "No, I like men just fine," she said in between bites. "Just not particularly interested in you. No offense. You're just not my type."

Lance gawked at her, unable to move. Unable to process what he was being told. It was as if he'd never been rejected before. Of course, with his looks and charm, he probably hadn't...especially if he only hit on women with an IQ lower than his pant-size.

She dabbed a napkin at the corner of his lips, took a few bites from the fries, and washed it down with the remainder of her Coke. She then laid a ten-dollar bill on the table and stood.

"It really was nice chatting with you," she said. "I hope you don't think me rude for eating and running, but I do have a town to look out for."

Lance Avery nodded. "I understand," he said, still staring at the place Becca had been sitting just a few seconds before. "But I really would like to speak with you some time soon. I have something important to talk to you about whether you want to go out with me or not."

She smiled at him, "Sure. Come by the station any time. I'll be happy to speak with you." She then waved at Alice and walked out of the diner without looking back.

If, however, she had glanced back, she would have seen another man, dressed in a pair of jeans and a Florida Gators t-shirt, slide from his own booth and stalk over to the seat across from Lance Avery. If she'd watched a few minutes longer, she would have seen the two men arguing, their arms gesturing wildly at each other. And if she'd decided to loiter just a while longer, she would have seen them both storm out of the diner, walking together as their argument continued while heading for the town's marina.

CHAPTER
FOUR

The radio crackled to life as Captain Brian Mallory stomped into the bridge of the 229-foot five deck *Jadewerft*-built superyacht, and rechecked their position. They'd been in this spot for the last half hour, but Mallory's obsessive personality kept nagging at him to ensure they were in the right spot.

The nav charts indicated they were directly over coordinates where the decaying remains of *The Lord's Vengeance* had rested undisturbed for the last four and a half centuries. The two salvage ships, along with the TV show crew, wouldn't be here until sometime tomorrow, but until then, it would be his job to guard the site.

"...I repeat, *Stately Lady*, do you copy?" came the voice over the radio. "I've been trying to reach you for the last half hour. Do you read me?"

Mallory's teeth grinded at the sound of Garrett Norris' voice. Ever since the captain's employer, Ilene Nebbles-Fielding, had reached out to Norris, the producer of *Mysterious Expeditions*, he'd been butting heads with the insufferable S.O.B. He supposed it was the nature of the job—producing, he was sure, was a stressful occupation—but the little weasel kept forgetting who the captain of Mrs. Nebbles-Fielding's famed yacht, the *Stately Lady*, was and that irked Mallory to the core.

He grabbed the mic off its perch and spoke into it. "I hear ya just fine, Norris. Calm yerself or I'll turn off the radio altogether. Got it?"

The radio squawked and the captain could imagine the ever-fashionable man with the dimpled chin and receding hairline nearly crushing his own microphone in his hand as he struggled to rustle up a comeback. A moment later, the producer replied.

"Is Lance out there with you?"

Mallory glanced over at his first mate, Tom Fletcher, who merely shrugged at the question. "Well, go check the rest of the ship," the captain said before keying the mic. "Ain't seen him since leaving the marina. But I've got my mate turning this boat upside down for him. If he's onboard, he's done so without my permission. This boat's got five decks, seven staterooms, two lounges, a ballroom, and a mess of places a layabout like Avery could be sulking." He paused. Something was wrong and he wasn't sure whether that tickled his fancy or irritated him. "Why you botherin' us for anyway? He's not scheduled to come out with us 'til tomorrow. We're just here to guard the site until the rest of the crew gets here."

"I'm bothering you, Captain..." Garrett Norris' voice hissed through the radio. "...because he was supposed to be at the marina an hour ago and he didn't show up. He's not in his motel room, and none of the local bars open until at least noon. Our entire production team can't do anything until he gets here. We're wasting daylight and money every second..."

"Cool yer jets," Mallory said. He wondered if the smile that had spread up one side of his face could be detected over the radio. "I ain't seen yer precious star, so don't take your frustrations out on me. I ain't one of your lap dogs you can take a rolled up newspaper to, you got me?" He glanced at his watch. "Now give us thirty minutes to search the ship. If he's here, we'll find him. I'll get back to you when we're finished lookin' for him."

Without waiting for a response, he hung the mic back into its bracket and stalked out of the bridge to join Tom and the others' search for the missing Lance Avery.

THE SUN WAS SLOWLY MAKING its way up across the horizon, and it was getting unbearably hot as Captain Mallory walked out onto the port side walkway of the third deck, and peered out across the sea. His eyes narrowed as two speedboats whisked away, in opposite directions from where the *Lady* was anchored.

"Blasted scavengers," he growled.

The area near the shipwreck was legally off-limits to anyone but Mallory's crew and the *Mysterious Expeditions* team. The governor himself had signed the permits to keep this area closed to all other boat traffic, and yet still, would-be treasure hunters tried to creep in to get to the wreck before Avery and his team did.

He lifted his walkie-talkie to his mouth. "Fletcher, any luck finding our boy yet?"

"No sir. All decks have been searched. The only ones on

board right now are our own crew, and that medic woman. She's in the sick bay, getting everything ready. Says she hasn't seen Avery since last night."

Mallory rolled his eyes. This job was going to be the death of him. He just knew it. "Fine. Fine." He sighed. "Look, we've got a couple of bloodhounds sniffing around our waters. Better call the sheriff's office and have them send a marine patrol out here to scare them off. Then, search the decks one more time."

"Aye-aye, sir."

The captain eyes moved between the two different boats as they disappeared in different horizons, then reached into his pocket, and pulled out a cell phone. He pressed down on the saved contact he wanted to call and lifted the phone to his ear. Someone answered the other end.

"It's me," he said, glancing back and forth to be sure no one was within earshot. "You sure about this, ma'am?"

He listened to the person on the other end, then nodded. "Okay. Fine by me. I just wanted to make sure you didn't want to back out now. It's not too late, ya know."

He listened to the irritated response.

"No, no. I'm not getting cold feet at all. You know I'd do anything you asked, and I know you need this. I owe you too much not to. I'm just concerned for you, that's all. This whole thing could blow up in your face if we're not careful, and..."

The person on the other end cut him off, mumbled a few choice words at him, then the call abruptly ended. He knew he'd taken a risk in making the call, but the stakes were too high. He had to be sure. If this went bad, everything they'd worked for would be for nothing. Besides that, if he was honest with himself, he'd admit that he wasn't particularly happy with this whole thing to begin with.

Talismans, curses, and magic never set well with him, and this artifact—or whatever it was—they were looking for scared the bejeezus out of him. Too much power in something like that, if anyone asked him.

But he hadn't lied when he said he wasn't having second thoughts. He hadn't lied when he'd said he'd do anything that was asked of him. That's how high he felt his debt was. He'd give his life, if he had to. So he knew he could easily endure something as small as babysitting this infernal film crew for a few days. After all, they were the ones taking the biggest risk, although the majority of them didn't know it.

Lighting up a cigarette, he made his way to the stairs, and headed down to the main deck to continue searching for the ridiculous TV show host that had already turned his world upside down.

SILAS MOT LEANED back in the passenger seat of the small speed boat that was crashing through the waves toward land. Dressed in a bright red, flower-printed Hawaiian shirt, Bermuda shorts, and flip-flops, he pulled his straw Panama Jack hat down over his eyes, and enjoyed the spray of salt water as it flew past him in the ocean air. His lips curled around a straw, he took a pull on a Death on a Beach—a concoction of strawberries, pineapple, and spiced rum topped off with a miniature umbrella and curly straw—and let out a relaxed sigh.

"Can't you go any faster?" he asked with a half-smile. He knew the question would drive Elliot Newman nuts, who happened to to be behind the wheel of their boat.

It was precisely why he asked.

Elliot turned his head and glared at him. Actually, Silas thought, 'glare' wasn't exactly the right word. In fact, there was probably no appropriate word in the English language that could describe the venom those milky gray eyes contained for him. He couldn't really blame the little man. Silas had, after all, stripped him of his Great Reward by bringing him back to life. It was only a temporary detour, of course, but Elliot had no way of knowing that—despite the fact that his body was already beginning to decay while his soul remained inside. Silas had no intention of telling him either, at least until he noticed the greenish-tinted veins spreading down his neck and arms, and the occasional clumps of hair that fell out at random here and there. Despite Becca's insistence that he have a talk with the little guy, to prepare him for what was happening, he figured he'd best hold off for the right moment. Elliot was such an excitable chap, after all. And Silas had no answer to his premature decomposition quite yet. It was a puzzle. So, for the moment, it was best not to bring it up until the archaeologist noticed his condition and asked about it.

"I'm not really sure why we even came out here to begin with," Elliot yelled over the roar of the engine and wind. "It was far too risky, considering the restrictions that have been put in place around the wreck site. If the cops had caught us, Becca would be none too happy.

And it's not like we haven't visited the shipwreck a million times before that Fielding woman got state approval for her little show. You and I both know, there's nothing left to find that will lead to the Hand."

Silas offered a casual shrug in response and took a deep sip from his drink.

He was right, to a point. But because of what Silas was—a spiritual being inhabiting an ectoplasmic body—and the nature of Elliot's reanimation, neither of them had risked actually diving down to the wreck to check for signs of the Hand themselves. Water and spiritual energies did not mix. Silas shuddered to even consider what would happen to his body should he become submerged in free-flowing water for an extended period of time.

"I mean, for crying out loud!" Elliot shouted. "We didn't even stay long enough to do anything anyway. You just had me zip around the *Stately Lady* as if you were trying to get their attention or something. Like you wanted to get caught." The little man blinked, then his eyebrows furrowed into severe arcs. "You weren't trying to get caught, were you? 'Cause that would be awfully dumb, if you did. I mean, I hate the idea of this excavation more than anyone, but there's certain rules and protocols we need to..."

Silas held up an open hand, then with his thumb and forefinger, mimed the closing of a zipper. Elliot's mouth shut instantly with the gesture.

"My dear Dr. Newman," he said, leaning his head back to let the rising sun's rays wash over his tanned face. "You talk too much. And you worry even more than you talk." Silas took a deep breath, and then leaned forward, shifting to the edge of his seat with his hands on his bare knees. "The truth of the matter was that I wanted to get a 'feel' for the place, if you will. Yes, we've visited the site on a number of occasions, but not since that ridiculous film crew started mucking about. Stirring the waters like that, if you will, could stir up other, more sinister things. I simply needed to see if I sensed anything around the wreckage of that accursed shipwreck."

"You mean, if you felt Baron Tombstone."

Silas nodded. "I know he's here. My darling ex-wife, Esperanza, basically told me as much last year. And he's been conniving, with the other lords and ladies of death, it seems to usurp me. I have no doubt he's behind this whole Hand of Cain fiasco, but I'm not sure how."

"Because immortals such as yourself aren't capable of using the device?" Elliot said.

"Can't even touch the thing, honestly. It was created by who-knows-who to give mortals the power over life and death. To strip me, as the Lord of the Psychopomps, of my authority, and to give it to whoever wields the Hand."

"Besides how it effects your oversized ego, why is that exactly a bad thing?"

Now it was Silas' turn to glare at his servant, but he didn't reprimand him. Truth was, he needed the archaeologist's knowledge of *The Lord's Vengeance* and its lore. It was the very purpose he'd returned his spirit to his decaying body to begin with.

"It's a bad thing, my young Padawan, because, like most mortals, you fail to understand what exactly my role is in the scheme of life and death," Silas said, tossing his now empty glass onto the deck, standing up, and moving over to his minion in a flash. His eyes burned with hurt pride, anger, and perhaps a little bit of fear. He hoped they'd intimidate Elliot enough to shut him up for a little while longer. "As I've told you, it isn't I who chooses who dies. I don't kill them. In fact, I take no joy in their deaths. And I'm certainly not out to 'collect their souls' like some macabre miser who goes around plucking up every penny he finds on the street.

"No, I have a more noble task than that. A greater purpose. I am Primary among the great psychopomps of the Nether. It is my task—and task of my numerous underlings and colleagues —to help guide the spirits of the dead to their Great Reward, whatever that might be."

"And?"

Silas rolled his eyes at the question. "And...the Hand of Cain doesn't care about the eternal destiny of the human soul or spirit. Its only purpose is to consume. Consume those spirits. Feed itself. Strengthen the might of its wielder. The stronger it is, the stronger the mortal who uses it is, and the spirits of those it consumes are simply digested to fuel the artifact." Gently, he smacked the side of Elliot's head. "Get it now?"

The undead archaeologist rubbed the side of his head, as he nodded, then looked up at his master. "Well?"

Silas blinked. "Well, what?"

"Did you sense anything when we passed by the shipwreck? I mean, that's the whole reason we risked prison and Chief Cole's wrath to begin with, after all. Did you get anything?"

Silas shook his head. "Not a thing," he said, returning to his seat near the back of the speed boat, and crossing his legs as his arms stretched to rest on top of the cushions. "Not a bloody th..." He paused, then stood up again to turn toward the distant dot that was, he knew, the *Stately Lady*. He looked back at Elliot with wide worried eyes. "I take that back. The Hand of Cain is at work as we speak. I can sense it. Someone is dying at this very moment."

CHAPTER
FIVE

Krista Dunaway, team medic for *Mysterious Expedition*, climbed down onto the primary dive platform at the first deck stern of the *Stately Lady*, and slipped the scuba tank and buoyancy control vest onto her back.

"Why am I doing this again?" she asked, glancing up at Captain Mallory. "I'm not scheduled for a dive until tomorrow during initial filming."

"Because your team leader has gone and gotten himself lost," Mallory growled at the good-looking blonde. The foul-smelling clod had been leering lasciviously at her ever since they'd first been introduced, and she'd been getting the heebie-jeebies from him ever since. But this change in demeanor was now even more unnerving. He glared at her now as if she carried the bubonic plague. "One of his crazy antique dive suits isn't in the locker, and the air pump is

30

running." He thumbed over his right shoulder where a compressor thrummed, pumping air down a rubber hose that fed under the surface of the water. "Ergo, it's pretty likely he decided to go ahead with his crazy little ritual I know he's famous for. Decided to take a sneak peek at the shipwreck before anyone else got a chance to in that suit of his. After all, since he's the only one allowed to use it, I reckon it's a good bet he's down there now."

"But he's no longer allowed to do that," Krista protested. "I saw to it personally."

"Well, that's between you and him. All I know is he's nowhere to be found in Summer Haven, that old suit is missing, and the pump's running." Captain Mallory chomped down on a stub of a cigar that had burned out at least an hour ago. "You do the math."

The captain spat into the sea in disgust, then continued to grumble. "Never mind the fact that I didn't even know he was onboard, I'm responsible for his well-being. It's my job on the line. Seein' as how I don't dive, and I ain't riskin' any of my crew, I decided to designate you as our search and rescue team."

"A one person team?"

"It's all that blowhard deserves, in my opinion. Idiot showboat's gonna get himself killed. I mean, what idiot uses a hundred year old dive suit? He's just askin' for trouble, am I right?" He pointed at the choppy sea. "Now get down there and find our big star. Let him know Norris is about to blow his top."

Krista now understood everything. When Garrett Norris gets anxious, life for everyone around him turns unbearable. Which meant that Captain Mallory was currently sporting one grade-A migraine right now after having to hear the show's producer moan and whine for God-knows-how-long.

She smiled a little at the thought. Served the old sea buzzard right.

Giving the captain a faux salute, she pulled down the full face mask, which came equipped with microphone and receiver for communication with the surface, and stepped off the diving platform into the warm Atlantic waters. The moment she submerged, a plume of bubbles welled up around her. She let herself sink until the BC vest she was wearing inflated just enough, and felt herself begin to rise. She then pressed down on a button on her BC, and listened as the air hissed out from the release valves in her vest. Once again, she found herself descending toward the ocean's bottom.

As she went deeper, her eyes scanned her surroundings until she found the feint shadow of the air tube that would lead directly to the idiot Lance Avery. Captain Mallory was a hundred percent right about one thing. Lance was a buffoon in more ways than one. But insisting on actually using his antique 'standard diving dress', built around 1915, complete with a large copper dome helmet, weighted boots, and an air hose instead of the much more reliable air tanks of modern scuba gear, was just one of the many things than classified him as such.

As a certified nurse practitioner and crew's medic, she had warned him against using his prized equipment more times than she could count. When he refused to listen, she'd forced the World of Wonders network to add a clause in his contract that prohibited him from ever using the suit without a properly equipped dive team nearby. He'd apparently decided he didn't care about his contract and went for his clandestine dive all by himself anyway.

Well, Garrett was going to hear about this, when it was all over. That much Krista knew. She wasn't going to work with someone who relied on her skills as a medic to stay alive, yet wouldn't listen to any of the medical advice she gave.

With a growl of frustration, she pushed her annoyance aside, and forced herself to focus on the task at hand. Keeping her eyes on the hose, she twisted her body toward the ocean floor and began kicking faster.

She hardly needed to follow the hose at all. She'd been studying the charts for the last week, and had committed the underwater terrain to memory. The sun was high and bright in the sky above. The water crystal clear. She wouldn't have much trouble finding the wreckage even if Lance hadn't left his little rubber crumb trail for her to follow.

She glanced down at her dive computer, checked her positioning, and moved twelve degrees southwest, all the while continuing to go deeper. The shore along the Florida 'First Coast' was typically shallow compared to other places she'd been. And where the ship had been known to sink, it was only about thirty-seven feet down. The water would be getting slightly dimmer the deeper she swam, but it would by no means be dark. The pressure would continue to increase as well, but as long as she paused every so often to clear her ears, she'd be fine.

Soon her eyes began to make out the skeletal frame of the derelict ship, its broken masts resembling the shattered spine of some great sea monster buried in the silt and sand below. As she drew closer, she saw that the wooden hull, which was partially obscured by a forest of kelp and seaweed, was nearly eaten through by rot and time. All that was left of the ship was the framework, covered in barnacles and a variety of aquatic plant life, and looking for all the world like the eviscerated carcass of the same sea monster with its ribs exposed to the sky.

Glancing to her right, she caught sight of the air hose

again, and followed it further down until she was a mere four feet off the sandy bottom. Numerous colorful fish fluttered past her, scurrying away from her unfamiliar human presence.

The hose was now almost horizontal with the bottom and disappeared around the other side of what had once been the ship's bow.

"Lance," Krista spoke into her helmet mic. "Can you hear me?"

She knew he'd retrofitted his antique helmet with a microphone as well, but static was the only response. Unconcerned, she kicked out toward the bow, taking in the immense splendor of the aquatic treasure that had once been *The Lord's Vengeance*, one of the most feared pirate ships ever known. She imagined the vessel, in all its former glory, riding the waves above. Its fierce—some say insane—captain standing behind the wheel, barking orders to his crew as they pursued merchant vessels along the Caribbean. Of course, she discounted the old stories about Baron Tombstone, the captain, being a reanimated corpse or that his crew was made up almost entirely of zombies conjured up by his voodoo black magic. Those were just stories after all, no doubt started by the Baron himself to increase the fear of his very name.

No, it was the very real man himself, not the myth, that excited Krista about this particular find. Quinn Bennett had been his real name. A former slave, turned pirate king. A real life rags to riches success story, even if it involved piracy and murder along the way. Ever since she was a kid, she'd been fascinated with tales of pirates, so this particular job had been a dream come true. When Lance and his estranged wife Laura had approached the team about it, she'd jumped at the chance despite a few of her colleagues who'd balked.

Truth was, Krista could hardly wait for her opportunity to

explore the vessel with her crew, and plunder the secrets these old rotten timbers might still be hiding. In fact, she...

She edged around the bow and came to abrupt stop. She'd spotted Lance, standing with his back toward her. He was swaying back and forth, but not really moving at all.

"Lance?"

He made no response. A swell of bubbles erupted up from the front of his helmet. He raised his hands to his face, frantically moving them where the round viewport of his helmet would be.

"Lance, are you okay?"

But he still didn't respond. He just kept working at whatever was going on in the front of his helmet that was causing all those tiny bubbles. Concerned, she pushed off the ocean floor, and glided toward him. As she approached, she felt the water around them grow warmer. She could now see that the bubbles weren't just coming from the front of his helmet, but were now forming along the rubberized canvass of his suit. Almost as if...

Is it boiling?

Just then, Lance spun to face her. His body stiffened. She could see from inside the front viewport that his eyes seemed to be bulging out from his head. Then, without any warning at all, fire erupted from inside the suit, consuming his body in flames. The window shattered, and Krista watched in horror as the blaze, now cast in an eerie blue-green hue, shot out from the front of his helmet, nearly singeing her where she hovered.

The heat was almost unbearable, forcing her to back away a few feet. By the time she turned around again, the fire was gone. It had dissipated as quickly as it had come. And the charred remains of Lance Avery, television host of *Mysterious Expedition*, stood buoyant in the water where he died. Charred beyond all recognition.

CHAPTER
SIX

SUMMER HAVEN MARINA
SUMMER HAVEN, FLORIDA
TUESDAY, 10:34 AM

Chief Becca Cole pulled her squad car into the gravel parking lot, along side the two other marked cruisers now blocking off all traffic to the marina. Their red and blue lights flashed in random patterns, nearly blinding her as she put her car in park.

"I know Brad," she said into her cellphone. "But this is a possible homicide. I'm sorry, but..."

"Don't be sorry, Becca," Dr. Brad Harris replied. "Just try to be on time, okay? You've had to cancel the last two dates we've had planned. I'd rather not shoot a hat trick this time."

She sighed. Of course, he was right. She hadn't been fair to him at all in recent days. Sure, he'd cancelled lunch yesterday because of his job, but that was nothing compared to the last couple of weeks she'd had to break away from date night. He'd been so patient with her, but he deserved to be treated better.

In reality, he deserved a much better girlfriend. She'd considered ending things with him altogether on numerous occasions, but just couldn't bring herself to do it. And she knew that today would not be the day she'd decide their fate either. She also knew she would do whatever it took to keep their date tonight. No matter what.

"Trust me, Brad. I'll be there. I might be a little late, but I promise you I'll be there..." She paused, then added, "...if at all possible."

It was his turn to sigh now. She just had to throw that last bit in, didn't she?

"Good," he finally said. "I just miss you, Bec. You know?"

"I know." She was smiling now. No matter how she felt about the handsome doctor, it was always good to hear those words. Then, she saw Commander Jeremy Tanner walking toward her car. A grim look on his face. "Hey Brad, I gotta go. But I promise. I'll see you tonight."

"Okay. You be careful," he said. "I love y..."

She'd already ended the call before he could finish his sentence. She couldn't bear to hear those words. Not now anyway. She got out of the car and made her way to the crime scene tape when Tanner met up with her.

"Chief, this is a crazy one," he said to her in greeting.

"That's what Linda said when she dispatched me," Becca replied. The two began walking toward the concrete boat slips, and toward the awaiting police boat. "Although she didn't give me any details."

The large cop shrugged as they hopped into the boat. "I haven't seen the body either," he said. "Just heard it's weird from Tim and Larry."

Tanner, dressed in his customary long sleeve blues and baseball cap, started the engine while Becca untied the boat, and they took off along the Intracoastal Waterway. The boat veered east, negotiated around a series of small sandbars, and made its way out into open waters in less than five minutes.

Becca glanced at her phone for the hundredth time. Silas Mot had yet to respond to her texts or phone calls.

"Have you seen Silas today?" she asked, while sending yet another text.

The commander—as her most experienced officer and second-in-command, she'd promoted him from sergeant to his current position only a few months ago—turned and sneered at her. "Why do you want that oddball involved? I'm tellin' you, boss, he ain't nothing but trouble. After Saturday night, I don't know why you don't give him the boot entirely."

She smiled at him, appreciating the officer's concern for her. "He's not so bad when you get to know him. Plus, like I've told you, he's on special assignment from the governor. There's not much I can do about him even if I wanted to."

The weathered cop grumbled a few choice words under his breath, then shook his head. "No, I ain't seen him. Which I'll go on record as saying I'm not sorry about. The guy's just plain weird. An albatross around your neck, if ya ask me."

"He's something alright, that's for sure."

The two rode in silence for the remainder of the trip until they arrived at the anchored superyacht, *Stately Lady*. Two other boats were moored to the yacht—a police boat and one she couldn't identify. When they finished tying their boat to the ship, the two clambered up the ladder to the main deck, where they were greeted by one of the *Lady's* crew.

He introduced himself as First Mate Tom Fletcher, then motioned for them to follow.

"Glad you're here," Fletcher said. "The captain is about to explode. Some people forced their way on board and refuse to leave. I'm half-expecting the captain to try to get me to throw them in the brig." He turned back to look at the two cops. "Which we don't have, by the way."

The trio shuffled along the narrow walkway toward the stern of the ship, when shouts of anger erupted in front of them.

"For the last time, I said get off my ship!"

A gunshot then rang out, bringing Fletcher to a halt. "Oh God."

With that, he began to sprint. Becca and Tanner followed close behind, until they came around a corner to see the ship's captain standing with his back to them, holding a gun. Someone laid face up on the deck, wearing what looked to be an old fashioned dive suit. Three other crew members hovered nearby, as well. Two of her police officers, Tim Sharron and Larry O'Donnell stood with their guns drawn, pointing them at the captain. But it was the two men standing in front of the captain that made the blood rush to Chief Becca Cole's head.

Silas Mot, wearing his ridiculous new fashion of tropical shirt, shorts, and flip flops, stood with his hands casually in his pockets as he grinned at the ship's captain. The formerly deceased archaeologist, Elliot Newman, stood next to his master. Unlike Silas, he wasn't nearly as calm, and Becca could see the small man's wax-like lips quiver as he stared wide-eyed at the .45 caliber Colt 1911 pointed at the two of them.

"Geez," growled Tanner. "What the heck are those two doin' here anyway?"

Becca didn't answer. Instead, she swept past the first mate, and moved around the captain while holding up her own hands.

"Easy, sir," she said to him. Her hand had already unsnapped her holster, and now hovered over the grip of her own gun. "I'm Chief Cole with the Summer Haven Police

Department. I'm going to need you to lower your weapon now."

"Not until these scavengers...these...these *pirates*...get off my ship!" the man said, never taking his eyes off Mot.

"Ooooh, pirates!" Silas' grin stretched even wider. "I like the sound of that."

"Ain't supposed to be any boaters in these waters. It's restricted," the captain said. "And I've seen these two twice already today. They're no doubt plannin' on lootin' *The Lord's Vengeance*, and I ain't about to let that happen."

"And I've been telling him, I work for the police," Silas Mot said, his smile never faltering. "But he doesn't seem to believe me." He glanced over at the chief. "Care to educate him, Becca?"

She glared at him, then turned her attention back to the captain. "He doesn't work *for* us, but he does work with us. In an *unofficial* capacity," she said. "I have no idea what he is doing out here, but I assure you, I'll be having a few words with him about it later. Now please, lower your weapon."

The captain looked from her to Silas, then back to her again. Then, slowly, he lowered the gun, and Commander Tanner rushed in to retrieve it from his hand. Officers Sharron and O'Donnell then holstered their own weapons and stepped back to allow their chief to do her job.

With everyone able to breathe easier again, she instructed Tanner to move everyone back away from the body, and took a few moments to examine the remains.

"My apologies, Chief Becca," Silas said, sidling up beside her. "I had no idea my presence would set Captain Mallory off the way it did. If I'd known, I would have waited for you."

She bent down for a closer look at the dead man in the dive suit, although she wasn't quite able to focus on the job at hand quite yet. She was seething. Still angry with Silas Mot for his antics at the celebration Saturday night—he'd intentionally avoided her ever since—she hadn't quite been ready to forgive and forget as it was. Now this. His presence in restricted waters, over the sunken vessel that he and Elliot have been so obsessed with since the days when she'd first met him, was inexcusable. She had warned him at least twenty times about coming out here now that Ilene Nebbles-Fielding had set her claws into the excavation. The old bat was not someone to mess with, and she was seriously a major hazard to Becca's own career.

"Not now, Silas," she whispered. "We'll talk about this later. Now tell me what you know about our victim."

He crouched down beside her and told her about the sensation he'd felt as he and Elliot were returning to shore. How he knew the Hand of Cain was at work, which is why he'd returned to the *Stately Lady* and ingratiated himself into the investigation before she'd arrived.

"Apparently," he continued, gesturing to the dead man, "this is Lance Avery."

Her mouth dropped at the declaration. While the exterior of the rubber-canvas dive suit seemed relatively unharmed, the corpse's head and shoulders were charred beyond all recognition. Trickles of crimson spiderwebbed the char-black surface of his head. The left side of his lips had been burned away to reveal soot-stained teeth in a death's head grin.

Beside the body was a copper helmet. The three glass viewports lining the thing all appeared to have melted away from intense heat. The butterfly nuts used to seal the windows were little more than molten slag now.

"What happened?" she asked.

"That's the interesting thing," Silas explained. "Apparently, he burned to death."

She glanced at him, cocking her head to one side. "How's that interesting?"

His infernal grin returned. "Because he was about forty-feet underwater when it happened."

Becca paused at this, and despite herself, her eyes widened. Then, she returned her gaze to the deceased television show host, and pondered the screwed up mess her life had become ever since the Grim Reaper himself came to visit her quiet little world.

"WHERE IS HE?" a female voice shouted from somewhere on the yacht. "Where's my husband?"

Becca stood from where she'd been examining the body of Lance Avery, and looked around when a tall, attractive blonde in a gray suit pushed past her officers, and into her crime scene. The woman's eyes were wide with worry, darting left and right, searching for something. When they came to the conflagrated body, she stopped mid-step and began to scream.

Officer Sharron rushed over to her, taking her by the arm in an attempt to maneuver her back to the other crew members, but she shrugged him off, and ran over to Becca. Tears streamed down her face.

"Oh God! Oh God! Lance!"

The woman dropped to her knees, and was just reaching out to take the dead man in her arms when Becca finally caught her bearings and jumped into action. She crouched to face the grieving woman and intercepted her hands before they could do any damage to evidence that might still be present on the body.

"I'm sorry, ma'am," she said in a soothing voice. "But you can't be here. It's an active crime scene, and..."

"I'm his wife!" the woman shouted. Tears streaked her mascara as it ran down her cheeks. "I'm his wife!"

Becca took a deep breath. She hadn't expected this. The way the TV show host had hit on her yesterday at the diner, she had no idea he'd been married. Of course, it shouldn't have been a surprise. Television personalities like Lance Avery weren't known for the marital fidelity.

Or are you stereotyping, Becca?

"I'm very sorry for your loss, Mrs. Avery," she finally said. "But I still..."

"It's Granger, actually," the woman said. "Laura Granger. I never changed my name. Bad for business, you see." She sniffed, wiping away the moisture from her cheeks with her jacket sleeve.

"I understand." Becca really didn't, but she also didn't understand the inner workings of Hollywood and popular television shows either. "But I'm still going to have to ask you to step back behind the appropriate crime scene parameters. I have a job to do here. When I'm done, we can talk and you can ask me anything you'd like."

A hand appeared on Laura Granger's shoulder, and Becca looked up to see a nice looking, older gentleman with salt and pepper hair and a dimpled chin. She recognized him from Saturday's celebration. The show's producer, if she wasn't mistaken. Garrett Norris, she believed his name was.

"Laura, honey," he said. "Let's let the police do their job, okay?"

Ms. Granger stiffened at the man's touch, then looked back at him before nodding. She climbed to her feet and allowed the producer to walk her back to the rest of the crew, giving Becca the space she needed to work. Of course, she hated conducting scene investigations in full view of citizens. It was unnerving, making it difficult to concentrate. But she'd done it enough times she knew she'd be fine. Besides, the medical examiner investigator had just arrived, and soon, the body would be carried off the ship, and she could begin interviewing everyone on board. It was where she shined as an investigator and would be where she was back in her element.

"Well that was awkward," Silas Mot said, once more crouching down with her near the body.

"What do you mean?"

Silas shrugged. "Grieving widow who refused to change her name."

"That's not unheard of in this day and age."

"And Dimples calls her 'honey' over the corpse of her husband?"

She paused, letting his words sink in. She hadn't caught it, but Silas was right. Although it wasn't necessarily something she'd consider 'suspicious', it was definitely something she'd be filing away to pursue later, she thought. Something told her that Laura Granger and Lance Avery weren't on the best of terms, and she instantly wondered how much of the grieving widow act had been sincere and how much had been staged.

First things first, Becca. For now, let's just finish examining Avery. Worry about suspects later.

CHAPTER
SEVEN

THE *STATELY LADY*
GALLEY, MAIN DECK
TUESDAY, 2:45 PM

Becca Cole was just about finished with her shipboard interviews, including the captain, first mate, and the four other shipmates. Once they concluded this last one, she and Silas could head back to Summer Haven, and as luck would have it, in plenty of time for her date later with Brad. A special underwater crime scene unit from the sheriff's office was already submerged, scouring the area where Lance's suit caught fire for evidence. The state attorney's office had been advised of the situation. The investigation had gone as smoothly and as efficiently as she could have hoped for. And now, she jotted a few lines in her notebook as *Mysterious Expedition* team medic, Krista Dunaway, finished recounting the discovery of Lance Avery's body for the third time.

"Like I said, Chief Cole," Krista said, "I'm not sure why Lance was even down there. He wasn't supposed to be. He was scheduled for production meetings in Summer Haven earlier this morning. And no, I never saw him on board when we headed out here this morning. It was a surprise to me when Mallory asked me to go look for him, if you want to know the truth."

"While interviewing the captain, he said he'd spotted two boats out in the water earlier today," Becca said. "We know one of them was my associate's." She gestured over to Silas. "But we have no idea who was in the other. Did you happen to see them today?"

Krista shook her head. "No, but I really hadn't been out on deck much this morning. Too busy in the sick bay, inventorying my supplies for the shoot tomorrow."

"Can you think of anyone who'd want him dead?" Silas Mot asked, as Becca continued to scribble in her notebook.

"You met him the other night at the party, didn't you?" she asked.

He nodded.

"Do you really need to ask then? The guy was a Grade-A jerk. An arrogant womanizer. Cocky as they come."

I can attest to that. Becca kept that thought to herself.

"He didn't have many friends," Krista continued. "At least, not *real* friends. Most just wanted something from him. The rest just secretly despised the guy."

"Including you?" Silas asked, offering her a shark-toothed predatory smile.

Krista shrugged. "It's a matter of public record how I felt about him. And how he felt about me. We butted heads all the time. The guy wouldn't listen to me for crap. It was my job to keep him safe, and he pretty much did whatever he wanted anyway, whether it made my job more difficult or not." She went on to explain his fascination with his two ridiculously stupid antique diving suits and how she'd managed to get the network to include a clause in his contract prohibiting him from using them unsupervised.

"Now, that's something I'm interested in learning more about," Becca said. "Those dive suits are big. Bulky. And from what I've been told, he wasn't attached to a crane line that would help pull him back up to the *Lady*."

Krista nodded. "Yeah, but that's nothing new. Because so many of the crew got tired of him taking risks with the suit, they just stopped helping him use it. So, he'd go it alone, and when he was done, he'd just remove it on the bottom, swim back to the ship, and go retrieve it later with proper scuba gear."

"Wasn't that dangerous? I mean, with the Bends and everything?"

The medic shook her head. "Nah. Depends on how deep he was, but as long as he steadily exhaled as he rose, it wasn't that dangerous. Especially at depths of less than fifty feet, and he at least had the good sense not to use that suit for anything deeper than that."

"One final question," Becca said. "What can you tell me about his relationship with his wife?"

Krista fidgeted uncomfortably in her seat at the question. "I...uh..."

"It's okay, Ms. Dunaway. Anything you say will be held in strictest confidence. I know she's the executive producer, over Mr. Norris, so I realize the spot I'm putting you in. But I need to know."

The medic shrugged. "Well, you have to understand, I like Laura. She might seem tough as nails in her expensive power suits and stern face, but she's really a sweetheart. Heck, she's practically a saint for putting up with Lance for as long as she did." She took a pull from the water bottle in front of her and wiped the excess from her lips. "But within the last year or so, they weren't that close. In fact, they'd separated from what I'd been told."

"Was she going to divorce him?"

Krista shook her head. "I don't think so. The way I heard it, she couldn't. Well, she couldn't divorce him and keep her job on the show anyway. There was some business hiccup from what I understand. She, Lance, and Garrett started the production company that created *Mysterious Expedition*. A divorce would throw everything out of whack. So, from what I hear, she stayed married to him for the company's sake."

"Very interesting," Silas said. "And what about her relationship with Mr. Norris?"

Krista's eyes shifted over to him. "I don't have any idea about that. They're friends, sure. But if there's anything else going on there, I haven't heard anything about it." She paused, as if thinking about something, then held up a finger. "Come to think of it though—and I'm not one for gossip, mind you—but she does have a reputation, I guess. As unfaithful as Lance was, the way I hear it, she could give just as much as she could take, if you know what I mean."

"Thank you for your time, Ms. Dunaway," Becca told the medic, gesturing toward the door. "If we need anything else, we'll be in touch. But for now, you can go."

They watched her walk away, then both leaned back in their respective chairs at the crew table in the yacht's galley where they'd been conducting their interviews. Elliot, who'd been silent during the interviews, just paced back and forth across the room, taking occasional confused whiffs of his underarms as if checking to see if his antiperspirant was working.

"So what do you think?" Becca asked, flipping through the pages of her notebook. "Any ideas?"

"Well, Krista's account of Avery's relationship with his wife checks out with what Laura Granger told us when we interviewed her. Looks like Ms. Granger wasn't trying to deceive us in that respect. And she did seem genuinely upset over the initial news of the death, but managed to pull herself together enough to talk to us."

"I was thinking the same thing."

"Kind of weird that the producer guy...what's his name? Norris? Kind of weird how he skipped out before we could interview him though."

"Not really," Becca said. "When Ilene Nebbles-Fielding asks to see someone immediately, everything else can be put on hold."

Silas shook his head. "I don't know why you allow that old cow to have such power in this town, Becca." He popped a Warhead candy into his mouth and grimaced at its sour flavor. "She's not an elected official. She's not royalty. And yet you allow her to run this town as if she was both. By calling Norris away, she's impeding a homicide investigation."

"Unfortunately, it's just the way the system works. Old school politics. I have little say in how our town is run. Especially these days." She gave Silas a glare as she spoke that last sentence, but he seemed oblivious to the implication. "Besides, we have time to interview him later. These are all preliminary interviews anyway. We'll have our turn with the producer later. Right now, I'm still trying to figure out just how Lance Avery was murdered."

"You mean about how a guy can catch fire underwater?"

"It could be the Baron's curse," Elliot interjected, breaking his uncharacteristic silence since Becca had arrived. "It's a well-known fact that Baron Tombstone placed vodou hexes on his ship to prevent other pirates and thieves from boarding it. Warding spells. Lance could have triggered one."

49

Both Becca and Silas stared at the little man in the rumpled seersucker suit, their mouths simultaneously dropping.

"Seriously?" Silas was the first to respond. "You're a scientist. You're honestly suggesting our dead man died from a voodoo curse?"

"I *used* to be a scientist. Now, I'm the undead henchman of the Supreme Lord of Death." Elliot quit his pacing, and looked at Silas with furrowed, angry brows. "Whose ex-wife is Lilith of Judeo-Christian mythology and Santa Muerte to the narco drug cults. Who's searching for an ancient artifact of unknown origin that has the power to give mortals control of life and death on a whim. And you're going to make fun of me for suggesting that a seventeenth century loa of the *Ghede*—the vodou spirits in charge of the dead—who possessed the corpse of an African slave to become the most feared pirate in the Caribbean wouldn't have the power to place protection spells on his prized ship?"

Silas' lips twisted in thought. He raised his index finger in preparation of an answer, then lowered it again before looking back at Becca, and offering her a sheepish shrug.

"Well, when he puts it that way, he kind of has a point." He then turned and wagged a finger at Elliot. "And for the last time, stop calling me the 'Supreme Lord of Death'. Only one being has that title, and he earned it over two-thousand years ago. I'm not in any position to draw his wrath upon me at the moment, thank you very much."

Becca rolled her eyes. As much as she would have liked to press Silas on his last statement—he was notoriously vague whenever it came to answering questions about God and the afterlife—she needed to bring her team back to reality for the moment.

"Well, for now, we're going to look for a more earthly answer with a flesh and blood mortal killer, if you don't mind," she said, standing up and gathering the paperwork she'd accumulated since starting her investigation. "Much easier to prosecute that way." She started making her way toward the galley door. "Now come on. We need to get back to Summer Haven. I've got a date to keep for a change."

CHAPTER
EIGHT

Silas Mot rode with Becca from the pier to the police department after sending Elliot on to Ankou Mot, the old Victorian mansion in which they'd recently taken up residence. There'd been very little conversation between the police chief and him during the drive. It had mostly been Becca unleashing her frustration and irritation over Silas' antics over the last few days.

And he'd sat in the passenger seat, taking it all like a champ. Didn't utter a word. Simply allowed the lead police officer in the city to vent and rage, and tell him just how he was systematically destroying her career.

He deserved it. He knew that much. Despite being among the Land of the Living for the past year, mortals were a peculiar breed with peculiar social customs, and he'd hardly made a dent in understanding them. After all, he was celestial royalty of sorts. *Rex Mortem*. The Death King. It was no easy feat to learn to be subservient to human etiquette. Besides, where was the fun in that?

But Silas liked Becca. Respected her a great deal. So, if she wanted to unleash her woes upon him for the short ride from the house to the police station, he could easily handle it. And then, things could go back to normal once more.

"Are you even listening to me?" Becca asked, taking a left on State Road A1A to head north.

"Every word." He plopped a strawberry flavored lollipop in his mouth and continued his gaze out the window. At the beautiful blue canvas of the ocean and the beachgoers enjoying a heavenly day in the surf.

"Well, do you have anything to say for yourself?"

"I can assure you, I have plenty to say," he replied. "But for now, I think the most essential thing I can say is 'I'm sorry'." He pulled his eyes away from the beach and looked at her. "I truly am. You're right. I wasn't considering your position in the community when I crashed the party Saturday night. I wasn't thinking of what it might look like—intoxicated, as I was, among your constituency. Which by the way, is rather a mystery to me since my body should not be able to get drunk. But anyway, accosting that old crone and that tiresome television show host—may his Reward be truly great—in front of the entire town was very inconsiderate of me. But I promise you, it was for a good cause."

Becca let out a frustrated breath, which rumbled in her throat like a growl. "And what would that be Silas?"

He leaned back in his seat, crunching down on the lollipop. "I wanted to see how Ilene Nebbles-Fielding would react."

She blinked at him, and he could see her face turning three different shades of maroon in an effort to process what he'd just said. A few moments of silence went by, and she was just opening her mouth to resume her verbal flogging when the police radio squawked to life, offering a moment of reprieve.

"HQ to Unit 101," the voice of Linda White, the police department's office administrator/daytime dispatcher said.

Becca glowered at Silas before picking up the radio mic and speaking into it. "I'm here, Linda. What's up?"

"Um, I think you should get back to HQ as soon as possible."

"We're almost there," Becca said. "Why? What's going on?"

There was a pause from the other end, then Linda responded in a hushed whisper. "You've got visitors, Chief. And they don't look very happy."

Becca rolled her eyes, then nodded. "Fine. We'll be there in two minutes. Go ahead and show them to my office."

"Trouble you think?" Silas asked, averting his eyes. He didn't dare look at her directly at the moment. He already felt three sizes smaller than when he first got in the car with her.

"Well, it's not much of a surprise. I was expecting this visit the moment I learned about our murder victim," she said, taking a right and traveling down a narrow one-lane road that led directly to the police station's tiny parking lot.

"Oh, in that case, you can just drop me off here, and I'll be on my..."

Her head whipped around at him, her fierce eyes telling him in no uncertain terms that now was not a time for jokes.

"Don't even think about it," she said. "If I have to deal with this, so do you. And you're going to be the picture of civility and grace. Got it?"

He couldn't help but grin back at her. It wasn't a sarcastic one, mind you, but that of genuine affection and respect for the woman. A year ago, she would have been somewhat fearful of unleashing her full wrath upon the Grim Reaper. The fact that she could so easily do it now meant she was finally growing accustomed to him. Starting to trust him. And becoming comfortable with their relationship. He appreciated it a great deal.

"As you wish," he said, bowing his head ever so slightly. As he did so, a dark mist began to encircle his body, wrapping its tendrils around his arms, legs, and torso. When it dissipated, he was now wearing his familiar jet-black suit, black shirt, and black tie. The only thing that remained of his more colorful, casual attire were the flip flops. They were just too darn comfortable.

SUMMER HAVEN POLICE DEPARTMENT
TUESDAY, 4:15 PM

THE STATION WAS a frenzy of activity when Becca and Silas strode through the front doors. Out of the eighteen uniformed officers that worked for the city, eight were in the office, fielding calls, taking notes, and scheduling interviews in regards to the murder investigation from earlier that morning. Five officers, Becca knew, were out on patrol. The rest were off-duty, resting up for their upcoming shifts. She'd left Commander Tanner back at the marina, to finish up initial interviews with secondary and tertiary witnesses.

"Chief Cole," Linda said, scrambling up to them with nervous energy. She kept looking over her shoulder as though the Boogey Man might be lurking behind her. "They're getting impatient. I've offered them coffee, coke, anything to placate them, but they're awfully on edge."

Becca smiled at the officer manager, patting her on the shoulder. "That's fine, Linda. I'll handle it."

She moved past Linda with Silas following close by, and the two of them stepped into the chief's office to be greeted by the stone-faced visage of the relatively new mayor, Nicholas Belker, who had replaced Ray Hardwick two months earlier after the morbidly obese man had died of a heart attack—a completely natural event, according to Silas. Belker had been Chairman of the City Council, and was acting as interim mayor until the special election coming up in a few weeks. He was determined to win that election too, at all costs, despite having an unprecedented number of candidates running against him. At the moment, the look he was giving Becca spoke volumes about how this murder was going to affect his candidacy, and it didn't look good.

The other person in her office, with an equally dour expression, was Ilene Nebbles-Fielding. She sat in the chief's own chair, her arms folded over the blazer of her pant suit, and her lips twisted in a scowl that reminded Becca of the magic mirror in Disney's *Snow White*.

"Get him out of here!" Ilene pointed to Silas and nodded toward the door.

"Excuse me? Becca asked.

"I won't discuss anything with that vile man in the room."

Becca glanced from her to Silas, then back, before straightening to her full height. "Then you won't discuss anything, I suppose. This is still *my* office, and he's not going anywhere."

The older woman bit down on her lower lip, then cast her gaze at Mayor Belker. "Nicholas?"

The mayor's eyes were fixed on Silas, then he pushed his wire-rimmed glasses up on the bridge of his nose and shrugged. "It is her office, Ilene. If she wants Mr. Mot to remain, I can't do anything to stop her."

"Look, I hate to be rude," Becca said. "But it's been a long day. I have a homicide investigation to conduct. And I'd like to get out of the office while I'm still young. What did you want to speak with me about?"

As if I don't already know.

"Why this tragic homicide, of course," Belker said, shaking his head in faux sympathy for the departed. "Lance Avery was a national treasure. The whole world will be mourning his loss once the news of his death hits the media. We've never been in this kind of spotlight before, Becca..."

"Chief Cole," she said.

His mouth went slack at the correction, then he continued.

"This doesn't look good for Summer Haven...Chief Cole." He said her name now with a sneer. "My constituents are demanding answers."

"That's funny," Silas Mot said. "If news hasn't hit the media, then how do your constituents even know anything to demand those answers?"

Mayor Belker's head whipped over at him, his cheeks flushing. "Well, I mean...I know they will be demanding answers. I'm trying to get ahead of this. I'm trying to be proactive. I'm..."

"Trying to save your hide in the upcoming election?" Silas' white teeth shined bright under the fluorescent light of Becca's office.

"Of course I am. I won't deny it. This looks bad for me." The mayor turned his gaze to Becca. "It looks bad for you as well, Chief. Your own police force can't even keep a minor celebrity safe in its own town. How is the common man on the street going to feel safe to visit us if we can't even offer a modicum of protection?"

"And what do you think it does to my project?" Ilene Nebbles-Fielding added. "The historic implications alone are a tragedy. Should the expedition be cancelled because of Lance's death, we may never uncover the true origins of that sunken vessel. We may never uncover its secrets."

Silas moved to Becca's desk, and bent down to look at the old widow eye to eye. "I'm curious about that, myself. Just what secrets could you be looking for in that old wreck, I wonder?"

Ilene gasped, flustered. "Why...why I'm doing this for the sake of posterity. For the sake of the town."

"Oh, really?" His eyes burned at the old bird in front of him. Becca had never seen him wield that particular expression before, and it worried her. "And it has nothing to do with a certain treasure Tombstone's old boat might have been carrying?"

"Silas, enough," Becca said, placing a hand on his shoulder to ease him back. Then, she turned her attention back to her guests. "Look. I appreciate your concern. I really do. I share them myself. However, we're going to work this case like any other. Slow, steady, and thorough. I'm not going to be pressured politically to do a rush job on this. We're going to find the killer the right way. We're going to prosecute. And we're going to see the culprit go to prison for a very long time. Any other way, especially for the sake of political expediency, is a sure fire way to either accuse the wrong party or get a case thrown out of court."

She then turned her gaze directly at Ilene Nebbles-Fielding, knowing she was the real power in the room at that moment. "The town hired me for my experience and record. Trust me to do my job the right way, and I'll trust you to do...well, whatever it is you do, the right way as well. But from now on, I'd appreciate it if you stayed out of my business."

The old woman opened her mouth as if to protest, then closed it again.

"Oh, and another thing," Becca said. "If you ever call away

one of my witnesses before I have a chance to interview them again, I'll charge you with obstruction. Do you understand, Mrs. Fielding?"

Ilene sat in Becca's chair silently for several uncomfortable moments, her lips twisting and tightening with every breath. Mayor Belker, for his part, only gasped at the chief's sharp words, and visibly tensed while waiting for the older woman to explode.

Then, in the most demure manner possible, Ilene Nebbles-Fielding sniffed, arose from the chair, gathered her purse and sunglasses, and walked out the door without a word. The mayor looked from Becca to Silas, his mouth still wide with shock, and quickly followed the old crone.

"Well, you certainly didn't make a friend with those two, did you?" Silas said, taking a seat and crossing his legs as he smiled back at Becca. 'I'll charge you with obstruction?' Really?"

"Oh, shut up." But she was smiling too as she took her own chair opposite her irritating partner and leaned back.

Silas chuckled, taking a handful of Warhead candies from the bowl on her desk, and stuffing them in his blazer pocket.

"I'm going to pay for that, you know?" she said.

"Oh, I know. I know."

"I just can't stand that woman. Her audacity. Her little power trip she's got going on."

"Preachin' to the choir, love. Preachin' to the choir."

She sighed. Then raised her right hand to eye level. It was shaking. Becca Cole wasn't afraid of a lot of people. In fact, she hated being afraid. But the effect Ilene had over her was something akin to terrifying and she didn't like it. The woman had way too much power in this town, and it was going to her head. And she was a dangerous person to have as a political enemy. There was no doubt about that.

"Tell me," she said suddenly. "Why have you been leaning so hard on her lately anyway? It's like you suspect her of having the Hand of Cain or something."

Silas unwrapped a piece of candy and popped it in his mouth, then shrugged. "Oh, that's because I do."

CHAPTER
NINE

E lliot Newman pulled into the parking lot of the city marina and turned off the ignition to his old '76 Volkswagen Beetle before turning to look at Silas Mot.

"So what exactly are we doing here?" he asked, rubbing the bridge of his nose as he did.

Silas knew the little guy wasn't going to like the answer. In fact, he was going to gripe about it throughout the entire evening. His little nasally voice was going to squeak and squawk about how unfair his afterlife was, and how other dead people didn't have to worry about running errands for the 'Supreme Overlord of Death', or whatever variation Elliot might use to mock his master. But Silas also knew that there was little that could be done about it. Lance Avery's death had hit just a little too close to home. Too close to the suspected final resting place of the Hand of Cain, before it was stolen by

61

whoever controlled it now. And he couldn't help but think that the murder might well be related in some way.

"We're going to perform our own little investigation into that television braggart's death," Silas said as he slipped out of the little round car. He gave a quick duck as a crash of thunder boomed somewhere in the distance. Lightning streaked out across the horizon, bringing the night sky to blazing life in bursts of white brilliance.

It appeared as though they were going to get a storm tonight.

"But why?" Elliot asked, getting out of the car and ensuring both doors were locked before scurrying after his master like a discount Renfield. "It's night. We've been told not to return to the *Stately Lady*. What good is going out there going to do us tonight?"

Silas stopped to allow him to catch up, then clapped him on the back with a laugh. "Have no fear, my little minion. Leave everything to me, and all will become clear." He gestured toward the boat slips. "Now get our boat ready for departure. The sooner we get out there, the longer we'll have to snoop around."

Elliot looked at him, opening his mouth as if to protest, then let out a breath of defeat and shrugged. "Whatever."

He trudged down the walkway leading to the boat slips, then stopped with a squeal. Silas, who'd been just about to open a new bag of Twizzlers, looked up to see what had elicited such a girlish cry.

More lightning lit up the sky, offering a better view of the dock.

If Silas Mot actually had blood running through his ectoplasmic veins, it would have frozen at the sight.

Two large canines, surrounded by a swirling cloud of coal-black smoke, stood on the concrete dock, snarling at his undead lackey. Both dogs, on all fours, easily came up to Elliot's chest. Completely hairless with ebony skin, they had long, narrow snouts and high pointed ears that looked as if they'd been removed from a couple of bats and surgically attached to their skulls. They were both emaciated to the point where their skin hung loose from their bones, and their long razor sharp teeth glistened with saliva as they sneered at the terrified little man before them.

"Wh-what are those?" Elliot asked from over his shoulder while keeping his eyes locked on the canid beasts.

"Shhhh," Silas replied. "Don't speak. Don't even move. They sense what you are, and they don't like it one bit."

This brought out a slight whimper from Elliot, but he miraculously held it together. Then, carefully, Silas walked down the gangplank, edged past his friend, and stared the dogs down with his most reproving gaze.

"Be gone, beasts!" he said, waving his arms in the air. "This man is under my sovereignty. He is pledged to me, and therefore under my protection. I have no time for you or your master this night! Be gone! I command you."

The two canines looked at one another, and just as suddenly as they appeared, they dissolved into nothing before Silas and Elliot's very eyes. As soon as they were gone, the undead archaeologist teetered on his feet, then instantly plopped down on his rear in a trembling huff.

Silas crouched down, patting him on his shoulder. "There, there. It's over. They're gone now."

"B-but what were they? I've never seen dogs like them before. Never seen anything like them before." Elliot's eyes stretched wide. "They weren't..." He paused to try to establish more control of himself when his voice began to squeak. "They weren't werewolves, were they?"

"Don't be ridiculous." Silas reached down to help Elliot to

his feet, then started leading him over to a bench on the edge of the dock and helped him sit down.

"Hellhounds?"

Silas laughed. "Not quite, but you're getting warmer."

"Then what were they?"

Silas sat down next to him, crossed his legs, and yanked off a piece of Twizzler with his teeth. "Have you ever heard of a *Xoloitzcuintle*?"

The thunder and lightning had ceased the moment the beasts had disappeared, but fortunately, the dock was equipped with rows of incandescent lights up and down the slips. He could see Elliot when he shook his head.

"A Pharaoh hound?"

"Nope."

"Well, those two creatures were ancient descendants of those two modern dog breeds," Silas explained. "In fact, you could say, they were the first domesticated dogs ever."

"Really?" His love for archaeology and human history was becoming aroused now, which eased his frayed nerves like a soothing salve. "What did they do?"

Silas chewed at his Twizzler, delaying having to answer for as long as he could. He knew it wouldn't last long. He knew he'd be pestered until he did. But he wanted at least a few moments to gather his thoughts while Elliot continued to calm down a bit more.

"I said, 'what did they do?'," Elliot repeated, obviously becoming impatient. "Early man domesticated dogs for work. They weren't considered pets until much later. I'm just curious what their jobs were."

"Oh, a little of this and a little of that." Silas pulled off another strip of candy, and bit into it while staring up into the sky.

Elliot glanced over at him. "What don't you want to tell me?"

Silas shifted in the overly hard seat and swallowed. "Well, I guess you could say they were used for hunting mostly."

Now it was the little guy's turn to fidget. "What exactly did they hunt, Silas?"

He cocked his head to one side, running through various possible ways to answer the question. In the end, he decided the best thing to do was just rip the bandage off quickly and get it over with.

"Lost souls and wandering spirits." Silas tried to offer a reassuring smile. "They belonged to Anubis, the Egyptian god of the dead. And they were primarily used to track down spirits that slipped out of the underworld and returned to the Land of the Living."

"So they were...they were..." Elliot licked his chapped lips. "They were after me?"

He nodded. "Think of Anubis as being sort of a bounty hunter of the dead." Silas chuckled suddenly. "Kind of like Dog the Bounty Hunter. Ha!"

Elliot glared at him, and he continued. "Anyway, those who escape the Great Reward—no matter what that might be—he is tasked with bringing back. This mostly includes ghosts, but the occasional bodily resurrections outside of divine providence can also be included in that as well." He tucked the package of Twizzlers back into his shorts' pockets and turned to face Elliot head on. "There was always a chance this could happen, I knew, but I believed my station—my authority—would buy us a lot more time. But with the Enclave convening soon, and my position..."

"As Supreme Lord of Death," Elliot offered.

Silas rolled his eyes. "Yes, that. As I was saying, with my

position being questioned, it seems like my spiritual street cred is being challenged by my lessers."

A cool breeze whipped around them from the bay, and while Silas could feel neither hot nor cold, he savored the sensation. There was always great comfort that came from the ocean breeze, he'd discovered.

"I can't believe this is happening to me," Elliot moaned.

"What? The fact that I stripped you from your Great Reward or the Death Dogs?"

The archaeologist glowered at him. "Both!"

Silas grinned. "Well cheer up! It's not as bad as it seems!" He stood up and extended his hand to Elliot, who accepted it, and stood from the bench. "But right now, we have work to do."

"Why exactly are we here, Silas? You never said."

"Well, originally I had planned to motor out to the ship-wreck for a little more clandestine snooping. Obviously something connected to the Hand of Cain is down there with Baron Tombstone's ship. It was triggered by the tragic Lance Avery. And I wanted to see if I could sense anything else from it before the television crew churns those waters up tomorrow." Silas gestured over to where the spectral dogs had just been. "But our encounter with Anubis' hounds has made me reconsider that for the moment. So for now, I think we'll play it safe and use our time here for something far less dangerous."

"And that would be?"

The two started walking down the length of the dock, while Silas searched the names and ID numbers of each boat docked there, one by one.

"You heard Captain Morgan," Silas said.

"Mallory," Elliot corrected. "His name is Captain Mallory."

"Morgan is a much more satisfying captain's name. But nevertheless, he mentioned the fact that there were *two* speed boats out on the water yesterday when our young television host was being murdered." Silas paused, crouching down near the bow of a high-end cigarette boat and scrutinizing it for moment before standing once more and continuing his search. "One of those boats belonged to us. I want to try to find the second one."

"How are you going to do that?" Elliot asked. "We didn't see it ourselves. The captain didn't identify the make or model. There's no way we can possibly know which boat—if any of these docked here—was out there yesterday."

Silas shrugged, ignoring the protest and continued to examine every boat in the marina. After another twenty minutes, he sighed, allowing his shoulders to slouch ever so slightly. His minion was right. He wasn't sure why he thought the results would be any different. Part of him had thought he'd be able to sense a telltale trace of the Hand of Cain on one of the vessels, but that would have only been possible if the artifact had actually been on it at the time of yesterday's murder. Silas had already surmised that it had been something on the ocean floor that had triggered the Hand. He knew it was going to be a long shot to find the other boat, but he needed to try nonetheless.

"You're right," he finally admitted. "This was a wasted, and almost catastrophic effort. Let's go home and pick this up tomorrow."

CHAPTER
TEN

MEDICAL EXAMINER'S OFFICE
ST. AUGUSTINE, FLORIDA
WEDNESDAY, 10:11 AM

Silas, Becca, and Elliot sat in the reception area of the Medical Examiner's Office, waiting to be called back to the autopsy room. Silas busied himself with practicing a variety of tricks he'd been learning on his yo-yo, while Becca skimmed her phone for emails and updates on the case. Elliot, for his part, was keeping his nose firmly planted in a book on pirate lore, mumbling from time to time as he read something of interest.

Becca was thankful that, once again, Silas had come more appropriately dressed in his black suit ensemble, and had even decided to wear proper shoes to go along with it. She couldn't decide whether that was because he was trying to put on a professional image, or if it was because the Hawaiian shirt and shorts motif had been the medical examiner, Dr. Peter

Lipkovic's shtick for the last thirty years. Either way, she was thankful.

After a few blissful moments of silence, Silas spoke.

"So, how was your date last night with Dr. Dullsville?"

Becca continued to scroll through her emails, but rolled her eyes.

"It was a perfectly delightful evening," she said. "And he's not dull."

Silas chuckled. "My dear Becca, if the man was any more dull, he'd be a cement block." He whipped the yo-yo in a perfect 'Around the World', then gave a sharp yank of the string to send it into 'Walking the Dog'.

If Becca had planned on protesting, she was interrupted before she could by the office manager.

"Dr. Lipkovic is about to start the autopsy now," the woman said, ushering them into the front office. "If you all would just sign in for me please."

The three of them moved over to the desk she indicated and jotted down their names. Becca checked to ensure that Elliot had used the pseudonym they'd given him to avoid anyone possibly recognizing the name of the deceased city archaeologist. After that, they followed the young office manager through the building, out a small covered breezeway, and into the morgue section of the complex.

"Ah, Chief Cole," Dr. Lipkovic said as he slipped on his blue plastic gown. "Mr. Mot. Good to see you two again." He turned to Elliot and cocked his head. "And you are?"

"This is John Clark," Becca told him before Elliot had a chance to speak. "An expert on...um, diving accidents. I've called him in to assist us."

Lipkovic smiled and nodded his head to Elliot, as he slipped on his Tyvek booties while leaning against one of the walls. "It's a pleasure to meet you, Mr. Clark. I look forward to hearing some of your theories on this one."

Elliot, whose nose crinkled at the myriad of smells permeating the room, waved the suggestion away. "Right now, my number one theory is that it's the curse of Baron Tombstone," he said without a lick of irony. "But I guess we'll see after we get this autopsy over with."

The doctor eyed him curiously, as if unable to tell whether he was joking or not. After a brief moment, they exchanged a few pleasantries while the autopsy technicians busied themselves with photographing the body before removing the dive suit carefully, and laying it on clean blue sheets covering an evidence work station. During that time, Becca explained the details regarding the case, filling in any holes the medical examiner investigator might have missed, and answering several questions the doctor had before proceeding with the autopsy.

Elliot, looking a little green around the gills, averted his eyes from the autopsy table. His hands and legs visibly trembled under his unsteady stance, and he unconsciously stroked the lines of the Y-incision scars on his own chest as he stared at the techs.

Silas, of course, could understand his discomfort. Among everyone present that morning, he was the only one in the room that had actually been autopsied before. He imagined the déjà vu would no doubt be rather traumatic to anyone, especially someone as excitable as his minion. Granted, there was no way Elliot could remember the ordeal personally, but it wouldn't take very much imagination to identify with the corpse currently lying naked on the table for someone who'd been there.

"And you have no idea how the fire started?" Lipkovic asked Becca, bringing Silas back to the present.

"Not yet. I'll be sending the suit to the Florida Department of Law Enforcement lab for analysis," Becca said. "Right now, my best guess is it was a chemical of some kind. Just don't know what."

"Or a curse," Elliot Newman repeated, followed by an immediate elbow by Silas Mot.

"Haha! Yes, we can't forget pirate curses, can we?" Lipkovic said, one eyebrow raising.

"Never mind him. It's an inside joke," Silas explained. "The ship Mr. Avery was exploring is said to be cursed by a voodoo *mambo bokor*."

"Ah!" Dr. Lipkovic said, as if the explanation was perfectly run-of-the-mill. He then turned to the autopsy table where Lance Avery now lay, and began to announce his initial observations—more to the tech who was jotting down notes than anything else. "The subject is that of a thirty-three year old Caucasian male. Height is seventy-four inches. Weight, a hundred and eighty-seven pounds."

For the next hour and a half, they watched as the doctor performed his autopsy. He explained how Lance Avery was severely charred from the head down to around the shoulders, then the heat damage became less severe the farther down the body. In fact, below the waist, there were hardly any burns at all.

"My guess is that the fire originated near the head and was pretty much contained there," Dr. Lipkovic told them. "It was obviously an intense heat, but more like a flash burn. It dissipated rapidly, I believe."

"That's pretty much what our eyewitness told us, yes," Becca said.

The doctor nodded. "Look here." He pointed to Avery's trachea, and with a quick slice of a scalpel, he opened it up for them to see. "Scorching along the upper tracheal wall. Means he was alive when the fire started. He literally breathed the flame into his body." His finger motioned further down the windpipe. "Like the exterior of his body, the heat damage gets less severe and shows only soot with no thermal damage. This helps to confirm my theory of an intense flash of heat confined to the upper extremity. More specifically the head and neck."

"Okay," Becca said. "So he was alive at the time of the fire, and it originated around the head. Good to know."

"Any other signs of trauma, Doctor?" Silas asked, bending over the autopsy table for a closer look. "I mean, besides the obvious burns, of course."

"None that I can see. My staff took x-rays of the body as well, and we found no non-thermal-related artifacts of any kind." Lipkovic pulled his mask off with a flip of his wrist. "Some suture fractures of the skull, but that's to be expected with a fire death. The heat literally boils the brain. Pressure builds and the skull pops. It's quite common."

With that, the three of them walked over to the evidence station containing the dive suit. The medical examiner motioned to the copper helmet sitting at the head of the table. "As you can see, burn marks on the helmet further confirm my theory." He pointed to the central viewport, and pointed at the butterfly nuts—or what was left of them—that kept the window in place. "They've been turned to slag. Pretty much soldering the piece to the dome."

Becca also noticed the absence of glass around the port. Although some of the glass still remained around the framework, it didn't appear to be shattered or broken. Instead, the edge was smooth, as if the glass itself had simply melted away.

"Of course, this is the most interesting aspect of the helmet in my mind," Lipkovic said, holding the helmet in both hands and turning it slightly at an angle. "Take a look at the rubber seal between the viewport and the helmet."

Both Becca and Silas leaned forward, scrutinizing the equipment.

"I don't get it, Doc," Silas said. "What am I supposed to be looking at?"

But Becca took the helmet from the doctor and brought it closer, her eyes widening. "The rubber isn't there. There should be a seal of some kind—whether made of rubber, silicon, or something else—but it's not there." She handed it back to the medical examiner. "Melted too?"

Lipkovic nodded. "But here's the thing...it shouldn't have. The rubber of the suit was hardly singed at all. Granted, most of the heat was concentrated inside the helmet, but if it was hot enough to melt the sealant, it should have at least melted some of the suit around the shoulders, I suspect."

"So what does that tell us?" Becca asked him.

The doctor shrugged. "I have no idea." He nodded to Elliot, who'd been trying so hard not to throw up since stepping foot into the morgue. "Perhaps your expert here can figure that out."

"Fine," Silas said, as his own stomach began to rumble. "But he'll do it after lunch. Right now, I'm starving."

CHAPTER
ELEVEN

GILDED GRILL DINER
SUMMER HAVEN, FLORIDA
WEDNESDAY, 1:05 PM

The three of them scrambled into Becca's favorite booth at the Gilded Grill Diner and continued their discussion of Lance Avery's autopsy under hushed tones. There'd been no big surprises, and the major mystery of how the fire had started to begin with hadn't quite been answered.

"I'm telling you," Elliot said, hunched over the table and looking at Silas and Becca who sat across from him. "It's Tombstone's curse. It's the only thing that makes sense."

"But you're a scientist," Becca protested. "Surely you can't possibly believe in things like curses."

"You're right. When I was alive, I would have never even considered such a thing." He held up his hands and thumbed back at himself. "But hello? Dead guy walking. It's pretty easy to believe anything when you've come back from the dead to be a lackey for the Supreme Lord of Death."

"I do wish you'd stop calling me that," Silas hissed. His nose was practically pressed against the menu. "It's pretentious, and everyone knows I'm a very humble reaper."

"All the more reason to keep using it," Elliot said, leaning back in his seat and crossing his arms in defiance. "At least until Anubis' dogs get a hold of me, and start using me for their chew toy."

Becca blinked at this, then turned to Silas. "What's he talking about?"

In response, he waved the question away with a swipe of his hand. "Pish posh," he said, directing his narrowed eyes over at the undead archaeologist. "Merely a trifle. Seems my minion has attracted the attention of the Egyptian god of the underworld. The matter is well in hand, and nothing whatsoever to worry about."

"Anubis?" Becca asked. "As in, *the* Anubis?"

Silas let out an exasperated sigh. "No need for the definite article. Anny has a big enough ego as it is. He'd be simply impossible to live with if he heard you add a 'the' in front of his name." He pointed at the menu. "Now can we all figure out what to eat please?"

Becca opened her mouth to reply, but was interrupted by a voice near the front of the diner.

"Hey babe," Dr. Brad Harris said as he sauntered from the door over to their booth. His million dollar smile seemed to illuminate the rather dimly lit diner as he approached.

"Oh swell," Silas muttered. "There's a doctor in the house."

Becca gave him a swift stomp on his foot, then turned to wave at her boyfriend. "Hey Brad," she said, standing up from the booth, and giving him a quick peck on the cheek. Her eyes glanced over the doctor's shoulder as she did, keeping an eye on the other customers in the restaurant. "What are you doing here?"

Harris shrugged. "Same as you," he said. "On a lunch break. Your office said you were here, so I thought I'd come and try to catch a few minutes with my lady love."

Becca blushed at this and knew Silas Mot would have a field day over the comment when it was all over. Nervously, she brushed a few strands of her hair behind her ear, and looked up at the tall, muscular physician.

"Brad, you know Silas and Elliot Newman, right?" she asked, attempting to divert attention away from herself.

The doctor glanced in their direction, nodded, and offered a sincere wave. "Hey guys," he said. "Good to see you again."

"Likewise," Elliot replied.

Silas, who was still perusing the menu, merely nodded with a slight grunt in response.

Brad turned back to Becca. "So what about it? Have you ordered yet?"

"Why no we haven't," Silas interrupted. "And I'm getting rather annoyed by that little inconvenience."

Ignoring the remark, Brad smiled down at her. "Want to have lunch with me, babe?"

She glanced over her two cohorts in the booth, then back to the doctor. Then she shrugged apologetically. "I'm sorry. I'd love to," she said. "But I can't. This is a working lunch. We're discussing our strategy for the case."

"That TV guy. The one who died in that scuba diving accident?"

"Oh, it wasn't an accident," Elliot chimed in. "We're pretty sure it was murd..."

"Elliot!" Becca hissed. "Hush."

The nerdy archaeologist stiffened at the rebuke, then picked up his own menu, and began imitating his master.

"Anyway, I just can't have lunch with you right now." She took his hand in hers and gave it a squeeze. "Rain check?"

Dr. Brad Harris struggled to contain his disappointment, but nodded, then attempted a weak smile of understanding. "Sure. No problem. We still on for tonight?"

She glanced over at Silas, who'd at least turned his attention way from lunch and now had his elbows on the table, cradling his chin in his hands, and offered her wicked grin. He batted his eyelids at her mockingly.

She turned back to Brad. "I'm not sure," she said. "After this, we've got to do interviews with the crew of *Mysterious Expedition*. Not sure how long that'll take. But if I finish in time, sure."

"Okay then," he told her, bending down and planting a kiss directly on her lips. "I'll hold you to that."

He then waved at Silas and Elliot, turned, and walked out of the diner without bothering to order anything at all. When Becca returned to her seat, Silas was still giving her that goofy school girl smile.

"What?" she asked.

"The man gets on *every* nerve in your body," Silas responded, stifling a laugh. "Admit it."

"No he doesn't."

"Oh yes. I rather think he does." Silas began to count off his fingers. "One, he insists on public displays of affection. Something you can't stomach. Two, he's needy and continuously smothers you. Always wanting to spend time with you. Three…"

"Okay, enough," she said, motioning for Alice Carpenter, the diner's waitress, to come over and take their orders. "I'm not saying you're right. Just that I wasn't interested in hearing all your inane points."

Silas chuckled, then greeted the waitress as she

approached. "Ah, the divine Alice!" He beamed at her with his most charming smile. "As always the very picture of beauty to this famished soul."

The gruff old waitress just rolled her eyes, then turned her attention to Becca. "Chief, did I hear right a minute ago? Was Lance Avery really murdered?"

Becca glared at Elliot long enough for the little guy to squirm in his seat, then turned back to Alice. "I'm sorry. I can't discuss an ongoing investigation."

The waitress glanced over her shoulders twice, then bent down closer to the trio. "Well, you know me, I ain't one for gossip and such." Silas once again let out an exasperated groan of frustration. Becca had never seen him like this. Heck, she hadn't even known he could actually get hungry. She knew he ate, sure. But never imagined that his ectoplasmic body actually needed food.

"...but I remembered something that might be important to you," Alice was saying when Becca mentally returned to the conversation. "...that is, if Mr. Avery was murdered and all."

"What did you remember?"

Alice crouched down at the table, her knees audibly popping as she did so, and looked at the police chief with wide eyes. "Well, remember the other day?" She paused. "I think it was the day before he died. He came and sat with you. He was hitting on you, in fact, but you shot him down."

Becca nodded. "I remember."

She also remembered the fact that even after turning him down, he'd insisted on still seeing her for something. He'd seemed genuinely concerned about something. Now that he was dead, she couldn't help wonder if she should have paid more attention at the time. Maybe she could have prevented his death somehow.

"Well, after you left, some guy started talkin' to him, and it got pretty heated, let me tell you. I thought they were gonna get into a fight right here in the dinin' area."

"Excuse me," Silas said. "But um, are you going to take my order any time soon? I'm famished."

Becca glared at him. "Seriously? What is wrong with you?"

He shrugged. "Not sure," he said. "At the moment, all I can think about is food. Couldn't we discuss this after she took our order and while our food was being prepared?"

She ignored the question and returned her attention to Alice. "Sorry about that. Do you know who he was arguing with?"

The waitress shook her head. "Never seen him before that day."

"Could he be one of the crew from the TV show?" Elliot asked.

"Yes, I would like your double cheeseburger, with cheddar, cooked medium—I like it pink in the middle—and everything on it, fries, and a large lemonade," Silas said, pointing to his menu.

"Silas!" Becca barked.

"But..."

She reached over and grabbed a packet of Saltines from the salt shaker holder and tossed it over to him. "There." She looked back at Alice. "Yeah, could it have been one of the crew?"

Alice shook her head. "Maybe, but I don't think so. I'm pretty sure they've all been to the diner several times, and I've never seen him."

There was a rustle of plastic as Silas worked at tearing the wrapper from the crackers with his teeth.

"What were they arguing about?" Becca asked.

"Well, I don't rightly know." The waitress looked up at the

diner's ceiling as if trying to remember. "The way it sounded, they were arguing over treasure."

"Treasure?" Elliot asked. "You mean Tombstone's treasure?"

"I dunno. Maybe. But the guy arguing with Lance seemed to think he was trying to double cross him or something. Of course, Lance told him he was worrying over nothing, but the guy wouldn't listen."

"But there shouldn't be any treasure in the remains of *The Lord's Vengeance*," Elliot protested. He looked over at Silas, who'd stopped munching on his crackers, and was now paying very close attention to the conversation. "My research into the ship indicated that any treasure that might have been there had already been picked over by illegal salvagers long ago. In fact, it was rumored that Baron Tombstone himself dragged his most precious cache to land and buried it somewhere on shore."

"Which is where Jacinto Garcia's crew found the Hand of Cain originally," Silas interjected.

"The Hand of what?" Alice asked, but he waved her question off.

"Until it was stolen from him anyway and found its way into the hands of its new master," Silas continued.

"Do you think we might have missed something?" Elliot asked.

"I think it would behoove us to take a closer look at that ship, yes," Silas answered.

"Guys," Becca cut in. "We'll discuss this later." She turned back to Alice. "This guy who was arguing with Lance...do you remember what he looked like? Could you describe him to a sketch artist?"

The waitress nodded. "Yeah, I think so. He certainly stood

out enough. Nearly as handsome as Lance Avery, I must admit."

"Good. Tell you what, when your shift is over, head to the police station. I'll have an artist waiting for you, okay?"

"No problem. I'd be happy to help." Alice stood up from the table and pulled out her notepad. "Now, what can I get you all to eat?"

"Ah, thank the heavens!" Silas gasped. "I'm starving!"

CHAPTER
TWELVE

SAND DOLLAR OASIS MOTEL
SUMMER HAVEN, FLORIDA
WEDNESDAY, 2:45 PM

The Sand Dollar Oasis Motel might not have been rated five stars by any newspaper in the region. Its Yelp reviews plunged in the one to two stars, in fact, and that was being generous. But truth be told, it was the only motel in Summer Haven, so it was the only place large enough in town to accommodate the production crew of *Mysterious Expedition*.

Any fans of the show, of course, would say that as far as places the M.E. team had been forced to stay in previous episodes—from run-down barns in the Siberian wilderness to grass huts on a desert island during a hurricane—the Sand Dollar Oasis was about as top notch as they'd ever spent the night. Of course, the crew, if asked candidly, would argue against this until they were blue in the face.

Becca considered this as she pulled into the motel's poorly

paved parking lot and stifled a chuckle. No matter how rugged they tried to appear in front of the camera, she knew these people were total Hollywood when it came down to it. And having made a few arrests on the premises in the past, she knew exactly what the accommodations here were really like. Heck, even Silas Mot had been stuck staying here until he managed to purchase an old Victorian manor on the outskirts of town a few months ago (he'd still failed to explain just how exactly that had happened, but she hadn't had much time to look into it).

"Oh, I don't feel so good," Silas said, his face grimacing as he held his stomach with both hands.

"I can't imagine why," she replied. "Three cheeseburgers, two chili dogs, fries, and two milkshakes will do that to a fella."

"I told you. I was...famished."

"And you're not exactly a regular 'fella' either," Elliot piped in from the back seat. He leaned forward to speak with Becca. "This shouldn't be happening, Becca. I don't think he should be able to be as hungry as he was. Nor should he be able to get sick from overeating. Silas doesn't exactly have the piping for that kind of thing."

She looked over at Silas, who was admittedly a bit green around the gills. She had to admit, Elliot's concerns had already crossed her mind. She'd never seen Silas like this.

"Silas? Are you okay?" she asked.

He waved at her dismissively. "Just because these things have never happened to me before, doesn't mean something is wrong," he said, taking deep breaths in between words. "It simply means I'm experiencing Life."

He turned to grin at her, but his complexion, which was normally golden tanned, was now pasty. Nearly gray in tone. Dark rings encircled his eyes.

She shook her head, reached over him, and opened the

glove compartment before pulling out a container of multi-colored Rolaids. "No, I don't think this is 'Life', as you put it. Looks more like one big case of food poisoning to me."

She handed him a few of the chalky tablets, and she watched as he crunched down on them with gusto.

"Nonsense. The Grim Reaper doesn't get food poisoning." After swallowing the tablets, he swiveled his head to glare at Elliot, and held up a finger. "Nor indigestion. I only ate those antacids to shut Becca up, and because they were tasty." He shook his head. "No, I'll be fine. I simply outdid myself this time and my ethereal-formed body is simply working at compensating. That's all."

Silas opened the passenger side door of the police cruiser, and climbed out on wobbly, unsteady legs. Becca followed suit, then opened the back door for Elliot.

"I think maybe you should stay here and recuperate, Silas," she said. "Elliot and I can do the interviews."

Silas looked at her, and the moment he did, his jet-black suit shifted and rearranged itself into his now customary Hawaiian shirt and cargo shorts. "Ah, much better suited for the beach, don't you think?" He waved his arms up and down at his new attire. "And no, I'm perfectly capable of accompanying you on your interviews, Chief Cole. I believe I'm already adapting to whatever malady had been affecting me. Nothing like the bright summer sun and a hardy beach breeze to beat back what ails you, eh?"

"Not to mention a few well-timed Rolaids," Elliot said.

She looked at him and had to admit, with the change of clothing, so too had the pale complexion he'd been exhibiting only moments earlier. He was once again tanned and ridiculously handsome with his Errol Flynn mustache and black hair.

Becca shrugged. "It's fine with me if you want to come, but

if you feel the need to hurl, get as far away from me as possible. I don't even want to think about what might come out of you."

He chuckled at this as the trio strode to the motel's main entrance and entered the lobby, before making a stop at the clerk's desk.

"Chief Cole with the Summer Haven Police Department, here to see..." Becca pulled out her notepad and scanned through the pages until she came to the right name. "Garrett Norris."

The crusty old motel manager, Elroy Lincoln, eyed Silas with a withering glare. "Is he with you?" he asked, pointing at Mot. "'Cause if he is, I'm holding you personally responsible for anything he does, Chief. He's up to no good, that one. I couldn't have been happier when he moved out of my establishment, and I ain't exactly happy to see him back here so soon."

"It's a pleasure to see you again too, Mr. Lincoln," Silas said, offering a slight bow. "Ever the gracious host, as always."

The manager sneered, then looked at Becca as if waiting for an answer.

"Oh, you're serious," she said, adjusting the body armor under her uniform unconsciously. "Sure. I take full responsibility for anything Mr. Mot does while in your motel."

Lincoln's eyes shifted from her to Silas to Elliot, and back to Becca again, pursed his lips as if considering this, then nodded. "Norris and his infernal group of hippie-types are in our conference room havin' a meeting or something." He nodded down the hall to the right.

"This dump has a conference room?" Silas laughed. "Couldn't get hot water in my shower for the first two months I was here, but you've got a conference room. Will wonders never cease?"

Becca elbowed him, waved her thanks to the old man, and

led the way down the hall. "I think I liked you better with food poisoning," she said. "At least then you were quiet."

"Yes, well if you prefer me to be..."

Becca cut him off as they approached the door of the conference room. It was ajar, and loud, angry voices could be heard coming from within.

"What gives you the right to do this, Garrett?" a woman shouted. "You had no right!"

"My contract with the network says different."

"But I'm executive producer," the woman said. "I outrank you. I should have been consulted."

The man, presumably Garrett Norris, laughed. "Obviously, the network doesn't see it that way anymore. Otherwise we might have a problem."

There was an uncomfortable silence for a few moments, then someone—it sounded to Becca like the team's medic, Krista Dunaway, spoke up.

"So you're just replacing Lance? Just like that?" Krista asked. She seemed just as miffed as the first woman. "No auditions? No maybe letting someone else on the crew take over as the show's host? You just up and decide our researcher and destination scout should replace Lance?"

"Geez, his body ain't even cold yet, Garrett," came a male voice. Another pregnant pause. "Oh, Laura. I'm so sorry. I didn't mean it like that."

"It's okay, Kevin," the first woman said. From how she was addressed, Becca assumed this was Laura Granger, Lance Avery's estranged wife. "I completely agree with you. What Garrett is doing is more distasteful than anything I could have imagined. And you're not wrong. Lance would be flipping out about this too if he were still alive."

Becca glanced over at Silas, who had a hungry smile on his face. Of course he was loving this. Silas Mot thrived on drama, and this little team meeting sounded about as dramatic as one could expect in a small town like Summer Haven.

She reached out to take the door knob, preparing to enter the fracas, but was waylaid by Silas' hand on her arm. When she looked at him again, his face was all serious. He held his index finger to his lips, then mouthed, "Just a few more seconds."

"Derek Drake is a consummate professional," Garrett said.

"You mean Derek Rosenbaum, don't you?" Laura Granger said.

"Hey! I had it changed legally." This was a new voice among the cacophony.

"We thought giving him a more 'piratey' name would work better for our viewers...especially with this particular expedition. Plus, you have to admit. The guy's got it where it counts." Garrett Norris sounded annoyed now. "He's got the looks, the wit, and obviously, the brains. Derek's got great credentials. A bachelor's degree in archaeology and a master's in communications."

"I've been telling you guys this from day one," the man Becca assumed was Derek Drake said. "But no one would listen. I've got all the connections. The contacts in foreign countries, and resources at my disposal that, quite frankly, none of you have. Lance never wanted to admit that'd I'd make a much better host than him because he was a self-absorbed ass!"

"Come on, man!" This sounded to be coming from Kevin again. "Her husband just died. Have a little respect."

"Oh, give it a rest," Derek scoffed. "We all know you're just coming to Laura's rescue to try to get back in Laura's pants again. You'll have to wait in line though. She hasn't gone through the entire cast yet!"

"Why you piece of..." There was a crash from inside the conference room. The sounds of a struggle.

It was time for Becca to step into action. She threw open the door and strode inside to see two men grappling on the floor beside a long conference table. Two women and another male worked at separating the brawling men, but were being shoved aside easily.

"All right, knock this off!" Becca shouted, coming into view of the others. "Summer Haven Police Department."

The struggling men—Becca guessed were Derek and Kevin —stopped instantly, though still embracing in a grapple that appeared more like a romantic tryst than an actual fight. Two heartbeats later, the men untangled themselves. Five heartbeats more, and everyone was sitting in their prospective places around the table.

"Okay, for those who haven't met me yet, I'm Police Chief Cole," Becca addressed them in her most formal manner. "These are my associates, Mr. Silas Mot and Elliot Newman."

Death and his undead minion offered quick waves to the crowd, but wisely allowed her to continue speaking without interruption.

"I'm not quite sure any of you care, but we're investigating Lance Avery's death," she said. "And I expect all of your cooperation. Is that understood?"

All but Laura looked sheepishly at Becca, her rebuke having its desired effect. The wife of Lance Avery, however, looked anything but contrite.

"How dare you imply I don't care about my husband's death," she said. "I'm not the one desecrating his memory by hiring his research assistant less than twenty-four hours after his death."

Becca shrugged. "Frankly, I don't care. My team and I are going to investigate his death. We're going to conduct interviews. And each of you are going to act like grown ups while we do so. I respect that you are…um, grieving, Ms. Granger, but I've got a job to do, and the sooner it's concluded, the sooner you all can get back to whatever it is you're going to do."

She wanted to add 'to my town' at the end of the sentence, knowing full well that the entire production crew's presence was going to do more harm here than good, but thought better of it considering Ilene Nebbles-Fielding's involvement in the project.

"Now," she looked at the group with a scrutinizing gaze, then pointed at the man she assumed to be Derek 'Drake' Rosenbaum. "Let's start with you. Shall we?"

THIRTEEN

B ecca left Elliot to watch over the rest of the crew in the conference room while she, Silas, and Derek Drake commandeered the motel manager's office for their interview. The police chief took the chair behind the desk. Derek sat across from her. And Silas stood ominously by the door in his ever-growing desire to play 'bad cop' whenever the two of them spoke with suspects.

It was becoming an annoying—if not altogether distracting—habit, but she was in no mood to argue with him at the moment. Besides, after the argument she'd just heard in among the *Mysterious Expedition*'s crew, she now had the first motive she'd discovered so far for the possible murder of Lance Avery.

"So you're going to be the show's new host?" She decided to cut through all the niceties and just get to the heart of the matter right from the start. The name of the interrogation game was "Keep 'em Disoriented" and she was an excellent player.

Derek sat up straighter the moment the words were out of

her mouth. Garrett Norris had been right about one thing. The guy was handsome. Light brown hair with a chiseled, well-defined chin. Unlike Avery, he was clean shaven and wore wire-rimmed glasses that gave him more of a bookish, but sexy vibe. He was also well-built. Not too muscular, but athletic enough, and appeared capable of being just as much at home in a crumbling temple as he was a library.

"I know what you're thinking," he said. His Adam's apple visibly wobbled up and down as he tried to swallow.

"Really?" Silas said, leaning closer to the show's newest host and offering him his most devilish grin. "So besides all those credentials Norris mentioned, you're psychic too, eh?"

Derek's eyes darted from Silas to Becca, as if unsure of what to say. "No, no. I'm just saying I know this looks bad. Lance is killed, and all of a sudden, I'm taking over his show. I know what it looks like, but you've got to believe me...I had nothing to do with his death."

Silas chuckled. "I always find it rather amusing when suspects tell us how much we *have* to believe them. I mean, that's not how this whole investigating murders thing works, is it, Becca? 'Oh, they say they didn't do it, so I guess they didn't do it. Let's move onto the next sap, shall we?'"

"Silas," she warned her partner before turning her attention to the newly minted Derek Drake. "But Mr. Mot has a point. We'll follow the evidence, then believe what *it* has to say."

Derek nodded his understanding at this.

"Now tell me...before you were chosen to be the new host, what exactly did you do for the show?"

"Head researcher," he answered, his voice wavering almost imperceptibly. "Occasional staff writer. And location scout."

"What exactly does a location scout do?"

"Basically, they travel to the region where the show plans

on shooting, ahead of the crew. Look around for the best locations to film. Dig up research on the area, book lodging, transport, and equipment. That kind of thing."

"So you were in Summer Haven before the rest of your team?" Silas asked.

Derek nodded.

"When did you get into town?" Becca asked.

"I've been here twice actually. The first time was about a week after Ilene reached out to us," Derek said. "I was supposed to find out as much as I could about the sunken ship, and report back whether or not it would make a good episode."

"And the second?"

"A week ago. About three days before the rest of the crew."

"What did you do that time?"

"Mostly coordinated with Ilene's people. Helped plan Saturday's big shindig." He looked over at Silas. "You're the one who almost ruined the whole thing, aren't you?"

"We're the ones asking the questions here, ya mug," Silas said in his best Humphrey Bogart voice.

Becca gave her partner the stink eye, silently sending him back to lean against the door. "So Mr. Rosenbaum..."

"That's Drake. I had it legally changed."

She nodded. "Mr. Drake, I'm curious. When did you hear you were in the running to replace Lance Avery as *Mysterious Expedition*'s host?"

He looked down at his feet, his fingers fidgeting on the arms of his chair.

"Mr. Drake?"

"Well, um..."

Once again, Silas pushed away from the door, glided over to the man and bent down to give him his most frightening glare. "I'd highly recommend you answer this question as honestly as possible, Mr. *Rosenbaum*. My stomach's been rumbling a bit of late, which means I'm getting hungry again. And trust me. You wouldn't like me when I'm hungry."

Derek raised his head and Becca could see his shoulders slacken with resignation. "Garrett started talking to me about it a month or so ago."

"A month? That's how you had time to legally change your name before it was announced."

He nodded. "Everybody on the crew knows he and Lance have been butting heads for a while now. Lance's contract was coming up for renegotiation, and Garrett was doing everything he could to make sure the network didn't renew it. He came to me last month, asking if I'd be interested in taking over as host, and I jumped at the chance."

"So, Garrett was looking to get rid of Avery?" Becca asked.

Derek nodded again.

"And how did you feel about it?" Silas added.

"I was ecstatic! I mean, who wouldn't be, right...oh, you're talking about the animosity between Garrett and Lance?" He paused. "Well, it's not like Lance was easy to work with or anything."

Silas remained uncomfortably close to their interviewee. "I take it you weren't much of a fan."

Derek shrugged. "I wasn't much of anything as far as Lance was concerned," he said. "He hardly knew I existed. Then again, if you didn't have boobs and killer legs, he'd hardly notice anyone existed."

Becca jotted down some notes, then let out a sigh. It was time to wrap this interview up for now. "Okay," she said. "One final question. Where were you yesterday morning around the time Lance Avery died?"

The show's new host glanced up at the ceiling in thought, then shook his head. "Not exactly sure," he said. "I was all over the place yesterday. Getting ready for today's scheduled shoot." He stopped, his eyes widening. "Oh! But I know who can vouch for me. I was with Kevin Aker, our team's sound engineer, most of the day."

"And that would be the guy we found you fighting with when we walked into your meeting?"

He blushed at this, but nodded. "Yeah. Believe it or not, we're pretty good friends. He was just surprised by the news Garrett dumped on everyone today. He'd taken Lance's death harder than most, so he was understandably surprised. I hadn't been able to tell him beforehand because of a non-disclosure agreement I'd signed."

"And your comment about him..." Becca glanced down at her notes. "...'wanting to get in Laura's pants again'? What exactly does that mean?"

Derek shrugged. "Exactly what it sounds like," he said. "They used to be an item. Way back in college. But to be honest, pretty much every red-blooded male on the crew has had there way with her." He let out a nervous cough. "She's not exactly picky when it comes to the sack."

"And does 'almost every red-blooded male' include you, Mr. Drake?" Silas asked, giving the young man a lascivious wink.

The new host glanced down at the floor, his shoulders sagging ever-so-slightly.

"Ah," Silas said. "Just what I thought. She apparently *does* have some standards."

The interview was soon concluded, and Derek Drake returned to his comrades with the instructions to send Laura Granger for her turn to discuss the case with Chief Cole. A few minutes later, Lance Avery's ice-cold wife strode into the room, and sat down at the proffered chair, her back as rigid and straight as her expression.

As with the first time they'd met, her straight blonde hair

was pulled back in a severe bun, and she was dressed in a dark gray pantsuit almost identical to the one from yesterday. Becca couldn't help wondering how the woman managed to maintain such a cool demeanor wearing it in the Florida heat. But if the woman was sweating—either physically or mentally—it wasn't showing.

"So how long is this going to take?" Laura said, crossing both her legs and arms before scowling at Becca. "We've got a busy schedule and this investigation is eating into it."

Becca blinked. "Do you mean this interview or our entire investigation?"

"Both," Laura said. "Either. Take your pick."

"You don't seem entirely upset about the death of your husband."

"Would you prefer it if I pretended to be grieving widow?"

"You certainly played the part on the *Stately Lady* yesterday," Silas chimed in.

"Because I was in shock. No one expects someone they know to die like that." She reached into her purse, shuffled around a bit, then withdrew a cigarette between two fingers and a lighter between the next. She placed the cigarette between her lips and prepared to light it.

"There's no smoking in public buildings in Florida, Ms. Granger," Becca said, waiting for the woman to put the cigarette back in her purse before continuing. "As to your question, both our interview and our investigation will take as long as they need to take to get to the truth of your husband's death."

The woman rolled her eyes. "I really do wish you'd stop referring to him as that. Yes, technically we were married, but we haven't been husband and wife in nearly two years now."

"Why didn't you just divorce him?" Becca asked.

"I couldn't. We started Treasure Trove Productions—the

production company that created *Mysterious Expedition*—together. Our contracts were intertwined." She shifted in her seat to keep a better look at both of them. "If we divorced, our production company would be in shambles. Our contracts with World of Wonders network would fall apart, and we'd have to start from scratch. So, we made do."

"So I take it your contract was being renegotiated right alongside Lance's?"

Laura sat up at this, cocking her head to one side. "I'm sorry, what?"

Becca flipped through her notes to ensure she had the information in front of her. "Derek said Lance's contract was nearly expired and was in the process of being renegotiated. He said that Garrett Norris was doing his best to see to it that Lance's contract wasn't renewed."

The woman's eyes narrowed as she bit down on her lower lip. Her face reddened, and she glanced away. "That son of a..."

"I take it you weren't aware of this?"

She turned back to Becca, her eyes now just as red as her face. Tears were beginning to run down her cheeks and she brushed them away with a disgusted sniff. "No. I wasn't aware of it."

"Ms. Granger, I hate to do this, but I have to ask...where were you..."

There were two raps at the door before it burst open and Ilene Nebbles-Fielding, with Mayor Belker in tow, stormed into the room, nearly bowling Silas over as they did so.

"What's going on here?" Ilene said, looking from Becca to Laura with a pinched expression. Becca could almost make out the throbbing veins underneath the woman's wrinkled, paper-like skin.

Becca stood up from behind the desk, struggling to keep her own anger in check. "I'm doing my job. Conducting interviews into the death of Lance Avery...just as you pressured me to do yesterday, I might add." She narrowed her eyes at the older woman. "An investigation you and Mayor Belker are currently interfering with, by the way, Mrs. Fielding."

"Nonsense," she said. "I've looked into the matter personally. It was a tragic accident. Nothing more. My own investigators have assured me there was nothing at all malicious in Mr. Avery's death."

"Your own investigators?" Silas asked, one eyebrow raised.

The old woman wheeled around on him. "Why yes," she said. "You know. Professional ones. Unlike you, who are simply busy poking your nose in everyone's business for some unknown reason."

"Actually, he's on special assignment from the governor's office," Becca corrected. It was technically not a lie. She'd spoken with the governor himself when she'd first encountered Silas Mot, and that's what she'd been told. Never mind the fact that the governor had owed Silas a little favor—apparently a bit of an extension on his life subscription—but as far as Becca knew, the deal as special investigator was still in effect. "I've already explained that to you several times. Explained it to both you."

"Be that as it may," Ilene said. "I won't have you harassing these people any longer. They have a job to do, namely exploring *The Lord's Vengeance* for the good of the town." The old crone looked at Laura Granger. "You may go now, dear. I'll take care of our police chief."

The executive producer of *Mysterious Expedition* looked from Ilene to Becca, then headed for the now-open door without another word.

Becca, now boiling, moved from behind the desk and stepped up to Ilene. "I should arrest you for that," she said, struggling to keep her cool. "Like I said, you're interfering with an official police investiga…"

"Nicholas?" the old bat said over her shoulder. "Would you care to inform Ms. Cole, or should I?"

"That's *Chief* Cole," Becca corrected, feeling petty the moment she said it.

"Oh, not for long, dear." Ilene's smile resembled a viper. "Not if you keep this up. Nicholas?"

The mayor stepped forward and cleared his throat. "Chief Cole, I've reviewed the report provided by Mrs. Nebbles-Fielding's private investigators, and I concur. Lance Avery's death, while tragic, appears to have been an unfortunate accident with no malicious intent involved."

"No malicious intent?" Silas barked. "The man burned to death."

The two newcomers stared blankly at him.

"Underwater!"

"The investigators at the Harrell and Dobbs firm—both highly trained in death investigations and forensics, I might add—feel that this fire was caused by nothing more than some malfunction of the dive suit," Mayor Belker said. "They've subpoenaed the dive suit from the medical examiner's office and will be conducting their own tests to back up their claims, of course." He turned to Becca. "But in the meantime, I insist you conclude your investigation at once, and allow the crew of *Mysterious Expedition* to proceed with their shoot immediately."

Becca stiffened at this. She'd never liked being told what to do, especially by bureaucratic lap dogs with no backbone. Besides, the mayor had no authority over her when it came to the investigation of crime. He had no right to do this.

"We'll see how the State Attorney feels about this," she said, placing her hands on her hips.

"I don't think she'll have much to say about it," Belker said, pulling a folded sheet of paper from the inside of his coat pocket and handing it to her.

Becca opened the paper to see the seal of the Florida Attorney General. She scanned the note twice, not believing what she was reading. Basically, it was a cease and desist order from the highest prosecutor in the state. She was being ordered to stop her investigation immediately by the one person who truly did had authority over her.

She looked up from the letter and glared at Mayor Belker. "And if I refuse?"

"Then it's really quite simple." Ilene practically purred the words. "We'll be forced to hold a special hearing in regards to your career here and whether or not we have further confidence in your ability as chief of police." With that, the two turned and started for the door. "Have a nice day."

CHAPTER
FOURTEEN

STATELY LADY
ATLANTIC OCEAN
23 MILES EAST OF SUMMER HAVEN
THURSDAY, 8:34 AM

Silas Mot materialized out of nowhere on the top deck of *The Stately Lady*, and he was nearly exhausted from the effort. It had taken him much longer to escape his ectoplasmic body than it should have. The molecules holding the shell together just hadn't wanted to separate, leaving him trapped for a time on shore, and away from his destination. After a while, however, he'd managed to pull together enough will to dissolve his body, revert to his normal spirit form, and sail out over the water to rendezvous with the crew of *Mysterious Expedition* before they'd embarked on their principal photography near the sunken pirate ship.

Silas wasn't sure what was happening to him, but knew that something was most definitely wrong. The intense hunger he'd felt yesterday—a ravishing lust for food—was a completely new sensation for him. The stomach pains after-wards, nearly doubling him over in Becca Cole's police cruiser, was something that should never have happened. He didn't have a stomach after all. Had no intestines or innards of any kind, in fact. And now it seemed his ethereal-born body was rebelling against him completely. It was something he would have to look into when this investigation was completed.

For now, however, with Becca sidelined by the Wicked Witch of Summer Haven, it was up to him to get to the bottom of Lance Avery's death. And he had no intention of failing.

Conjuring a quick 'Death on the Beach', he strode across the wooden deck in the direction of voices near the bow. Given his unofficial capacity at the gathering, he'd opted to demateri-alize in his standard black on black suit in case his presence there was to be questioned, and strolled at a leisurely pace.

"I'm still having problems taking direction from a location scout," a man—Silas believed it was Kevin Aker, the sound engineer—said. "I'm telling you, he doesn't have a clue about being in front of a camera."

"And I'm telling you to get over it or take a hike," Garrett Norris replied. "We're already horribly behind schedule, and our budget—even with Mrs. Fielding's generous donations—is quickly depleting. We need to get our shots today as quick as possible and move on with the excavation." The producer pointed across the starboard bow at the two large salvage ships anchored nearby. "So stop complaining and pitch in. Got it?"

Silas moved into view of the others, leaned against the gunwale, and took a sip of his cocktail with an amused grin sliding up one side of his face.

"Ahem," he said, causing the crew to spin around to see him.

Garrett Norris straightened. "What are you doing here?

You're not allowed to be here," he said, stalking over to him, and poking an index finger into his chest. "Ilene Nebbles-Fielding said the case was closed."

Silas looked down at the finger still pressed against his chest, then eyed the annoyed producer with a glare that would have wilted a rhino. Norris took a step back from the gaze while Silas straightened the lapel of his suit, took another sip of the umbrella drink, and cleared his throat.

"The old biddy might have twisted an arm or two to get the local police department to stop their investigation." He reached inside his coat pocket, pulled out a folded piece of paper, but didn't open it. "I, on the other hand, don't work for Nebbles-Fielding. Nor do I work for the police. This piece of paper authorizes me, by order of the Florida governor, to conduct any and all investigations I deem necessary."

In reality, the paper was nothing more than a photo-copied take-out menu from Silas' favorite barbecue joint. Truth was, Governor Tyler had refused to take his calls after the verbal altercation he and Becca had had with the deceased senator's wife. Her pull, apparently, hadn't just reached the Attorney General, but the governor's office itself. So, without Chief Cole's knowledge, Silas had decided to take matters into his own hand and continue the investigation on his own. And he was more than willing to lie through his ectoplasmic teeth to do it.

Silas stuffed the menu back in his pocket before anyone could ask to see it, pushed himself from the gunwale, and strode over to the crew while looking each one up and down with a scrutinizing gaze. There was no sign of Lance Avery's estranged wife, Laura Granger, but everyone else seemed present. There was Krista Dunaway, the team's medic, who had stopped packing her gear to watch him as he walked by. The sound guy, Kevin Aker, who currently had a hand with a screwdriver in it inserted into one of the team member's dive helmets and installing a new transmitter. The camera man—Silas hadn't seen him with the rest of the crew yesterday, nor did he know his name—was busy waterproofing the camera equipment. And finally, the show's brand new host, Derek Drake; his jaw slack and dumb as Silas walked past.

Once he'd walked by each of them, he spun around, finished the rest of his 'Death on the Beach', then whipped his hand around like a magician, and the empty glass disappeared for all to see.

"So," he said, clapping his hands excitedly, "what's on the agenda for today?"

"I'm calling Ilene right now," Garrett Norris said, pulling his cell phone from his pocket and squinting at the screen. He raised his arm up, and moved it right to left, as if trying to find a better signal.

"Geez, Garrett," Krista Dunaway said. She'd resumed packing her gear in a waterproof bag and zipped it up. "Stop being such a jerk. He's trying to find out what happened to Lance, and I, for one, would like to find out myself."

"Yeah. You're being a bit weird about this whole thing," the cameraman said. "Let the man do his job, and we'll just go ahead and do ours. Okay?"

Silas eased over to the camera man, his arms behind his back, as he bent down for a better look at the hard-shelled Pelican camera cases. Each of the cases were labeled with the name Gabe Williams.

"So, you must be Gabe," he said.

"Yep. Nice to meet ya." He held out a hand, and Silas politely shook it.

"You weren't at the meeting yesterday?"

"Nah, bro. Had to go to Jacksonville for some gear.

Someone got some potassium hydroxide smudged on some of my lenses. Completely ruined them."

"Potassium hydroxide?" Silas asked. "Is that common compound to find on camera equipment?"

The cameraman laughed. "Man, you wouldn't believe the kind of crap I find on my stuff on a regular basis. Nothing ever shocks me anymore." Gabe shrugged. "But I think the potassium stuff came from some new dive equipment Lance was working on before he died. It's the only thing that really makes sense to me."

Silas nodded, deciding to file this information away for further questioning. He then turned to Garrett Norris, who'd given up trying to find a signal and tucked his phone back into the pockets of his shorts. "Fine," he said. "But you'll have to stay out of our way."

"Oh, absolutely!" Silas grinned from ear to ear. "I have no intention of hindering your shoot today whatsoever. I'm merely here to observe. Maybe talk to a few of you here and there. I'll be a proverbial fly on the wall. You shan't even know I'm here."

"Good. That's what I like to hear."

"So tell me," Silas said, rubbing his hands together and looking around the deck. "Where do I get my scuba gear?"

"Dude, I can't believe you pulled the rug out from under Norris like that," Gabe Williams said as he led Silas into the yacht's locker rooms where the dive equipment was being stored. "He never saw it coming. It was awesome!"

"You mean about the dive?"

"Oh yeah! The look on his face when you asked for scuba

gear was priceless! I can't believe he agreed to let you go down with us."

Silas took a look around the large open room. To his right, sat a handful of normal-looking air tanks, BC vests, and regulators, already prepped and ready to go. Masks, flippers, weight belts, and wetsuits were piled on a bench running parallel to a row of lockers.

In one tiny corner of the room, sat a work bench with two much smaller tanks, tools, and an unusual looking mouthpiece that Silas couldn't identify. He nodded over to the bench.

"What's that?"

Gabe's eyes lit up at the question. "Oh, that's the experimental equipment Lance had been working on." The cameraman walked over to the gear and let his hands hover reverently over it as if reaching out to Eden's forbidden fruit. "Basically, Lance got the idea from equipment used by miners who go deep, deep underground, as well as submarines, and spaceships. Potassium superoxide is used as a condensed source of oxygen. Not only does it give a longer breathing time in a much smaller tank, it also scrubs the air your breathing of contaminants. Pretty amazing stuff really, although I don't think Lance ever got all the kinks worked out."

Gabe moved from the workbench over to the regular dive gear and picked up one of the neatly folded wetsuits. He then placed a pair of flippers and a mask on top, and held it out to Silas, who hesitated.

Truth was, Silas had very good reason to be nervous about submerging himself into the Atlantic Ocean. In his time in the Land of the Living, although spending a great deal of time at the beach, he'd always avoided the water as if it were a vat of flesh-eating acid. The reason was simple. To someone like him —a creature of the Netherworld—flowing water of any kind could be disastrous. Unknown to most humans, reality was filled with fissures between the material and spirit worlds where energies on both sides converge. For some reason, however, water had a unique way of dampening such energies. Weakening them. Even eradicating them altogether.

Want to break a spell or a curse? Cross a freely flowing body of water. It was a well-known folk remedy in almost every part of the world. Even Baron Tombstone, at the height of his power, was forced to conjure up an entire island in the Caribbean to do his infernal voodoo for that very reason.

And Silas' body was made up of those same spiritual energies. Water—in such large quantities anyway—and he weren't going to mix. And yet, in order to conduct his investigation, he had to get down to Tombstone's sunken ship. To see it with his own eyes.

Taking a deep breath, he took the equipment from the camera man, and moved over to the bench to start to put it on.

"I take it you don't much care for your boss," Silas said, unbuttoning his shirt like any mortal would instead of simply allowing it to dissolve into ectoplasm. It wouldn't do to let Gabe see that happen.

"Nah. He's just kind of a creep. That's all. But they're all pretty much like that."

"Your team?"

Gabe shook his head. "No. Producers. All producers are cut from the same cloth. It's all about money and schedules. The art is completely lost on them. It all boils down to the mighty dollar with them, and they'll do whatever it takes to get the job done under budget for that little bit of extra profit."

Silas pondered this for a few moments. "I suppose that's simply part of their job description."

"I guess."

Silas removed his shirt, then his shoes, and pants, all the while searching the locker room, still anxious about his upcoming dive. He had no idea what was going to happen to him once his ectoplasmic body submerged into the embrace of the ocean, and he was trying to distract himself more than anything else. But soon his eyes locked onto a small alcove where a mannequin stood naked. Apparently, it had been used for the antique dive suit Lance Avery had been wearing upon his death. He knew this because of the thing standing directly next to it.

Silas smiled.

"Is that...?" He nodded to the object. Gabe's eyes followed the direction he'd indicated.

"Oh yeah," he said. "He had a bit of a collection."

Suddenly, Silas stood up from the bench, and walked over to it. "This," he said. "I'm going to wear this."

Gabe Williams shuffled over to him. "Uh dude, I'm not sure they're gonna..."

Silas turned a fierce and determined gaze on the camera man. "I'm wearing it."

THE LOUDSPEAKERS on the main deck squelched, and Garrett Norris's voice boomed throughout the entire 129-foot yacht. "May I have everyone's attention? The first dive begins in five minutes," he said with a reverberating screech in the speakers. "Report to the dive platform immediately."

Soon, the crew, who'd been milling about in various parts of the ship, returned to the stern, grabbed up their own gear and tanks, and began preparing for the dive. They chatted amongst themselves, as they did so. Laughing every now and then, ignoring the tragedy that had just taken place a couple of days earlier below the waves.

The moment Silas and Gabe stepped into view, however, the chatter stopped. All eyes turned, gawking at him as he lumbered carefully along the walkway toward the dive platform in a vintage dive suit identical to the one Lance Avery had been wearing two days earlier.

"You've got to be kidding me," someone among the crew muttered.

"That's just in so bad taste," said another.

"You can't be serious," Garrett Norris said, as he strode up to Silas. "You must have some set of cojones on you to wear that. Cold-hearted, man. If Laura finds out you wore Lance's suit, she's going to have a fit."

Silas beamed at them, as he opened the front viewport of his helmet to address their protestations. "I'm terribly sorry for any discomfort you might feel about this," he said, knowing full well that the smile he was giving them proved he was lying. "But as an investigator, I found it imperative to use as close to the original equipment as possible so I can truly get into Mr. Avery's mind at the time of his death."

Krista stepped out from among her peers. "Then I'll tell you the same thing I told him. That suit is old. It's not as old as the one he was wearing, but only by about ten years. It's unreliable. Dangerous. As team medic, I can't be responsible for you if anything goes wrong."

"Have no fear, Ms. Dunaway." Silas motioned over to Garrett. "Seems I had to sign my soul away to your stalwart producer. A liability waiver in exchange for authorization to go down with your team."

Garrett nodded. "Absolutely. None of you are responsible for this man," he said, holding up the legal document for everyone to see. "If something goes wrong...if he gets himself in any trouble, you are not to put yourselves in danger by helping him. Got that?"

The entire team looked from Garrett to Silas. All of them but Krista nodded in understanding.

"Krista?" Garrett said.

"It's just that..." She eyed the antique suit with suspicion. "I don't know if I can accept that. I don't trust that suit. Any number of things can go wrong with it, and..."

"And it's none of your responsibility," the producer said. "Mr. Mot agrees."

"I insist, in fact!" Silas said. "If something goes wrong, just ignore me. Just let me go about my experiment as I see fit. I promise, I'll be fine."

Krista blinked, but seemed unable to turn her gaze from the suit.

"Trust me," Silas Mot said, stretching out his waterproof canvas-clad arms, and giving her a wink. "I'm a professional."

She was still staring at him when Garrett Norris turned to the rest of the group, clapping his hands loud for everyone's attention. "Alright everyone, there's nothing we can do about this idiot," he said. "So get to your places!"

As one, each of the team scrambled down the short ladder to the dive platform. Silas waited for Gabe Williams to reach the platform, then carefully lowered himself. He found that getting his lead-booted feet into each rung was more difficult than he'd anticipated, but after a few minutes, he managed to descend without so much as a slip. Then, he walked over to the air pump, and let Gabe hook the hose and winch up to his helmet. While Silas was being prepped, Garrett Norris continued to address the crew.

"Okay everyone." Garrett, still on the main deck, glanced down at his watch. "It's now 10:20. The sun will be at its highest in just an hour or so, and because *The Lord's Vengeance* is as deep as it is, we need as much light as we can get. So, we need to get moving." He looked at Silas. "So you're still insisting on this charade of an investigation?"

Silas nodded. "I'd like to see exactly where Mr. Avery died. I figure Ms. Dunaway can point the location out to me." He watched as the medic offered him a hesitant nod. "Other than that, who wouldn't want to see a supposed cursed pirate ship sunk off the Florida coast centuries ago?"

"Fine with me." Garrett once more held up the liability waiver. "Your funeral."

Silas let out a burst of laughter. "Aye, you've no idea!"

"Okay, everyone." Garrett seemed to ignore his comment. "Let's do this while we still have good light."

Without another word, each of the crew members gathered their kits—most of which were kept in mesh bags designed for underwater carrying—slipped on their dive helmets which were all equipped with mounted cameras, and jumped into the water one by one.

Gabe, with the help of the yacht's crew and supervised by Garrett Norris, lowered a small remote operated vehicle into the water as well. Garrett, using a PC tablet, controlled the ROV from the surface, and watched it descend with the others by the non-reflective screen.

Silas, still standing on the platform, took a deep breath, closed the front window panel and locked it in place. Then, he peered into the water and fidgeted. The vintage dive suit, despite its age, had one advantage over the modern wet suits being worn by the crew. It was airtight. No water could get in, therefore, no water should be able to disrupt the energies that were holding Silas together. It was the main reason he'd chosen to use the suit despite what he'd told the others.

He knew he should be safe now. He understood the mechanics of it all. And yet now, on the precipice of this superyacht, he was having trouble believing it.

"Are you going to go today?" Garrett asked with a scoffing laugh. "Or would you rather come back next week?"

Silas scowled at the man, who'd just helped make up his mind instantly. Without another thought, he stepped off the platform's ledge, and plunged into the warm Atlantic waters as his air hose reeled out above him.

FIFTEEN

SUMMER HAVEN POLICE DEPARTMENT
SUMMER HAVEN
THURSDAY, 9:15 AM

Chief Becca Cole jumped at the sound of her desk phone buzzing. She'd been absorbed in paperwork, attempting to appeal to the attorney general's office in regards to the Lance Avery case, and hadn't realized had engrossed she was in it. When she picked up the phone's receiver, she was immediately greeted by the warm friendly voice of her office manager, Linda Green.

"I have Dr. Lipkovic on the phone for you, Chief."

"Thanks, Linda." Becca took a breath to calm her racing heart. "Put him through please." She held the receiver to her ear, heard a click and a couple of tones, and then the call was transferred. "Dr. Lipkovic? This is Becca."

The Slavic man on the other end cleared his throat. "Chief Cole! I hope you're having a glorious day."

He sounded happy, which was nothing really new. The

county's medical examiner was always, for lack of a better word, enthusiastic. And verbose, if she didn't corral him to his point quick. She liked him a lot, and had tremendous respect for him, but the man could small talk you to death if you gave him the chance.

"So far so good," she said. "What can I do for you, Doc?"

"Well, as you might know by now, the dive suit belonging to Mr. Avery was requested by a private investigation firm in Jacksonville. They supplied a court order for it, so I had no choice but to provide it to them."

"Naturally," she said. "I understand."

"But I wanted to tell you, I think I might know what caused the fire."

She sat up at this, gripping the receiver tighter in her hand.

"Really?"

"Well, I can't be positive, mind you, because I am no longer in possession of the evidence," he said, his accent growing thicker the more excited he became. "But before it was taken, I procured a few swabs of the helmet. It's not really in the scope of my job, of course, but I decided to run some tests on it myself—with the meager lab we have here in our small office."

Verbose, Becca thought. *As always.*

"And?" There was a tap on her door. "Hold on a sec, Doc."

Still keeping the phone pressed to her ear, she looked up to see Commander Jeremy Tanner at the door. She waved him inside, and when he complied, he gestured behind him to Elliot Newman, who followed him in. She nodded her consent for the little guy to stay, then resumed her conversation with the medical examiner.

"Sorry about that," she said. "You were saying?"

"Yes, well..." She could hear a rustle of papers on the other end of the phone. "One of the things I discovered on the head-gear was potassium hydroxide."

She sat there for a moment, waiting for the punchline. "And?"

"Potassium hydroxide, Chief Cole. It shouldn't be there."

"And that's what you think started the fire? Under water?"

The doctor laughed. "Heavens no! Potassium hydroxide would hardly be flammable in the best of circumstances. However, pure potassium is downright explosive in water. And as it burns away, it leaves a potassium hydroxide residue."

Becca scribbled a few notes down on a notepad. Elliot swept around the table to see what she wrote, and his eyes went the size of Volkswagen tires. "So you think someone put potassium in his helmet and it combusted. But that doesn't make sense. Those helmets are airtight. There's no way for water to get inside."

Elliot suddenly became excited, waving his arms frantically to get her attention. She waved him away and concentrated on what the medical examiner was telling her.

"I can't tell you how they did it. I know that if it had been placed on the outside, it would have burst into flames almost immediately when touching the water. And, we wouldn't have seen the thermal damage to Mr. Avery that we did. It might not have killed him at all as the helmet would have been a buffer to the heat."

Elliot continued waving his arms, now jumping up and down.

"Doc, thank you for this information," she said, gesturing for the little guy to calm down. "I need to look into this. I'll call you back later if I have any other questions."

"Certainly," he said. "I'm glad I could be of assistance to you in this time..."

But she had already hung up the phone and was glaring at Elliot. "What is it?"

"I've got a theory!" he said, holding up his index finger. "Hold on! I'll be right back!"

He took off before she could protest, running out her office door faster than she could imagine him being able to move. She looked up at her second in command with a shrug.

Tanner offered her a scowl in return. "I just don't know why you put up with those two weirdos," he told her.

"Because they can be brilliant." She paused, then pinched at her nose with a sigh. "Sometimes. Speaking of which, have you seen Silas this morning? He's been uncharacteristically quiet today, which is weird because he was none too happy with our investigation being nixed."

"Sorry boss." He shook his head and leaned in, placing his hands flat on her desk. "Haven't seen that lunatic today, thankfully."

She looked down at his hands, her eyes slowly roving up his wrist, and at just where his long sleeve cuffs were fastened in place. She noted the blue ink of a tattoo just beneath the sleeve, triggering a memory.

Becca pointed to the tattoo. "You know, I've always known you had ink, but I've never seen them."

Tanner glanced down, self-consciously pulling his sleeves over the tattoos before standing up straight and putting his hands in his pockets. He blushed. "Well, you know. Our regulations and all. If an officer has tattoos, we're required to keep them covered from the public."

She smiled at him, but it was a nervous one. She didn't particularly like where her thoughts were going. Last year, while investigating the murder of Andrea Alvarez, Silas Mot had been attacked by three masked men. They supposedly had killed a local bartender too, who had tried to warn him about the danger he was in. The only thing Silas could say about his attackers was that they each had Celtic-inspired tattoos on their arms. He'd suspected that at least one of them had been one of her police officers, but she hadn't taken him too seriously at the time.

But the bartender's murder had now long gone cold. The St. Johns County Sheriff's Office, who'd been assigned to the case because her own department had been stretched too thin at the time, had moved onto other, more pressing cases. And Becca had hardly given the case much thought ever since, although she knew the same wasn't true for Silas Mot, who blamed himself for her death.

"It's just weird," she said. "I've been to your house...the barbecues that you and Maxine do every weekend for the guys. Even at home you wear long sleeves."

Tanner shrugged. "The wife doesn't like them much. Embarrassed for company to see them, I guess. She makes me cover up too."

She considered asking him to roll up his sleeves so she could take a look, but wasn't sure how to do that without raising an eyebrow from him. No one but her knew about the tattoos on Silas' attackers. It had been left out of the official report on Silas' own insistence—presumably to protect her. But now, there was an overwhelming need to take a look at the ink that marked her second-in-command's arms.

"Uh, do you need anything else, Chief?" Tanner asked, reaching for the door. "I need to get back out on patrol."

She stared past him for a moment, lost in her own thoughts, then latched onto his question and shook her head. "No Jeremy," she said. "I'm fine. Be safe out there, okay?"

He grinned back at her. "Will do, boss." Then he opened her office door and strode out.

CHAPTER
SIXTEEN

REMAINS OF *THE LORD'S VENGEANCE*
23 MILES EAST OF SUMMER HAVEN
THURSDAY, 10:24 AM

Silas Mot sunk fast. Much faster than he'd imagined going actually, and with the heavy copper helmet mounted to his dive suit, it was impossible to look down to see where the water ended and the sand-covered bottom began. Impossible to know when his lead-laden boots would find land and buckle his ectoplasmic knees with the impact.

The good news, however, was that so far, the archaic dive suit had proved to be, indeed, waterproof. Not a drop of sea water had entered into his oxygen-rich domain since plunging into the ocean, and he found great solace in that.

There was a crackle inside the helmet, then the voice of Derek Drake entered his world.

"Everybody good so far?" he asked.

"Good here," Kevin Aker replied.

"All clear," Krista Dunaway said.

"10-4, everything's A-okay on my end," said cameraman Gabe Williams.

Bubbles streaked past Silas' window to the aquatic world around him. He could just make out the ROV diving deeper to his left, churning up a trail of more bubbles as it descended.

He cleared his throat and willed his voice not to crack.

"So far, so good on my end," he said. "If anyone cares, that is."

"Mr. Mot, I still don't think it's a good idea for you to be here," Krista said. "That suit is an antique. I don't know the last time it was tested. Maybe you should..."

"Cut the chatter everyone!" Garrett Norris' voice cut in from the deck of the yacht above them. "You've got a job to do. Let Mr. Mot worry about himself."

Easy for him to say, Silas thought.

Although there wasn't much in the physical world that could really do him harm, he wasn't so sure that the Atlantic Ocean wasn't one of them. And it wasn't just his temporarily constructed body that concerned him this time. The energy-sapping effects of the water could potentially have the power to rip his essence back to the Land of the Dead, crippling him enough to prevent his return to the Living any time soon. And that would end any chances of recovering the Hand of Cain, which could have devastating consequences for the world at large.

A splash here or a drop there was no big deal, but the entire weight of the ocean rushing in on him could be bad news for everyone. It was enough to make even the most Devil-May-Care soul hesitate.

His feet soon hit the bottom, and he was pleased to discover that the descent had been slow enough and the sand thick enough to absorb the impact without so much as a sprained ankle—if he was even capable of such a thing.

Silas looked out across the aquatic horizon. Besides schools of fish swimming through forests of kelp, there was little else to see. He began turning around. Slowly. Carefully, since he'd not quite become accustomed to his cumbersome suit and didn't want to even think how difficult it would be to pick himself up if he tripped. Soon, as his body began to twist around, he saw it. The decaying carcass of Baron Tombstone's accursed pirate ship.

What was left of the hull was now overgrown with barnacles and algae. Kelp, about as tall as Silas' head, swayed back and forth, concealing most of the remaining structure. Swimming just above the deck, he could see the crew of *Mysterious Expedition*, filming various shots while they explored the exterior of the vessel, taking measurements, and various readings as they did. The small ROV zipped by each of them, came about, then took in a wide panoramic view from above.

Silas knew from the crew's schedule that today's shoot—what they call principal photography—was video only. No sound. So he would be free to talk with them as he strode around the perimeter of the ship.

"Ms. Dunaway?" he said into his helmet's transmitter.

"I'm here." He glanced up to see a lone figure swimming toward him, a stream of air bubbles cascading behind her. In a matter of minutes, she hovered just in front of him.

"Can you show me where you found Mr. Avery, please?"

She glanced over her shoulder nervously, then turned back to him and nodded. "Sure. Follow me."

Silas stomped after her, learning real fast the importance of fully picking up one foot and moving it forward before picking up the next. His weighted boots were heavier than he'd expected, making movement slow and painstaking, but soon, he got into the rhythm of walking, and it became a little easier. He followed her toward the rotted remains of the ship's bow. The ship's figurehead had long ago ceased to be recognizable, and was now confined in a cocoon of vegetation and silt.

A shadow loomed above them, distracting Silas for a moment. He looked up to see two medium-sized sharks, a handful of pilot fish circling them, swimming overhead. For the moment, the predators were of no concern, so he pushed forward, rounding the corner of the bow while still looking up at the toothy fish, and nearly bumped into a waiting Krista Dunaway.

"It was right there." Ignoring the near collision, she pointed to a spot about ten yards away from the hull.

Although there was no visible sign of any thermal damage around the area where she indicated, Silas could sense the residual power of the Hand of Cain in the area. He wasn't entirely certain how the artifact could have worked so far down in the ocean's depths. He would have figured that such energy as it utilized would have suffered the same fate as any magical energy in free-flowing water. It should have dissipated long before it hit its target. And yet, from the sensations he was feeling, he knew that it had indeed been the artifact that had taken Lance Avery's life—with the help, of course, from more mundane elements as well.

He had long suspected that the wielder of the Hand hadn't quite developed skill enough to use it with precision. Whoever it was, they were still learning. Still trying to master it. And while some of its victims—such as the newspaper reporter, Spencer Blakely—were intentionally targeted, most were random casualties. Collateral damage.

"We good?"

He looked around to see Krista looking at him. He gave her

the 'okay' sign, and she took off again to join her compatriots in their filming.

SUMMER HAVEN POLICE DEPARTMENT
SUMMER HAVEN
THURSDAY, 10:33 AM

"SORRY IT TOOK SO LONG," Elliot Newman said as he barged into Becca's office without so much as a knock. "Do you have any idea how hard it is to get a sample of pure potassium on such short notice?"

Becca looked up from the notes she'd been scribbling for the past forty-five minutes, and tried not to look surprised by the sudden outburst. Truth was, she was getting jumpy. First Dr. Lipkovic's phone call, now Elliot. Her nerves were beginning to fray, and surprisingly, it had less to do with the Lance Avery case than it did her growing suspicions regarding Jeremy Tanner, and his possible involvement with the person who currently possessed the Hand of Cain.

The notes, that she now covered with a stack of folders, had documented everything she knew about the man who'd been a loyal and trusted officer of her father's. Granted, Spencer Blakely, the deceased owner of the town's newspaper, had often accused her father's administration of having rampant corruption among its officers, but she'd never once believed any of the accusations. Now, she wasn't so sure.

"What are you doing?" she asked as Elliot moved over to her desk and pushed all the folders and papers away to clear space. "I was working on those."

"Trust me," he said, setting a large paper bag down on the

desk, and rummaging through the contents. The stuff clattered and clanked as he shifted the objects around inside the bag. "You're going to want to see this."

He pulled out a round glass bowl, a gallon bottle of water, a small tube of putty, and a small jar containing a clear liquid. Floating in the center of the liquid was a chunk of silver-gray metal. After he arranged everything to his satisfaction, he reached into the bag and withdrew two safety goggles and pair of tongs.

"I'm assuming this has to do with your theory on how Avery was killed?"

He held up a finger. "Forgot something in the car. Don't go anywhere!"

He scrambled out of her office like a miniature tornado. With a sigh, she picked up the jar containing what she assumed to be the chunk of potassium and gave it a good once over. She wasn't entirely sure how how a piece of metal could torch someone the way it had Lance Avery. After all, the element was practically everywhere in the wild. The human body was even composed of large amounts of the stuff—or at least, it was considered essential for proper health anyway. In the clear liquid, it certainly seemed harmless enough. She just couldn't see it being all that combustible.

Her door flew open, and Elliot, huffing with exertion, stomped in carrying a miniature diver figurine in a similar vintage suit as Avery had been wearing. She recognized the figure as something one would find in a fish tank alongside a miniature treasure chest standing on a bed of multi-colored rocks.

"You ready for this?" he asked as he placed the new objects next to the others.

"I'm not sure."

Ignoring her, he filled the round fish bowl with the water

bottle, then picked up the diver figurine, gave something on its back a little twist, and came away with a round plastic cap. Becca recognized immediately what she was looking at. It wasn't a fish tank decoration at all, but rather a piggy bank of sorts. As she examined it, she could see the slit at the top of its helmet where a child might drop her pennies inside.

"I gave this a bit of a test before coming over here," he said. "Except for the coin slot, this baby's pretty much watertight."

He unscrewed the jar with potassium, reached in with the tongs, and picked it up. "The metal is best contained in mineral oil," he explained. "Prolonged exposure to oxygen can ignite it too. But we should be good for this little experiment."

Carefully, he placed the chunk on a piece of glass, and cut into it with a pocket knife. "See? It's malleable. You can pretty much mould it into any shape you want...such as a circle around a viewport." He nudged the soft metal into the hole in the back of the figurine and screwed the cap back on. He then opened the tube of putty, squirted a small amount onto the blade of his pocket knife, and covered the coin slot with a thin layer.

"This stuff dries quick. Shouldn't take long."

Becca still wasn't sure what he expected to happen, but she was now more curious than annoyed, so there was something to be said for the little man's enthusiasm.

After a few quiet moments, he picked up the figure with the tongs and held it over the lip of the fish bowl. "You might want to back away," he said. "No telling how long this might take."

He waited for her to get up out of her chair, and back away a safe distance. Then, he opened the tongs, and the figurine fell into the water to slowly drift to the bottom. They waited a moment. Then two. Becca glanced at her watch, then back at the bowl. Nothing was happening.

"Elliot, I'm not sure..."

"Shhhh!" he hissed. "Give it a minute. The putty has to get soft enough. I might have put a little too much on it."

"But..."

"Look, this is what I think happened," Elliot said, cutting her off yet again. "I think the killer put the potassium around the inside portion of the viewport *after* replacing some of the silicon sealant around the rim with putty or some other substance. After a while, the water dissolved the putty, letting water leak inside, and igniting the potassium."

The two of them continued to stare at the bowl. Becca was far less patient, or excited, than her cohort, but she decided to hear him out.

"But why go to all that trouble?" she asked. "If they rigged the helmet to leak, why not just let him drown? Why burn him up?"

The archaeologist shrugged, his eyes never shifting from his experiment. "Who knows? Maybe they were betting on the curse as a possible explanation for it? Maybe they couldn't guarantee the leak would start on queue, leaving an opportunity for Lance to get back to the ship before he drowned? I'm just telling you how I think they..."

There was a sudden bubbling of water, following by an explosive pop, and a blinding flare of heat and light. The fish bowl on her desk shattered, sending nearly a quart of water billowing over her paperwork.

Becca let out a slow growl as she watched the liquid pour out over the sides of her desk, and she turned to glare at the little man, who looked nervously back at her.

"Ta-da," he whispered, nervously raising his arms above his head like a stage magician.

Two of her uniformed officers, having heard the explosion burst through her door, their guns drawn.

"You okay, Chief?" one of them asked, looking around her office for signs of trouble.

She held up her hands, allowing a begrudging smile to form on her otherwise tense face, and nodded. "Just a little science experiment from Mr. Wizard here," she said. "No trouble at all. Thanks."

The two officers eyed Elliot suspiciously for a moment, then backed out of the office and closed the door behind them.

"Alright, Dr. Newman," Becca said, walking toward her desk to assess the damage. "You've made a believer out of me. This is now officially a murder investigation. I don't care what Ilene, the attorney general, or the mayor says. We've got a killer to catch." She paused, looking quizzically at Elliot. "We just have to find Silas and get the ball rolling again."

CHAPTER
SEVENTEEN

REMAINS OF *THE LORD'S VENGEANCE*
23 MILES EAST OF SUMMER HAVEN
THURSDAY, 11:04 AM

Silas Mot stepped closer to the area Krista had indicated as being the general spot where Lance Avery had died. Though the dive suit was very inflexible, he managed to drop to his knees, a plume of silt wafting up around him from the impact, and lowered himself carefully on all fours. Something was bothering him about this place. The presence he'd been feeling—the sensation of the Hand's residual power—seemed far too strong. Too potent.

Avery's death was two days ago. Even if the Hand of Cain had been responsible for it, its energies should have long since dissipated. And yet, it was near. It wasn't ebbing either. The energy, in fact, seemed constant. Not powerful, mind you, but strong enough.

He searched the sea floor, swiping his right hand back and forth to brush the sand and silt away with frantic gestures. As the detritus began to settle, he caught sight of something green, slightly phosphorescent, glowing up from the sand. Intrigued, he dug deeper until exposing a chunk of stone that seemed to radiate its own supernatural energy. He reached out to touch it, and instantly regretted it. The moment his gloved fingers caressed the jagged stone, a jolt of pain shot through his arm, reverberating down his spine. His hand snapped back, and he cursed.

There was only object on earth that could have reacted to his touch like that.

The Hand of Cain.

Only, it wasn't the entire Hand. It was just a fragment. A single chunk of the eldritch object that had been vexing Silas for so long now.

So the Hand of Cain isn't complete. That's why its wielder hasn't been able to master it yet. It's not because they can't focus it enough. It's that it's not all there.

Could it have been a coincidence that Lance Avery was standing over this very spot when he died? Had he known about the object? Had he been searching for it himself? These were questions, of course, for another time. For now, he needed to figure out a way to retrieve the piece. It was far too dangerous to allow it to remain where it was. If he found it, so could others. But only mortals could touch it. Only mortals could...

With a struggle, he clumsily managed to get to his feet, and he glanced around through the small periphery of his viewport, searching for movement from the team above him that were still busying themselves with their shoot.

"Ms. Dunaway, I could use your assistance again," he said into his microphone.

"Mr. Mot," he heard her voice in his helmet. "Are you okay? Is everything okay?"

"Yes, yes. Everything is fine," he said, spotting her a few dozen yards off to his right. He waved her towards him. "I simply have need of your hands for the moment, if you don't mind."

"My crew doesn't have time to help you, Mot," came Garrett Norris' irritated voice. "I told you, you're on your own."

"And you can expect a lump of coal in your casket when you go onto your Great Reward, you knuckle-dragger," Silas growled into his mic. "This is far more important than your ridiculous television show."

Fortunately, Krista hadn't seemed to heed her boss, and kicked toward him quickly. She reached him in seconds.

"What do you need?" Her voice was concerned. She seemed hardly put out at all for being distracted from her work.

Silas hesitated. He hardly knew the girl, and she was still, technically, a suspect in a murder investigation. And it was a murder investigation no matter what that old bat Fielding said about it. He was sure of that. And Krista had been at the scene of that murder when it was happening in real time. Had she known about the piece of the Hand down here? Had she used it to trigger the blaze that burned Lance Avery to a crisp?

She didn't seem the type, but then, greed and the promise of power had corrupted even the most saintly of people in the past. He'd seen what it could do first hand just a few months ago when the prospect of immortality by the wielder of the Hand had turned an upstanding college student into a cold blooded killer.

Still, he couldn't allow the piece to remain on the ocean floor. Unguarded. Unprotected. He'd have to trust her if he hoped to keep the relic safe.

"Do you see that green glowy thing?" he asked her, pointing down to the sand.

She looked down, then back at him. "Glowy?"

"Yes, yes," he said, jerking his index finger in the direction of the illuminated object. "Right there. Green and pulsing with light. How can you miss it?"

Krista cocked her head curiously at him.

"Oh, for grave's sake!" He collapsed to his knees again, swatted away the sand to clear the chunk of stone once more, then brought his finger down to within a half-inch of it. "Right there."

She lowered herself to the sea floor, her entire body just inches above the sand, and peered at the piece. "I see it, but it's not glowing."

Silas blinked, then he banged his hand against the side of his helmet for how dense he'd been. Of course, a mortal unfamiliar with the Nether—to the workings of the Land of the Dead—would be unable to see the power emanating from the object. It was arcane. The illumination outside the scope of the mortal realm. He'd been such a fool.

He smiled at her with a stupid, lopsided grin. "My mistake. Sorry. But yes, that object is what I'm talking about. Could you please retrieve it for me and keep it among your things until we get topside?"

"Is it important? Do you think it has something to do with Lance's death?"

He pursed his lips, mulling the question over. "Absolutely. I think it's most definitely an imperative piece of the puzzle," he said. "Of course, I'd collect it myself, but this blasted suit is ridiculously cumbersome." He held up his thick-fingered gloves. "And naturally, no pockets."

She nodded at him, then picked the object up and placed it in her mesh scuba bag for safekeeping. Satisfied it was safe for now, Silas scrambled back up to his feet with Krista's assistance.

"Thank you, my dear," he said. "Your assistance has been inval..."

He was unable to finish the sentence because his helmet—around the front viewport—had suddenly sprung a leak. At first, it was merely a drop or two, wetting his face. He considered whether it might merely have been sweat, but then he remembered his body was incapable of perspiration, which ruled that theory out right away. Then, sea water began to trickle into his helmet with a bit more force.

"...ah, nutter butter!" he growled. "This is gonna suck."

"Mr. Mot," Krista shouted. "Your helmet!"

"I know, I know!" he shouted, shooing her away with his hand. "Better get back in case this thing goes Death Star on me like it did to Avery."

As if the Universe had perfect comic timing, the space around the helmet's viewport began to simmer and boil. Tiny bubbles erupted outside the copper sphere, followed soon after by larger, more—to Silas' mind anyway—disturbing ones.

Frantically, he scrambled to find the butterfly nuts connecting the helmet to his suit, then realized the task would be impossible since a few were bolted down around the back.

"I take it this wasn't a suit Lance used to discard on the ocean floor?" he asked Krista, who was a considerable distance away now.

She shook her head. "Helmet has mounts around the entire upper torso," she said. "No way to get it off on your own."

So, the helmet was on for good. It was far too dangerous to ask the medic to assist him at this point, or she'd be put far too close to the blast radius. There wasn't much he could do now but dissolve his ectoplasmic body, return to his spirit form, and hope the boiling sea water surrounding him wouldn't send him back to the Land of the Dead with his proverbial tail between his legs.

Silas' eyes drifted from the window's frame, which was now beginning to radiate an intense burning heat, to see Krista still hovering far too close to him despite the distance she'd already put between them.

"Ms. Dunaway, you need to go now!" he shouted. "There's nothing you can do!"

She gave him one last look, then swiveled around and kicked off toward the rest of the crew, who were now all staring in his direction. Once she appeared to be a safe distance away, Silas turned his back on them, hoping that if the fire exploded out through the viewport the way it had Avery, they'd all at least be safe from its heat.

Once he'd positioned himself where he wanted to be, he willed his being to depart from his body.

And nothing happened.

He blinked.

"Okay, this isn't good," he muttered to himself, before closing his eyes, and concentrating on the need to eject from his ectoplasmic shell.

And more nothing continued to happen.

He took a deep breath. The heat from inside his helmet now seemed like a steaming lava pouring down his throat as he inhaled.

"Nope, not good at all."

He suddenly remembered the strange things that had been happening to him lately. The difficulty he'd recently developed in shedding his body. His ravenous hunger just yesterday, and the subsequent upset stomach. These things should not be happening to him, and yet they were. And now, he appeared trapped in his mortal visage, unable to escape entirely.

The question at the moment was why? Why had these problems developed? Was it because his station as Supreme Lord of Death, as Elliot liked to put it, was being challenged?

Was it the Hand of Cain, slowly chipping away at his power with every death it caused? Or was it something else entirely?

All fine questions, Ankou, he thought to himself. *But none helpful at the moment.*

He once more began fidgeting with the nuts bolting down his helmet, frantically struggling to undo as many of them as he could. The heat continued to increase as more water began to pour inside. Then, there was a tiniest flicker of light. Silas Mot stared at it for what seemed to be a millennium. The light flared out, blazing brighter and brighter as it barreled toward his face.

"Ah, crap..."

The flash was blinding, radiating through the confines of the helmet for one finite moment. Then, the visor shattered, and a streak of flame, the color of lilac, shot out into the ocean water for the briefest of seconds. Then faded to nothing but a seltzer-like mist of bubbles and heat.

Silas Mot's dive suit crumpled to the sand like an empty husk.

CHAPTER
EIGHTEEN

SUMMER HAVEN MARINA
SUMMER HAVEN
THURSDAY, 1:15 PM

"I warned him!" Krista Dunaway told Becca Cole during their interview once the crew returned from their calamitous first shoot. "I told him that suit wasn't safe, but he wouldn't listen."

"And my production company can't be held responsible either," Garrett Norris interjected while holding up the liability waiver Silas Mot had signed. "It wasn't our fault. He took full responsibility."

Becca glared at the TV show producer, then looked over at Commander Tanner. "Jeremy, get him out of here. I'm trying to talk to Ms. Dunaway now. I'll get to him in a minute."

She was irked. She hadn't known where Silas Mot had been all morning, but that wasn't new. She'd assumed he was off doing whatever Grim Reapers do when they're not butting their noses into her murder investigations. So imagine her annoyance when, finally getting Alice from the Gilded Grill diner to describe the man arguing with Lance Avery the day before he died—and just after the same waitress had delivered her a plate of her world famous grilled cheese sandwich and fries—she'd gotten the call about the incident that occurred at the site of the shipwreck. About how the same thing that had happened to Lance Avery had just happened to Silas. How after the fire, there had been nothing left but the charred remains of yet another antique dive suit.

He'd been investigating on his own, without her knowledge, and that's what irked her. At this point, she wasn't too concerned about the man himself. After all, he wasn't a 'man' per se. He was Death. The Grim Reaper. An immortal being with no real physical body of his own. She'd seen first hand how he could leave his fabricated form at the blink of an eye, and had seen just how quickly the leftover matter—something he'd called 'ectoplasm'—simply dissolved into nothing after a few minutes. She had no doubt, her friend, even now, was lurking somewhere, constructing a brand new body to annoy the crap out of her with.

Either way, she'd sent Elliot Newman out to search for him, leaving her alone to conduct the investigation into his disappearance.

"Ms. Dunaway, I'm curious." She pushed thoughts of Silas' well-being aside for the moment, and focused again on her interview. "Why were you so sure his suit was going to do the same thing it had to Lance?"

Krista's eyes shifted, and she looked down at her feet. She shrugged when she looked back up at Becca. "I didn't think that. Not really," she said. "Like I told you the first time we talked, I've been..." She paused for a moment. "I *had* been fighting with Lance over those stupid suits ever since he bought them. If he wanted them to be displayed as collectibles, that would be perfectly fine. But they weren't up to any safety code around. They were death traps just waiting to snap."

"And you didn't expect the suits to burst into flames?"

The show's medic threw up her hands in exasperation. "How on earth would anyone expect that? That's not supposed to happen at all. Ever. There's nothing combustible in those suits."

"Except for a healthy portion of potassium."

Krista's eyes widened. "What?"

"It's been confirmed. Traces of potassium hydroxide were discovered in Lance's helmet. It's a byproduct of..."

"Of combusted potassium, yeah. I know." She looked around, eyeing her fellow crew members as if trying to figure something out.

"Ms. Dunaway, do you know something about this?"

She still continued to watch her team, moving from one to the next, while biting down on her lower lip. After a moment, Becca's question seemed to register, and she looked over at her. "Uh, no. Not really. It's just that..."

"What? It's just what?"

"Well, both Lance and Garrett purchased some potassium recently for an experimental dive suit they were working to develop for the show. Really high tech stuff. Miners have been using something called potassium superdioxide in their respirators. It essentially works to store oxygen within the compound, and offers a larger amount of breathable air within their tanks. Lance had been trying to design a new scuba tank from a similar principle, and Garrett was supplying him with the equipment to do it."

Becca glanced over at Garrett, who was now leaning up against the trunk of a squad car looking angry and dismissive. Commander Tanner hovered nearby, keeping a wary eye on the man.

"Okay, good to know," Becca said, still watching the producer from the corner of her eyes. "You're free to go. For now."

Without a second glance, the medic scampered off. Becca turned to look around the marina's parking lot to see who she was going to interview next. After a moment, she smiled, pointed at Derek Drake, and gestured for him to come to her. The show's new host stiffened, glanced around at his fellow crew members, then shuffled over to her without argument.

ANKOU MOT MANOR
FIVE MILES SOUTH OF SUMMER HAVEN
THURSDAY, 1:40 PM

ELLIOT NEWMAN WALKED down the winding brick walkway leading up to the dilapidated Victorian mansion that Silas Mot had purchased just a few months earlier with a sense of intense dread. The twenty-three room home with wraparound porch, two second-floor balconies, and a domed turret at the apex of the east wing seemed to appraise the little man approaching it like a meal it was preparing to scarf down if he got too close.

Truth was, Elliot had never liked this place. Once a prominent funeral parlor in the early 1900s, the house made the Addams' Family home look like the abode of Strawberry Shortcake, and the all-too-real, but intangible presence within had always chilled him to the core. In short, it was haunted, and the entity within had never much cared for Elliot since the moment he first stepped foot inside.

Silas, of course, seemed oblivious to it all, and would tease

Elliot's superstitious fears of ghosts and hauntings as childish. It didn't matter that the Grim Reaper openly conceded to the fact that ghosts and spooks were real, and that they could, indeed, harbor a grudge or dislike for someone. But he argued that they were mostly harmless—especially while in his presence—and there was nothing whatsoever for the archaeologist to worry about while he lived there. Elliot, for his part, had never truly accepted Silas' reassurances. After all, feeling somewhat unholy himself for the undead creature he currently was, it made sense that ghosts—who had no bodies of their own—might feel a little animosity toward him from time to time.

No, Elliot was convinced the house didn't like him much despite what his master Silas Mot said.

Despite that, if Silas had survived the ordeal in his dive suit, this was precisely where he would have come to retake human form. It was his sanctum. His place of refuge. He loved this old, piece of rotten timber and nails more than anything else in the world.

The wooden step up to the porch creaked under the weight of Elliot's shoe. When his feet were firmly planted on the porch, he patted the nearest Corinthian column reassuringly, and looked up at the house.

"Okay House, it's just me," he said. "I'm looking for your master, so no funny business, okay? Just want to make sure he's okay."

He stepped toward the front door, which opened wide like a Venus flytrap waiting for its prey.

"This is serious." He inched closer to the gaping doorway. "Silas might be in trouble. I'm worried about him."

The door remained open and didn't appear to have grown any fangs, claws, or anything else that might slice Elliot to shreds, so he stepped through the threshold while holding his breath. The moment he was through, the door slammed behind him and he exhaled, feeling the tension in his body slacken infinitesimally.

"Shew," he mumbled, moving past the foyer and toward the sprawling staircase. "So far so good." He glanced around. "Okay, where is he, House? Do you know?"

There was a low snarl coming from Elliot's right—from the direction of the dining room. He tensed, trying to decipher the sound and not particularly liking what his brain was telling him. The tension doubled when a second snarl joined the first. He kept his eyes fixed dead ahead, not daring to turn and look into the dining room. He already knew what he would see when he did, and it wasn't going to be a pleasant sight.

"Elliot Newman," came a cold deep voice from the direction of the hounds. The voice itself wasn't as much audible as it was reverberating in his skull. "I have been waiting for you. Come in. I promise, my pets will not harm you."

Elliot turned slowly, readying his legs for a hasty retreat if the need arose, and looked into the dining room. The same two, grossly emaciated hell hounds stared back at him with red glowing eyes, their unnaturally long fangs bared. Behind them was Silas' dining table, cut from walnut with intricately carved reliefs of Celtic geometric patterns, an assortment of lilies, and skulls. The table was large enough to seat twelve people, with room left to spare. Today, only one being occupied it. On the far end, at the foot of the table, a man—if that is what you could call him—dressed in a long flowing black robe sat stiffly in the tall wicker-backed chair. His spine almost perfectly straight. Shoulders squared. The face underneath the hood was obscured by shadows which, because of the lighting in the room, should not have been there. But Elliot could make out the slightest traces of canid features. A long snout, but not quite that of a real dog. It reminded Elliot of what would happen if a human and dog could mix, in fact. His long teeth jutted out unnaturally from his mouth, reinforcing the canine resemblance. To top off the ensemble, he had beady red eyes that glowed in similar fashion to that of the preternatural hounds.

"Are...are you here for me?" Elliot asked, feeling his throat constrict as the words left his lips.

The two hounds looked back at their master, as if anticipating his answer. When the figure offered the slightest shake of his head, the dogs whined, then trotted back to him, taking their seats on each of his flanks.

"No, Elliot Newman," the figure said. "At least, not this day. Your master has made it clear that you are under his sovereignty. Therefore, I will honor that. For now."

Comforted to some extent by this, he stepped into the dining room, then swallowed.

"Then may I ask why you are here?"

The being leaned forward in his seat, resting his elbows onto the table, and casting his red-eyed gaze directly into Elliot, who wanted nothing more than to melt into the floor from their scrutiny.

"My reasons to be here are two-fold, Elliot Newman." The thing's voice, which continued to reverberate inside his head, was unnerving to say the least. "The first is a warning for my brother."

Elliot blinked. "Your brother?"

"Ankou. The great Mot."

"You and Silas are brothers?"

Anubis dipped his head in the affirmative, and Elliot couldn't quite see any family resemblance whatsoever. Especially when it came to their demeanor. Never once had he seen Silas so grave. So sinister. For a moment, he wondered which was the older brother, but decided it was irrelevant.

"What is your warning?" Elliot finally thought to ask.

"The being known to you as Silas Mot has been sanctioned to see the sting of death."

Elliot opened his mouth to respond, then closed it abruptly. He tilted his head slightly as he pondered that bit of news, then opened his mouth again to speak.

"Um, how...how exactly is that supposed to work exactly?" he asked. "Silas is immortal. A spirit. Do you mean his weird ectoplasm body is scheduled to die? 'Cause that's happened quite a few times already. He just always seems to make a new one, and..."

"Silence!"

Elliot's mouth clamped up. He bit down on his lower lip, while his shoulders wilted at Anubis' command.

"Ankou has taken far too long to recover the Hand of Cain," Anubis explained. "Even now, it increases in power, while he decreases. He struggles between the realm of spirit and the realm of life. The incident at the bottom of the sea—the reason for your visit here now—nearly destroyed him already. He will survive this encounter, but not without consequences."

"But how? How could that possibly happen to someone like him?"

"Just as a watch lost in the desert accumulates sand. As each day passes, more and more sand invades the watch, covering the cogs. Clogging the gears. Until eventually, the watch is unable to function as it should. So too is what is happening to my brother Ankou. The sands of mortality have invaded his being. He has partaken of the pleasures of this world in excess. Has tasted one too many fruits of life, and he has changed irreparably because of it." The being known as Anubis stood from his chair, and Elliot marveled at just how tall he was. The top of his hood grazed underneath the twelve foot ceiling with very little room to spare. "Add to this the growing power of the Hand, which exsanguinates him of his own power, and he will become lost! He will cease to exist. His days are now numbered, just like any other mortal being."

Elliot cleared his throat. "But what can we do to stop it?" He suddenly realized the implications for his own continued existence if Silas Mot were to actually die. His un-death would be forfeited as well. "If this is a warning, then there must be a way to stop this from happening, right?"

Anubis reached down to scratch both of his hounds from behind their ears. The dogs looked up at their master, their tongues lolling from their mouths excitedly with each scratch just like any other mutt might.

Finally, the being spoke again. "It all rests on the convening enclave, and the decision that is made."

"You mean, Baron Tombstone's attempt to toss Silas off the throne, don't you?"

Again, Anubis offered an almost imperceptible nod.

"You said there were two reasons for you being here," Elliot said, realizing he would get no more help from Silas' larger, darker brother on the enclave. "What's the second?"

The strange canine-like being stopped petting his hounds, stood to his full height, and folded his arms across his broad chest.

"Seek out Lilith, the Lady of Death," Anubis said. "There you will find your master. Or what is left of him."

Then, in a swirl of black smoke, Anubis and his two starving hounds were gone.

CHAPTER
NINETEEN

SUMMER HAVEN MARINA
SUMMER HAVEN
THURSDAY, 1:41 PM

"So," Becca said, smiling at Derek Drake. "I wanted to have a chat with you again because I don't think you were completely honest with me the first time." She glanced around the marina's parking lot. "And there's no Ilene Nebbles-Fielding around to stop me from fully doing my job this time."

Derek looked back at her with wide round eyes. "I don't have anything to hide. I'll be happy to talk to you about anything you'd like."

Pursing her lips, Becca nodded, then reached into her pocket and retrieved her cell phone. "So let's talk about this." She brought the phone to life, clicked on the 'Photos' icon, followed by the picture of the police sketch Alice provided of the man seen arguing with Lance Avery the day before he died.

"Tell me if I'm wrong, but this looks an awful lot like you, doesn't it?"

He leaned forward, peering into the phone's screen. "Um, what am I looking at here?"

Becca shrugged. "Seems Lance Avery got into a bit of a tiff at the Gilded Grill on Monday." She pointed at the screen. "That's a sketch of the person he was arguing with."

Derek averted his eyes from the screen, and looked at her before nodding with a shrug. "Sure. That's me. And I'd like to point out, I wasn't arguing with him. He was arguing with me."

"Why?"

"Why do you think?" He didn't give her a chance to guess. "Jealousy. Plain and simple. He found out I was Garrett's top choice to replace him if his contract negotiations didn't go through. He thought I was working to sabotage everything. I went to him to try to clear the air, and he lit into me."

"Why would that matter? According to you in our first interview, Lance hardly acknowledged your existence on the team. Hardly gave you the time of day. What did you care what he thought?"

His shoulders sagged for a moment, and he tucked his hands deep into his short pockets. "Doesn't mean I didn't idolize the guy. He was my hero. I wanted to be just like him." Derek sighed. "Last thing I wanted was to take his job, but my aunt kept pushing for it...kept pushing Garrett to make me host. Kept pushing me to accept the offer."

"Your aunt?"

His head slumped, his eyes looked up at her and he blushed. "Ilene. She's my great aunt. It was my connection to the show that got Lance and Laura onboard with coming to Summer Haven to investigate the shipwreck to begin with. Garrett didn't want anything to do with it. Said the wreck was already too well-documented, and that it wouldn't make for good TV. But as you know, my aunt doesn't take no for an answer, so she eventually got him to agree to come here anyway."

Becca struggled to keep a neutral face over this revelation. She'd had no idea that Ilene had been intimately connected to the show through a nephew, which made her constant interference in the investigation even more suspect than it already was. The question was, why did she care so much about *The Lord's Vengeance*? Given the community's disinterest in tourism or publicity of any kind, the old woman's public explanation had never quite sat well with Becca. In fact, it had never sat well with most of the citizens in town, causing a great deal of flack for the most powerful woman in Summer Haven.

Could Silas be right? Does Ilene have the Hand of Cain? Unconsciously, she shook her head at the thought. *But that doesn't make sense. If she has it already, why the need to investigate Baron Tombstone's sunken pirate ship? The Hand, after all, is its most notorious treasure.*

"I'm curious, Derek, has your aunt talked to you about any possible artifacts you might find down there?" Becca asked. "Has she specifically told you to be on the lookout for anything of particular interest to her?"

He cocked his head in thought, his eyes squinting as he did so, then he shook his head. "Not that I recall, no. She just seems mildly interested in the ship as a whole. Hasn't mentioned anything specific at all."

As he spoke, Becca watched him carefully. Watched his eyes, which kept shifting downward and to the left. Watched his hands, which fidgeted in and out of his shorts' pockets. His feet, which couldn't quite seem to find a comfortable spot on which to stand. All signs he was being dishonest with her about something. She made a mental note to take a closer look at Derek and his activities in the future.

After a few more questions, Becca released the show's new host, and called in her next witness, Kevin Aker. She hadn't yet been able to talk with the show's sound engineer, and while there'd been nothing in her cursory research on him to suggest anything sinister in his past, he had certainly seemed passionate about Derek's promotion to host so soon after Lance's death. She couldn't help wonder if he had his own aspirations toward hosting duties.

For his part, Kevin was certainly handsome enough to stand in front of the camera as opposed to holding a boom mic over the star's head for hours on end. He was tall, though of average build, with a mop top of unkempt black hair and a neatly trimmed mustache which was topped off by a soul patch under his lower lip. His face was long and lean with cheekbones that could easily slice through a block of ice if given the chance.

Seemingly unfazed by talking to her, he casually leaned back on the trunk of her patrol car with his legs crossed near his ankles and his long arms crossed over his chest.

After a few perfunctory comments to the man, Becca dove straight into the interview.

"So my background check on you said you and Lance went to college together," she began. "I take it you were close?"

"Not just him. All three of us went to school together."

"Three?"

"Yeah, me, Lance, and Laura. We all met at the University of Miami," he said. "And we all became best friends there. Have been ever since, so yeah...we were pretty close."

"So his death hit you pretty hard, huh?"

Kevin straightened up at this question, pulling himself off the trunk of her car, and squaring off at her. "What kind of stupid question is that? He was my best friend!" He was shouting, catching the attention of Commander Tanner and two other officers. Becca watched as they slowly started moving toward her, but she held up a hand to them in a silent statement that she was fine.

"I'm sorry," she said, understanding that antagonizing him wasn't the right move for now. His actions against Derek yesterday were proof the guy was a bit of a hothead. So, a different tack was needed. "That was insensitive of me. But I'm assuming you're still close to his wife, Laura?"

He visibly relaxed, then nodded. "Yeah, we've stayed pretty tight."

"Even despite their marriage problems?"

Surprisingly, he laughed at the question. "If I had to stop being friends with one of them every time they were having problems, I would have lost both of them back in college. Those two have never seen eye to eye on anything." He looked up into the blue sky as if reflecting on a string of memories. "You've heard that opposites attract? Well, they're a walking example. When they work, they're amazing together. But when they don't..." He paused. "...well, you better hope you're not in the blast radius. I learned a long time ago to play Switzerland when it came to them."

"Why'd they stay together? If they were that volatile, why go through that over and over again?"

"I'm surprised you didn't ask Laura that yourself."

"I did. Now I'm asking you."

He seemed to think about that for a moment, then shrugged. "Well, I'm sure her answer to your question seemed pretty pragmatic. Something about how she couldn't divorce him without risking her own career or something like that."

"Almost precisely."

"Well, what she doesn't want anyone to know...the big bad

secret of everything...was that those two were crazy about each other. They were like water and vinegar, except there was no way to separate them. They were bound together for life, no matter what anyone said or did to convince them otherwise."

"Even despite Lance's cheating?"

He laughed again. "Don't let her fool you, Chief. That woman doesn't take her marriage vows any more scared than Lance. Trust me on that."

She asked a few more questions of him. He seemed open. Honest. Relaxed. Then a thought sprang to mind.

"Since you were so close to Lance, maybe you can help me with something," she said. "The day before he died, he came to me. Wanted a moment to talk to me privately about something."

Kevin laughed. "Oh, I bet he did." He looked her up and down. "You're exactly his type, I'd say. Hot and smart."

She blushed at the comment, focused more on the 'smart' part than her looks, but shook her head. "No, he definitely hit on me," she said. "But when I turned him down, he still insisted on talking with me about something. It sounded important. Official. Any idea what he might have wanted to discuss?"

He thought about it for a moment, then shrugged. "Well, come to think of it, there *was* something going on with him lately." The sound man looked around, checking to see if anyone was within earshot, then leaned in to her. "Lance had recently gotten himself in some hot water. I don't know the deets, but way I hear it, he'd been dealing in some black market antiquities garbage. Stuff he might have stolen from some of our shows and smuggled out of the country. Last I heard—not from him, mind you. He refused to talk to me about this stuff—was that the cops from various other countries were onto him, and he was considering turning himself in."

"And how would that affect the show and his contract, do you think?"

Kevin shrugged. "That's a question to ask Garrett or Laura, I'd say. I really don't have a clue." He paused, looking over at Garrett Norris with narrowed eyes. "But I heard Lance and Garrett arguing about it several times in the last few weeks, I can tell you that. Dude was P.O.ed at Lance about his little crime spree and the danger it put the whole show in. Ask me, that's one of the reasons Garrett wanted to give him the boot so bad, and slap that weasel Derek in his place."

Becca jotted a few notes down in her notepad, then released him before searching for the next person to interview. She was just about ready to call Garrett Norris himself over when a long black town car rolled into the gravel lot, and parked. A moment later, a chauffeur scrambled out of the front seat, opened the door to the back, and a scowling Ilene Nebbles-Fielding slithered out of the car with murder in her eyes.

CHAPTER
TWENTY

U-STORE-IT
GRUENWALD COMMONS
THURSDAY, 3:45 PM

E lliot pulled his little Volkswagen Beetle into the gravel parking lot of the dilapidated old self-storage facility off Wilkshire Boulevard, cut off the engine, and shuddered. If there was any place on earth he hated more than Silas' mansion home, it was the gang-run industrial district of Gruenwald Commons, and the creature that called U-Store-It home.

After all, she was the being that had planted a kiss on him just before he'd stepped back into oncoming traffic to be struck and killed by a tour bus bound for Daytona. And the gang inside—*Los Cuernos del Diablo,* or 'The Devil's Horns'— protected her with the fanatical lunacy of zealots. The fact that they were part of a notorious drug cartel didn't help matters either.

But Anubis had told Elliot to find 'Lilith, the Lady of Death', and no one fit that bill more than *Nuestra Señora de la Santa Muerte*, or simply Santa Muerta for short. Otherwise known as Esperanza, Silas Mot's beautiful and deadly ex-wife.

Taking a deep breath, he turned toward the abandoned building that had once acted as the storage facility's business office. The building itself seemed to be barely standing as it canted ever so slightly to the right. The windows had long since been shattered and now were boarded up. A myriad of graffiti and gang tags were displayed prominently over the entire façade, at least in the places not completely overrun with vines and creepers.

Steeling himself for what lay ahead, he shuffled over the gravel to the front entrance. Expecting it to be locked, he was surprised to find that the door swung freely when he gave it the slightest pull, and he walked inside while repeating to himself that he was already very much dead and there was little to nothing a gang of cutthroats could do to change that. The mantra emboldened him, and he stepped deeper into what had once been the front office. With the windows boarded up, there was very little light within, and the few streams of sunlight that made it past the cracks in the plywood provided dust-moat filled beams wherever he looked.

Once he was satisfied he was far enough in, he cleared his throat. "Hello?" he shouted. "I know you're here and I know you're aware of my presence. I'm here to see your mistress!"

There was a long moment of nothing but mostly silence. Perhaps the patter of tiny mice feet scurrying away at the sound of his voice. A kerplunk or two of water droplets falling from somewhere within the interior of the building. But other than that, nothing more.

"I really..." His voice squeaked an octave higher than normal. He cleared his throat again and continued. "I really must insist upon seeing the Lady of Death." He stiffened his spine, clenched his fist, and added, "Now."

For a few long moments, there was nothing. For all intents and purposes, it felt to Elliot like he was the only man left on the entire planet. If he still had a heartbeat, he was certain it would be thumping against his eardrums by now.

Then someone behind him spoke.

"You are pretty brave for a mere minion of *mi esposo*, aren't you, *nino*?"

Elliot wheeled around toward the front door and his blood ran cold. She was every bit as lovely as the day she'd planted an open-mouthed kiss on him that had sent him to his doom. Long curly black hair that cascaded down her back. Darkened skin, as smooth as almond milk. Emerald green eyes that burned with a strange mixture of rage and sensuality, and thick pouty lips that even now curled up one side of her face in a condescending smile.

"Your master's not here to protect you," she said. "It was unwise of you—the man Ankou stole from my coffers—to come here."

"I...uh...was told to come see you," he stammered, taking a step back from her. When he did so, he bumped into something big and sturdy. He craned his head around to see a large black man glaring down at him with a scowl, an AK-47 clutched in one hand and gang tattoos running up and down his arm. Two more goons, equally as muscled and equally armed, stood a few paces back. Elliot had heard none of them enter the office space.

This brought Esperanza up short, and she stiffened.

"Really? I have it on good authority that my husband is... unavailable at the moment," she cooed. "Who would dare send you to me?"

Elliot gave a couple of quick looks over his shoulders, then back at the Mistress of Death. "Uh, well...it's kind of long story, but I was searching for Silas and..."

"Who sent you?"

"Anubis. Anubis told me that you would know where Silas was. That he was injured, and that I would find him with you."

If he'd thought Silas' ex was tense before, she pretty much fell into rigor mortis at the mention of the bounty hunter's name. Now it was her turn to look over her shoulders. She fidgeted slightly from foot to foot, before scrambling over to the entrance, and peering out the door as if fearful of some supernatural police raid.

"And you came here?" She wheeled around, and her eyes now glowed with a blazing green fury Elliot had never seen before. "You fool!" She bolted past him, heading toward the back of the building. "Bring him! We haven't a moment to lose!"

The goons grabbed Elliot by the arms and began dragging him to the back without a word. His feet dragged the floor behind him, as they walked past a chamber containing hundreds of lit candles surrounding a large statue of what, to most people, resembled the western ideals of the Grim Reaper. As an archaeologist, however, Elliot recognized the globe in the statue's hand and knew that he was now looking at a representation of Santa Muerta, the female patron saint of death to the people of Central and South America.

Of course, he didn't have time to study the statue any further as the gangbangers continued to drag him away and into a long winding tunnel leading down into the earth itself. Soon, they found themselves in front of a set of large double doors surrounded by two armed guards. At Esperanza's appearance, the guards opened the door, and they strode into a vast underground warehouse. The walls were made of rusted corrugated metal with seven sheets teetering dangerously close to falling completely off. Twelve heavy duty pylons acted as columns, supporting the roof that stretched nearly twenty-five feet above them. In the center of the room, surrounded by several lit candles sat an ornate throne that, from what Elliot had been told, was intended for one of the scariest men in all of Florida...Omo Sango, the *Babalowa* of Santeria and servant of one of the most tyrannical of *Orisha* gods among his religion's pantheon, Sango.

Today, however, it wasn't Omo Sango who sat in the ornate chair. Elliot could discern that easy enough as all accounts of the Babalowa was that he was also one of the fattest men in all of Florida as well. The man sitting on the throne today, although shrouded in a black cloak similar to that of Anubis', was extremely thin. Tall. Well-built. The man, who's head was covered by a hood, leaned back in the throne, one leg cast up on the armrest in a relaxed repose.

Elliot was dragged directly in front of the throne, and dropped just outside the circle of candles. The cloaked figure's head turned to the smaller man, then over at Esperanza.

"My dear minion." His voice was low, little more than a harsh whisper. It sounded weak. Pained. But Elliot knew it nonetheless.

"S-Silas?" He tried to peer under the hood, but could see nothing. "Is that you?"

In answer to his question, the man reached inside his cloak and withdrew a bright red strip of Twizzler before popping the cord in the shadows of his hood, roughly where his mouth would be. Elliot gasped at the sight of the licorice-wielding hand. It was blackened. Charred nearly beyond recognition.

"Silas, what happened to you?"

The cloaked figure twirled his burned hand, and the string

of licorice, in the air with a nonchalance that only his master would attempt over his own disfigurement.

"Life!" Silas chuckled at this, then doubled over in the throne as if wracked with terrible pain. "Life happened to me, my friend. Seems where Man is unable to escape the clutches of Death, I am destined to be snared by my opposite."

Esperanza rolled her eyes at this before moving over to Silas Mot's throne and wrapping an arm around his shoulder. She looked at Elliot.

"He's been like this ever since attempting—and failing miserably, I might add—to reassemble his body. He's become a regular pity party as you mortals say."

Silas threw her arms off his shoulders, and bolted up in his seat. "And do I not deserve to revel in my misery? I am hedonistic to the core. Is it unfitting of me to embrace the misfortunes of life as much as the pleasures?" He turned to look at Elliot. "Would you not wallow in misery if you looked like this?"

He pulled back his cloak's hood to reveal his face for all to see. The first thing that struck Elliot, after the initial shock began to wear off, was just how similar Silas now looked to, not his old self, but rather, *Mysterious Expedition*'s late host, Lance Avery. Complete with sandy blonde hair, as opposed to his customary ebony mane. The second thing he noticed was that he looked like Avery as he'd appeared on the autopsy tray at the medical examiner's office yesterday.

His face, like his hands, were charred. One eyelid had been burned away revealing a pinkish eye with cloudy, cataract-filled iris and pupil. The skin of one side of his face had burned away completely, leaving only strands of tendon and muscle, and the right side of his lower jaw and teeth fully visible.

Elliot brought a hand up to his mouth. "Oh Silas."

"Exactly!" Silas roared, whirling around manically in the

abandoned warehouse. "'Oh Silas', is exactly the correct response! Try as I might, minion, I am unable to reconstruct my body as I formerly knew it. Try as I might...every single attempt I've made...I resolve into this!" He laughed. To Elliot, it was a desperate, angst-filled laugh. "Worst of all, I can no longer seem to shed my body at all. Can no longer seem to return to the spirit form in which I thrive!"

"The warning," Elliot said, but it was barely a whisper.

"I'm sorry, what?" Silas asked, stalking closer to him. Elliot involuntarily cringed at his approach, something he'd never even considered doing before. It was something he never felt the need to do before since Silas' typical jovial and bombastic personality precluded any sense of real dread. At least, to his friends anyway.

"I said, it's like the warning..."

"Warning?"

"From Anubis."

Silas' charred jaw clenched tight, then he wheeled around to Esperanza for an explanation.

"That's why I brought him here immediately, *mi esposo*. I'm afraid your simpleton pet has led your brother right to us."

"No, no," Elliot said, shaking his head. "Anubis was trying to help. He knew I was looking for you after the incident down at *The Lord's Vengeance*. He said I'd find you with her." He pointed at Esperanza.

Silas spun back around to face Elliot. "And this warning?"

"He said you were in danger. Said that, because of your lust for Life and the growing power of the Hand of Cain, you were becoming mortal, and that you were now destined to die just like any other mortal."

Silas glanced over at Esperanza. "The Enclave. It has already begun."

"That's impossible," she said. "I would have been

informed. I have a seat on the council. They surely would not have excluded me."

"Nonetheless, the Enclave is convening, and my brother seeks to apprehend me for my trial."

CHAPTER
TWENTY-ONE

SUMMER HAVEN MARINA
SUMMER HAVEN
THURSDAY, 2:14 PM

"I warned you about continuing your investigation in this, Ms. Cole," Ilene spat, while getting dangerous close to using her gnarled index finger to poke her in the chest. "This is it! You're through here. I will have your badge. I will have you run out of town! I will..."

Becca held up a folder in one hand, and her cell phone with a sketch of her nephew in the other, bringing the old woman's tirade to a screeching halt.

"First of all, I'm *Chief* Cole. I shouldn't have to remind you of that again." She nodded to the folder. "Know what that is?"

Ilene Nebbles-Fielding bit down on her lip angrily, and shook her head.

"That is a report from the medical examiner." She could hardly contain the smile on her face as she spoke. "It's a chemical analysis of what was found on Lance Avery's helmet.

157

Potassium hydroxide. The residual debris remaining from when pure potassium is burned up. A metal, by the way, not found in dive gear...making Lance Avery's death not accidental. Ergo, it's looking more and more like murder. Which means, I have every right to be investigating this as I see fit." She waved the folder in the air a bit. "It also contains a letter from the attorney general stating I can proceed as well."

The old woman raged silently before her, but Becca wasn't about to let up now. This was vindication a long time coming, and she was going to savor it as best she could.

"Know what this is?" She shook her cell phone with the police sketch of Derek Rosenbaum, now legally 'Derek Drake'. She watched as Ilene swallowed, but refused to answer. "Seems your nephew..." She paused, waiting for the old woman's reaction. She wasn't disappointed. At the mention of the word 'nephew', her eyes snapped away from the phone screen and directly at her. "...had himself a heated argument with Lance Avery the day before he died in the Gilded Grill Diner. Lots of witnesses. Almost came to blows. Words were said. Loud, angry words." Becca slipped the phone back into her pocket. "Any idea what their argument might have been about, Mrs. Fielding?"

"Are you accusing my nephew of something, *Chief* Cole?" Her use of the word 'chief' was laced with venom.

"Not yet. But I'm questioning you now, aren't I? Not him."

The old woman's brows buckled, waving along her forehead like two rearing vipers. "Me? You're accusing me?"

Becca shrugged. "Not enough evidence to accuse anyone just yet. I'm just trying to get a sense for everyone's place in this drama. And I'm curious...why were you so bent on getting the *Mysterious Expedition* show to come here? The state of Florida has a number of archaeological teams at their disposal. Heck, the city of St. Augustine has a full time archaeologist who would love to come and excavate a sunken pirate ship. So why have a circus come to town? Why put on a show? What's in it for you?"

Ilene mumbled something coarse and offensive, but it came out as little more than a low growl.

"I'm sorry," Becca said. "What was that?"

"I don't have to answer these questions. You're harassing me and I won't stand for it."

"Mrs. Fielding, we can discuss this openly, here and now, or I can have you escorted to the police station. You'd be free to request your attorney to be present, if you'd like, but I'm well within my right to ask you this." Becca leaned in closer to the old woman, turning her head conspiratorially as if waiting for her to whisper the answer in her ear. "So, what's your game in all this? Really?"

The old woman sighed. "My position on that has been on record since day one, Chief Cole. I hope that the public display of the ship's excavation will put our quaint little town on the map and reinvigorate our economy."

"Even though most residents in town are against this?"

"Even so. This is what is best for Summer Haven. That's the only thing I care about."

"Uh-huh. And what about any treasure they happen to find?"

Ilene scoffed. "Any artifacts of significance have more than likely already been absconded with by would-be treasure hunters over the years," she hissed. "But I've already assured the state that if anything is found, we'll gladly hand it over to them for study, and then allow them to place it in museums of their choice. I have no financial vestment in this whatsoever."

Becca eyed her warily. Although she didn't feel like Ilene was outright lying to her, she couldn't help but think she wasn't telling her everything either. The old crone was holding something back, and she was pretty sure it had something to do with her pushing for her nephew to become the new host of the show.

"Fine," she said, offering a friendly wave at the old woman. "You're free to go. For now. But if I have any further questions..."

"I'll direct you to my attorney," Ilene said, turning away and stalking toward her idling car. "Good day."

SUMMER HAVE POLICE DEPARTMENT
SUMMER HAVEN
THURSDAY, 3:56 PM

"Argh!" Becca plopped down in her desk chair, wishing she had more time in the day. She had several phone calls to make, and knew that a number of places she'd planned to call would be closing up in the next few minutes. On top of it all, she hadn't seen Silas all day, and now Elliot was M.I.A. as well.

She leaned forward, and pressed the receptionist button on her phone.

"What is it, Chief?"

"Linda, have you finished with your research into Lance Avery yet?"

She heard a shuffled of papers on the other end of the phone. "Yep. Just finished the background check with NCIC. Just a sec."

The phone clicked, and a moment later, there was a soft tap at her door. The door opened, and Linda walked in waving the folder with a thick sheaf of papers inside. "Here ya go, boss."

She handed the folder to Becca, and made her way out the door. "Hope it helps!"

"Thanks!" she shouted in reply, hoping for the same thing. At the moment, they had a whole lot of nothing. Plenty of suspects. A few oddities. But so far, no clear motive for why Avery was killed, unless it had something to do with the antiquities thefts Kevin told her about. But she didn't know enough about that at the moment to do her any good. And without a motive, finding the culprit would be like finding a needle in a haystack.

With the folder firmly planted on her desk, she picked up her phone and dialed a number by heart.

"State Attorney's Office. This is Donna," said a friendly voice over the phone. "How can I help you?"

"Donna, it's Becca."

"Becca! Great to hear from you. From what I've seen on the news, you have a humdinger of a case up there."

"It's something alright." Becca forced herself to laugh, despite not feeling exceptionally jovial, or chatty for that matter. But the best way, she knew, to get in good with Donna McNichol, the state attorney's office manager, was to dish on the latest gossip. "A real head scratcher, I can tell you."

The two discussed the case for a few minutes—as much as Becca felt comfortable with anyway—and when she felt she'd managed enough 'girl talk' with the sweet, but talkative woman, turned her attention to the reason for the call.

"Is he still in?" she asked.

There was a pause. "...Uh, I'm not sure. Hold on." When Donna's voice was replaced by the shrill sound of electronic Muzak, Becca turned open the file Linda had placed on her desk, and started thumbing through the pages. A moment later, Donna picked up the phone again. "Mr. Henry was just about to leave, but he said he's always up for taking your calls."

Becca laughed. "I guarantee he won't after today. Thanks, Donna. Put me through."

She waited as Donna transferred the call. It was answered by Assistant State Attorney Gavin Henry before the first ring could even finish.

"Becca!" Gaven said. "Good to hear from you again. I take it you got the Attorney General to see things your way finally?"

"Yep. We're back on track. Ilene wasn't happy about it, as you can imagine."

"Ilene Nebbles-Fielding needs to be taken down a notch or two. It'll do her some good, I think."

Becca squeezed the phone receiver tight in her hand, and fidgeted nervously in her seat. She cleared her throat. "Well, I'm glad you feel that way, 'cause that's kind of what I'm calling you about."

There was an audible intake of breath from the other end. "What? What are you about to ask me?" He no longer sounded happy to hear from her, which is precisely as she predicted.

"My investigation is pointing me in her direction."

"No, nope...no. No. No. Uh-uh."

"Oh, come on, Gavin. You just said..."

"I know what I just said. I said it the same way a kid tells the bully down the street that 'my dad can beat up your dad.' You never expect to be called out on something like that. It's like an election promise."

"Says the political official with plans to run for State Attorney some day."

"Exactly! We can't be trusted. The entire lot of us."

She smiled at this. Despite Gavin Henry's protests, of all the assistant state attorneys within the Circuit 7 office, he was the one with the most backbone. It was one of the reasons she'd forged a pretty good friendship with the guy over the last couple of years.

A second later, he proved her assessment of him when he let out a deep sigh. "What do you need?"

"I need to look into Ilene's financials." She was still flipping the pages in the background material on Lance Avery, and came to an abrupt stop. "Well, I'll be..."

"You'll be in hot water if you don't have a good reason to be poking around in that woman's money."

She lifted the paper up for a closer look, ignoring her friend's snarky comment. She'd just discovered something mighty interesting on the dead host, coming from INTERPOL, no less.

"Becca, you still there?" Gaven's voice brought her back to reality.

"Oh, yeah. Sorry." She could hardly pull her eyes away from the page she'd been reading. "I need to check into her financials to look for connections. She brought this television crew to Summer Haven for a reason, and I don't think she's being honest with why. I want to know what she's been spending her money on lately."

"Geez, I don't know. It's going to be hard to convince a judge to grant a warrant for that without some good reasons. Just because you have a hunch isn't good enough." He let out an audible sigh. "Give me something. Anything to connect her to something shady, and I'll get you that warrant quick as a whip."

Becca nodded in response, knowing full well Gavin couldn't see. "Thanks. I'll get you something in the next day or so. Thanks again."

"No problemo. Talk to you soon."

The phone went dead, leaving Becca a brief respite to fully study the report from INTERPOL. If what she was reading was true, it threw a whole different light on the *Mysterious Expedition*, and what Kevin had told her about his criminal activity abroad. It was, in fact, a clear answer to her question about motive. Most importantly, it gave her a clear direction in which to take their investigation.

"Now, if I can just find my two partners, we'll be in business."

She turned to her computer, searching the Internet for INTERPOL's website, then picked up her phone to make another call.

CHAPTER
TWENTY-TWO

"Are you sure this is such a good idea?" Elliot asked Silas while pressing the accelerator to his VW down as far as it would go. "I mean, we're kind of like sitting ducks out here in the open like this, aren't we?"

Silas, still concealed in the immense fabric of his ebony cloak, peered at the speedometer, and tapped his fingers impatiently on the door panel. "Can't this contraption go any faster?"

Elliot shook his head. "It needs a tune-up. The timing's all out of whack. But you didn't answer my question. Going to your house? Anubis obviously knows where you live, and doesn't have any qualms about making himself at home there. I mean, the dude was just sitting at your dining table like he was king of the freakin' ball or something."

Silas chuckled at this. "Ah, my dear brother to a 'T', I'd say.

165

Never could read the room and tell when he was unwelcome." He rolled down the passenger window, hung his burned arm out it, and glanced up at the bright blue sky overhead. "But for now, Ankou Mot Manor is the safest place for us to be. At least until I'm able to...*ahem*...pull myself together, as it were."

He looked over at his minion, and smiled. While Esperanza had been furious with the little man for potentially leading the bounty hunter directly to her doorstep—had practically wanted to flay the skin off his bones as a result—Silas couldn't help but be even more pleased with his choice for confidant and, as crude as it sounded, servant. *Perhaps amanuensis would be a nobler term?* He shook his head at the thought. It was far more enjoyable teasing Elliot about being his minion than to do something like that. But truth was, despite the fact that Elliot was a milquetoast male of the uber-beta variety, he had marched himself right into the thick of *Los Cuernos del Diablos'* main headquarters as quick as you please, demanding to see him.

Now that was loyalty a *Supreme Lord of Death* just couldn't buy.

"Do you have your cell phone handy, Elliot?"

The little man nodded, reached into his shirt pocket, and pulled it out.

"Good. Be a sport and call Becca. Let her know we're..." His voice almost caught on this next word. "...fine, and we'll reconnect with her tomorrow. Try to find out if there's anything new to the case we need to know."

Elliot eyed him. "You don't want to talk to her yourself?"

He shook his head solemnly, and returned his gaze out the car window. Truth was, at the moment, he couldn't bear the thought of either seeing or talking with the police chief until he resolved the issues he was currently dealing with. His loss of control over being able to leave his body at a whim. His current appearance and disfigurement. His strange devolvement into mortality. It was all so much to take right now.

As he'd feared, the rushing sea water filling his dive suit earlier that morning had played havoc with his essence, ripping his ectoplasmic body to shreds before the suit even had time to catch fire. The flame never touched him. All of this—this new charred body resembling that of Lance Avery—had been because of the flow of water disrupting the spiritual energies of the cosmos. One minute, he'd been in the suit, fully aware that his helmet was beginning to smolder. The next, he was ripped from the mortal world in a blinding flash, amid agonizing pain, and found himself for the briefest of moments, in the presence of...

He shuddered involuntarily at the thought. That meeting had not been an unpleasant one, mind you. For someone like him, never destined to stand before that great Throne, it had been a strange blend of perfect peace and terrible fear. Perfect calm, while at the same time, complete shame. Contentment at his very core, yet longing for more. He had not wanted to return, and yet, he knew he couldn't stay without being utterly destroyed.

For the life of him, Silas couldn't remember any specifics of the encounter other than those few dichotomous emotions. Couldn't even begin to recall the things that were said. But he knew with certain clarity that he was on the right path. That despite the Enclave's misgivings into the reasons he'd sequestered himself here among the mortals, he was precisely where he was supposed to be.

Now, if only he could understand the reason for his current appearance...that would make his day complete.

"Alright, Becca," Elliot was saying when Silas' mind drifted back to the here and now. "We'll see you then." The little man turned to look at him. "She has some news for us. Big news. She's coming over."

"No! She can't!"

Elliot kept his eyes fixed on the road, as he navigated the path to the ancient manor he'd recently begun to call home. "Too bad. She's coming. She wouldn't take no for answer." He flicked on his turn signals, and began driving down the long winding dirt road lined on both sides with palmetto bushes and lush vegetation. Soon, the old Queen Anne Victorian loomed into view, its cracking wood siding begging for a fresh coat of paint and an appearance on *Extreme Makeover: Home Edition.*

But Silas had no time to worry about that at the moment.

He sighed, wrapping his cloak tighter around him as the Beetle pulled up to the front of the house. Elliot leapt from the car, scrambled to the passenger side door, and opened it. Silas slid from the car without a word, and limped up the front porch. The house's door opened for him instantly, and he stalked through it, moved to his left, and into the old comfortable parlor. He plopped down into his Chestfield high back reading chair, and kicked his feet up on an ottoman with a languid sigh.

A few moments later, Elliot scrambled into view. "Can I get you something? You know, to help you feel better."

Silas held up his hand, palm up, and scrutinized its charcoal-like hide. He concentrated on it for a moment, drawing energy from the Nether to conjure up a Death on a Beach, but nothing happened. He sighed again, this time offering the slightest trace of a growl. "A beverage, please," he said. "You know the kind."

Elliot nodded, and scurried from sight, leaving Silas alone with his thoughts. He'd never felt so powerless before. So injured. Scarred, and alone. The melancholy he was currently feeling was more alien to him than anything he'd endured in centuries. It was so unlike him to be this way, and yet, how else could he react? His entire existence was in jeopardy. There was a conspiracy to usurp his throne, a concerted effort by the other psychopomps of the cosmos to drive him from his station. His powers were weakened, if not altogether stripped from him. He was now detached completely from the Netherworld, unable to connect with the other reapers under his charge or to glean the knowledge that only the world of the spirit provides. And all the while, he was stuck in this hideous and deformed body, unable to leave it behind save for the way all mortals leave their bodies behind —to die.

He belted out a single, derisive laugh at the cruelty of the universe, and sunk deeper into his reading chair with a moan. As he did so, something shifted within the pockets of his cloak, and fell to the floor with a thud. He glanced down to see a bright red yo-yo lying near the clawed feet of the ottoman.

Silas stared at the toy a moment, narrowing its eyes at the infernal contraption. It was the very reason for his current dilemma. It, as well as Deaths on a Beach, comic books, television, and all the joys and wonders of the World of the Living. Besides the waxing power of the Hand of Cain, it was also his amorous affections for such things that had bound him to the mortal world. That stripped him of his powers, if not wits altogether. It was the curse of Life...

He shifted in his seat, bent over, and picked the device up, feeling the smooth round plastic in the palm of his hand. With his other hand, he carefully uncoiled some of the string, and unconsciously slipped the hoop over his finger before slowly whipping it though the air with a flick of his wrist. A slow smile began to form on the unblemished side of his face. He forced the thoughts of the exposed jaw and teeth on the other side, as well as his cataract-filled eyes, away for the moment, and allowed himself to enjoy the yo-yo's challenge.

By the time Elliot returned with the tall umbrella-laden glass, Silas was in much better spirits, performing a near perfect Eiffel Tower yo-yo trick while leaning comfortably back in his chair. His minion carefully set the drink on the end table beside his master, then disappeared from the room without a word.

ANKOU MOT MANOR
THURSDAY, 7:34 PM

BECCA WASN'T sure what to expect when she walked up to Silas' door and knocked. From the way Elliot had described Silas' current condition, things sounded bleak. He hadn't told her much over the phone, which only made her trepidation grow during the course of the drive over. She couldn't imagine anything happening to the Grim Reaper of any real significance. After all, he was an immortal spirit being. Seriously, what could possibly happen to someone like that of any real consequence? And yet, Elliot had sounded so grave over the phone.

She tensed when the door swung open, and Elliot greeted her with a dour expression on his face. "Glad you're here, Becca," he whispered, gesturing for her to come inside. "Just so you know, he didn't want you to come. Didn't want you to see him like this."

"What's going on, Elliot? What's wrong?"

He shifted his shoulder a bit, drawing his head to one side as if struggling with how to answer her question. "Better for you to see for yourself. Better to let him tell you." He took a single step toward the parlor, then stopped. "Oh, one more thing." Elliot looked up at the ceiling, then around the foyer. "The House has been a little out of sorts lately too. It doesn't like what's happened to Silas at all, and it's been kind of acting out."

"Acting out?" Becca blinked. "But it's just a hou..."

The door slammed behind her, and she spun around, hand on the hilt of her gun. Elliot gestured to the door. "Yeah, expect more of that." Then, he shouted up into the ceiling. "It's being mighty rude today!"

There was a creak of straining timber, then a low moan from somewhere in the bowels of the house. Something upstairs crashed with the sound of broken glass.

"And that mirror was expensive!" he yelled again.

This was only the second time Becca had stepped foot in the old mansion. Elliot had warned her in the past of its haunted status, but she'd just laughed him off. Now, she wasn't so certain.

"Good to know about the house," she said, trying to swallow past the lump in her throat. "Now, take me to Silas."

He gestured for her to follow, and directed her toward the parlor. There were thick velvet drapes covering the doorway, and hindering her view from inside.

"He insists on keeping the lights dim for now," Elliot explained. "He seems to be in a bit better spirits, but...well, you'll understand soon enough."

He reached to one drape panel, and pushed it back for her to enter the room. She squinted, trying to adjust to the dim light.

"I'll be right out here," Elliot said before closing the curtains behind her.

Becca glanced around, trying to get her bearings in the darkness.

"Silas? Are you there?"

There was an odd sound just off to her left. A familiar sound of a yo-yo whirring through the air, and she turned in its direction. Her eyesight now adjusted better, she could make out the form of a man covered in a cloak and hood seated in an antique Victorian-era leather chair, a yo-yo spinning from his fingers. In all the time she'd known Silas Mot, she'd never once seen him dressed in the stereotypical Grim Reaper attire. In fact, he'd always scoffed at the very notion of the medieval depiction of him and his cohorts. Even in spirit form, he'd appeared as little more than a foreboding cloud of shadow, more than what the legends said he should look like.

And yet now, here he was, shrouded in a cloak of black velvet.

"Silas? What's going on? What happened to you?"

"Oh," he said, "a little of this...a little of that. Nothing much. Just the potential end of me as I know it."

She rolled her eyes. "That's not an answer. I can't help you unless you tell me what's going on."

The yo-yo suddenly ceased it's erratic movements, and disappeared into the folds of the cloak. Then, the enigmatic figure of Silas Mot stood from his chair, and glided over to her. He moved with such intensity, such determination, her hand instinctively went for her gun. But he stopped before she felt the need to draw it.

"Answers, you seek," he said. She couldn't tell if she heard a faint trace of Silas' old smile in his words or not. "Answers, you'll get."

Then, he proceeded to tell her everything. He told her about his investigation at the shipwreck and the subsequent near catastrophic conflagration that threatened his unnatural life. Of his inability to shed his fabricated body, and his strange encounter with a being that Becca could only assume was God. And then he told her how he'd returned to the mortal world in the disfigured mess she now saw before her, of course, without actually showing her the disfigurement he was alluding to. Finally, he explained how Anubis was currently seeking him out to take into custody to face the Enclave, and the trumped-up charges they were about to levy against him.

"And after all this," he added, "I'm nowhere closer to knowing who killed Lance Avery, how it was connected to the Hand of Cain, or who possesses the accursed object to begin with." The shrouded hood turned to look at her. "And my time is quickly running out, Becca. If I don't get to the bottom of all this, I'm afraid I won't be able to stave off any more attacks to my station, and the entire realm of the psychopomps will be ruled by a madman."

"Baron Tombstone?"

He nodded.

"And now, for the *piece de resistance*." He gestured for her to sit down on a nearby settee. When she took her seat, he moved in front of her, about three feet away, and removed his hood.

She had tried to steel herself for what was to come, but nothing could have prepared her for the crisp blackened half-face that stared back at her. The sandy blonde patches of hair that dotted his head. Or the gaping hole in Silas' right cheek that revealed the interior of his mouth. She gasped involuntarily, then covered her mouth apologetically.

"Oh, Silas..."

He laughed. "That's pretty much word for word what Elliot said when he saw me too."

"And you can't...?" She left the question unfinished when he shook his head.

"At least, not yet. Whether it was the ocean water wreaking

havoc on the ectoplasmic energies of my body, or something else, at the moment, I'm stuck this way. For better or worse." He harrumphed at this. "Who am I kidding? It's all for the worse at this point, eh?"

He skulked over to the reading chair, and sunk down into it. His elbow on the armrest, he placed his chin on a balled up fist, and looked over at her.

"So, that was my day," he said, and Becca caught the slightest glimpse of a grin. "How was yours?"

CHAPTER
TWENTY-THREE

ANKOU MOT MANOR
THURSDAY, 11:56 PM

S ilas walked down the steps of the mansion, pulling on a hoodie, and slipping the hood over his head. They had work to do, and sulking about the miseries of the day was getting him no closer to solving his problems, or the case, any faster. It had been Becca who'd suggested a more mainstream form of clothing. However, since he'd learned to manifest his own clothes using ectoplasm, he'd not had anything practical to wear within his wardrobe. But a quick run by Elliot to Walmart had taken care of that, and now he was, at least by some standards, presentable to the outside world as long as he kept his face in shadows.

"You look a million times better," Becca said as he stepped into the foyer. The House rumbled under his feet, seeming to agree with her.

Offering a necessary half-smile, he pulled out the yo-yo again, and began spinning it nonchalantly. A moment later,

Elliot appeared from the back of the house carrying three rather unwieldy suitcases.

"Uh, here's the rest of the clothes I bought you," he said, pushing his glasses up on his nose. "You sure we need to take all of them?"

Silas nodded. "I'm agreeing with you, minion. Until I've had time to deal with my brother and the Enclave, this house won't be safe. I need a much more appropriate abode—one of which, I have perfectly in mind—and would prefer to have everything I need on hand. So yes. I'll be needing all the clothes."

He turned to the door, which opened once again of its own accord, and stalked out of the house with Becca close behind. Elliot, still fumbling with all three suitcases, staggered clumsily outside, and waited for the door to close behind him. When it didn't, he turned to the door, and waited some more.

"So are you going to close or not?" he said to the house, which naturally did not respond.

He waited another five seconds, then with a sigh, dropped the suitcases, and moved toward the door. The moment he reached out for the knob, it slammed shut on him, nearly smashing into his outstretched hand.

"Argh!" he growled. "I hate this House!"

Silas chuckled. "No you don't. It's a fine house. And it enjoys playing with you. How many houses do you know that can play with its residents, eh? That's a house with character, right there."

Elliot spun around, swooping up the suitcases again, and glaring at his master. "When this is all over, I want my own place." He stormed past them both, and waited at the trunk of Becca's patrol car for her to pop it open. He then tossed the suitcases inside, and slammed the trunk down with a grunt.

"Heh heh...I know it's horrible, but torturing Dr. Newman

has a way of always cheering me up," Silas whispered to Becca, as they climbed in the car, and waited for Elliot to clamber into the backseat.

Becca smiled back at him, started the engine, and began driving them back toward town.

"So tell me," Silas finally said once they were back on A1A. "What have you learned of the investigation."

Although Elliot had already explained to Silas the method by which Lance Avery was killed, they spent some time focused on his own incident, and speculated on why his own suit had suffered a similar fate.

"I already have a theory about that," Silas said. "Once Elliot told me about the potassium and its explosive nature in water, it dawned on me that the killer might not have known which dive suit Avery would be using that day. Stands to reason that their only option would be to treat both suits in the same manner to ensure it would work."

"And since the *Stately Lady* has been out to sea all this time, and all eyes would be on anyone tampering with the team's equipment for the foreseeable future, the killer had no time to dispose of it properly," Becca added. "Makes sense."

"Which places my sights squarely on Ms. Krista Dunaway," Silas said.

Becca glanced over at him. "Really? Why?"

"Because she was adamantly against me using the suit yesterday. She became very agitated upon seeing me wearing it, and kept her eyes fixed on me almost the entire time I was down there."

"Yeah, but from what you told Elliot, she was also right by your side when things went wonky. Sounds like she was trying to help you."

"Or ensure all evidence of her treachery burned up in the fire."

Becca seemed to think that over for a moment, then shook her head. "I don't know. I talked to her afterwards," she said. "She seemed genuinely upset. And I've checked her story. She really had made a number of complaints to the network about those antique dive suits. She really did think they were a hazard. Her concern for you wearing them could simply be from not trusting their safety."

Silas mulled this over in his head and shrugged. Her argument sounded reasonable, but he wasn't completely convinced. "So tell me more about what you learned today."

She filled them in on the interviews she'd had with the crew after Silas' incident, and of the discovery that Derek Drake was none other than Ilene Nebbles-Fielding's nephew. This, of course, brought about a chorus of 'ah-ha's!' and 'I see's', yet they held their tongues for her to continue the story.

"But it was my conversation with the sound guy, Kevin Aker, that really hit pay dirt." She told them about the rumors that Lance Avery had been suspected of stealing artifacts and antiquities from sites the show had visited all around the world, and about how he was considering turning himself into international police. "I found that interesting, obviously. But it was when I got back to the station that I discovered something really interesting." Still keeping her eyes on the road, her right hand drifted down to the center console where she fumbled with a file folder between her seat. A moment later, she withdrew a piece of paper, and handed it to Silas. "It's a report from INTERPOL."

Silas held it up, but since they were driving at night, there was very little light to see anything on the page.

"I'll summarize it for you," she said. "In four of the last nine places he's visited for the show—Iraq, London, Rome, and Cairo—Lance was an official person of interest in a string of thefts at archaeological sites. He was being investigated for circumventing national antiquities laws, smuggling, and selling artifacts on the black market."

"Intriguing."

"But we already pretty much knew that, thanks to Mr. Aker. What we didn't know was that the various law enforcement agencies involved also believe he has a partner working closely with him," she continued. "But at the moment, they have no idea who it is."

"So you're thinking maybe he had some kind of tiff with his partner?" Elliot chimed in. "And they decided to sever their partnership? Permanently?"

"That's what I suspected at first too," Becca nodded. "But after reading this report, and talking with someone at INTERPOL, I not only know what that tiff might have been about, but why Lance had come to me to talk the day before he died.

"Seems that not only was he planning on turning himself in, he'd already worked out a deal with detectives with Scotland Yard. He was going to return the stolen merchandise. Or at least, the merchandise he still had. And had promised to name his accomplice or accomplices."

Silas raised an eyebrow at this. "Very enlightening, I'd say. If his partner found out about this little plea deal, it would certainly be motive enough to kill him. Especially before they wrapped up their shoot here and Lance could rendezvous with international authorities."

"Exactly," Becca said as she steered her patrol car into the parking lot of the Sand Dollar Oasis parking lot. "Silas, are you sure you want to stay here? Of all places?"

He grinned at her. "It's open, and very public. Anubis would be very cautious about attacking me here." Silas chuckled. "Plus, it'll drive that old curmudgeon Elroy Lincoln into a conniption."

Becca rolled her eyes. "Wait here."

She got out of the car, and walked into the hotel lobby to be greeted by said curmudgeon with his usual lemon-faced hospitality. After a few minutes of assuring the hotel manager that, despite asking specifically for Room 113, Silas Mot would not be the one staying in his motel—his original room when he first came to town, and therefore had a nostalgic place in his heart—she secured the key, and trotted out to her car. She drove around the ocean-side wing of the place, and they all scrambled out of the car, and into Silas Mot's old room.

Once inside, Silas held a hand to Elliot. "Pocket knife?"

The undead archaeologist looked at his master quizzically, reached into his pocket, and produced a Swiss Army Knife. Once the knife was in Silas' hand, he crouched down at the air conditioning vent, and began to unscrew it from the wall. A moment later, he reached in, pulled out an old comic book, and plopped down in the bed with his legs crossed.

"Ah! The Big Red Cheese!" Silas said, opening a vintage Captain Marvel comic book. "Oh, how I've missed you."

Although Becca was glad to see her friend in a semblance of his normally childlike self, she had to ask. "So you hid a comic book in the wall of your motel room?"

He shrugged. "Never know when one will be forced to return. Wanted to ensure I had adequate reading material when I did."

Grinning, she took a chair next to the room's table/writing desk, and crossed her legs. "So, now that we're here, we need to make a game plan. Need to figure out what's next."

"You mean, besides figuring out how I can return to my former glory while avoiding an evil faction of psychopomps looking to overthrow me?" He thumbed another page in the book casually.

"Nothing I can do about that," she said. "I'm talking about the murder case."

"Seems to me, we need to figure out who Lance's partner was," Elliot said, who'd taken a seat on the other side of the table.

"Also, I'm still trying to figure out what Ilene's role in all this is," Becca said. "She could have requested real, professional archaeologists to excavate that ship. Legitimate scientists. Yet, she chose to invite a sensationalized reality TV show to do it instead."

"A TV show where the now-deceased host was suspected of stealing priceless artifacts from the sites he investigated," Elliot added.

"And a show that now features her own nephew as its newest host," Becca said.

Silas closed the comic book, and sat up at this. "Now that little tidbit...about Derek Drake...that intrigues me most of all."

She looked at him. "Why's that?"

"My suspicion that Ilene Nebbles-Fielding is in possession of the Hand. The shard I found near the shipwreck. Things are falling into place, I believe."

"Care to share?" Elliot asked.

"Not quite yet, dear minion. I'm still working through a few possibilities. Wouldn't want to skew the good detective's objectivity with my speculation."

"That's the problem," Becca said. "We have an embarrassing amount of facts, suspects, and possible motives. The over-abundance of clues beginning to bog us down down." She shook her head. "No, we need an edge. We need a..." Her eyes snapped up. "Wait a minute. Something you said while we were driving here...about the Dunaway woman."

Silas swiveled his feet around and was now seated on the edge of the bed. "You mean how she was adamant about me not wearing the dive suit."

"No, no...not that. You said she seemed to be watching you the entire time you were down there in the suit."

"She was. And I have to say it was a bit...disconcerting."

Becca grinned back at him. "And that's given me an idea for the next phase of our investigation. Gentlemen, I think we're about to break this case wide open."

She was just about to tell them her idea when a series of howls erupted from outside the motel, sending chills down Becca's pine.

"What was that?"

Elliot, whose eyes were now as big around as bowling balls, stared at Silas. "Anubis. He's here."

Becca stood up, her hand going to her gun. But Silas raised his own hand, shaking his head. "Easy. Easy. That pea-shooter will do no good against Anubis' hounds. Besides, they haven't found me." He looked at his minion. "They've found you, Elliot."

The little guy tensed at that revelation. "Me?" He thumbed back at his chest. "Why me?"

"Anubis' dogs have no power to track me, even in my weakened position." He paused. "Actually, less so now that I'm slowly approaching the threshold of mortality. No, they can only do what they were bred to do. Track down the souls of the departed who've returned to the Land of the Living. In other words, you. It was you that Anubis tracked to the mansion. It was you that he would have tracked to Esperanza's. And it is you that they are tracking now...in hopes of finding me."

"What should we do, Silas?" Becca asked.

"Leave. For now. Take Elliot with you, and drop him off at the mansion." He looked at the little guy. "Don't worry. The House, whether you believe it or not, will protect you. Not that Anubis will do anything to you. After all, you're still under my protection, and he can't get to me without you. So you'll be safe there."

"What about you?"

Silas smiled again, then seemed to remember the hideous disfigurement of his face, and pulled his hood further down over his head before once more laying back down in the bed, and opening the comic book. "Me? I'm going to enjoy the Captain's battle against the vile worm genius, Mister Mind, then call it a night."

Becca smiled, then nodded. "Okay. I'll be by to pick you up first thing in the morning. Then, we get back to our investigation."

Silas gave her a casual salute with a wink, then returned to reading the comic book as Becca and Elliot left him alone in his room.

CHAPTER
TWENTY-FOUR

SAND DOLLAR OASIS MOTEL
SUMMER HAVEN
FRIDAY, 7:34 AM

S ilas Mot answered his door before Becca had knocked the second time. He was up, dressed in a pair of black trousers, his black hoodie, a pair of wayfarer sunglasses, and a black silk scarf that he'd swathed around his face to hide his disfigurement.

Despite the fact he was no closer to figuring out how to fix his hideous appearance, he was in much better spirits this morning than how he'd been the night before. The colorful panels of the superhero of Faucet City, a few reruns of Firefly, and two and a half hours of sleep had worked wonders for his mood.

"Good morning," he said, as he stepped out into the beautiful morning sun and breathed in the fresh salty air. "No Elliot?"

Becca shook her head. "With Anubis hunting him to get to

you, we thought it best if he stayed away for now." She held up a cup of Dunkin' Donuts coffee, and he took it.

"Thank you," he said. "As for Elliot, we would have been safe for the time being either way. Although he's quite capable, Anubis wouldn't make a move in the light of day. Not really his style, ya know."

"Still, better safe that sorry."

Silas nodded his agreement at this, lowered his scarf just below his lips, and carefully took a sip on the less damaged side of his face. Two creams. Four sugars. Just the way he liked it. He let out a satisfied sigh as it slid down his throat.

"You going to be okay? I mean, being seen like this?" Becca waved a hand around his garb.

"Better like this than what lies beneath the layers, wouldn't you say?"

"I suppose. But let's face it. You're nothing if not vain."

He laughed before finishing the coffee, and pulling the scarf up over his nose again. The two started walking toward the motel's main office.

"I called ahead," Becca told him. "The *Mysterious Expedition* team is gearing up for another shoot, but I convinced Garrett Norris and Laura Granger to meet with us before they left. They weren't happy about it, but now that their benefactor, Ilene, is powerless to do anything, they had no choice." She held up a folded sheet of paper.

"What's that?"

"The ticket to getting some answers."

They strode through the lobby, then navigated the halls until they came to the conference room where they'd met the team two days earlier. To their word, the producer and executive producer of the show were already seated, and waiting at the conference table.

"Finally!" Garrett said, rising from his seat. "We've been waitin..." He halted at the sight of Silas. "Who's that?"

"My dear Mr. Norris," Silas said. Becca could swear she heard his mischievous grin under the fabric covering his face. "Don't you recognize me?"

"Mot? But...but that's impossible!"

"Obviously not," Laura said, leaning back in her seat, and glancing at her watch. "Now can we get on with this? This production has already been far more costly than the network likes, and we need to get back out to the wreck as soon as possible."

"Costly? As in, your husband's life?" Becca asked, moving over to the table, and laying the folded paper down in front of the two of them. "Yeah, that's pretty costly, I'd say."

"What's that?" Garrett asked, nodding to the paper.

"That, Mr. Norris, is a warrant. For the video footage your team shot yesterday."

The producer blinked. "Why on earth would you need that?"

"That little piece of paper," Silas said, "means that she doesn't have to explain her reasons to you." He was beginning to understand Becca's plan, and he approved.

"No way," Garrett said. "That footage..."

"Will be returned to you," Becca said. "And it's not like I'm asking for the original stuff. Your team was wearing Go-Pro cameras, weren't they? Digital? I'm just asking for copies."

"Unaltered copies," Silas added. He dipped his sunglasses just a bit, and gave the man a wink.

"But..."

"Geez, Garrett, just give them what they want," Laura said. "The sooner we do, the sooner we can wrap this up, and get going." She held up her hands. "You're the one complaining about being stuck in this one stop-light town all the time. Geez!"

The producer glared over at her, his face twisting in a disgusted look before turning back to Becca, and shrugging with a nod.

"Fine. I'll get you the files. Anything else?"

"Were you two aware of the several international police investigations into Lance Avery?" Becca asked.

The two exchanged furtive glances at one another. After a moment, Laura Granger uncrossed her legs, and sat up stiffly in her chair.

"It's a matter of public record," she said. "And it was entirely unsubstantiated."

"Unsubstantiated or not, you *were* aware of it."

"Yes," Laura said.

Garrett nodded.

"And his *unsubstantiated* partner?" Silas asked. "Any ideas on who that unsubstantially might be?"

"How are you even alive?" Garrett asked, cocking his head to one side. "I saw the video footage. Saw the fire. Your empty suit."

"Disappointed?" he asked.

"Just confused. That's all."

Becca waved her hands in the air to get their attention. "Let's get back on track. Answer Silas' question. Any theories on who the partner is?" She eyed both of her suspects. "And keep in mind, I'm not an idiot. If you knew about these investigations, then I know you've had discussions with Lance about them. If you say you don't know who his partner was, then I'm going to think one or both of *you* were."

Garrett let out a disgusted snort. "If I had to guess, it would be Kevin."

"How dare you!" Laura said, slamming the flat of her hand down on the table.

Silas' spine tingled with the impact, and he chuckled. "Oh, this is getting good." He swept up to Laura, put his arm around her, and leaned in. "And why does his suspicion that a mere sound engineer might be involved rankle the feathers of an executive producer, I wonder?"

She slung his arm off, and moved out of his reach. "Because he's trying to smear him. Everybody on the crew knows the truth." Laura pointed at Garrett. "He just doesn't want his new big star to get caught up in this scandal, so he's blaming my friend!"

"Ha! Your friend, is it?" Garrett roared. "Is that what we're calling it now, eh? Wish I had a friend like you." He paused, then sneered. "Again."

"Whoa, whoa, whoa!" Becca said. "Hold up." She looked over at Laura. "Are you saying that Derek Drake..."

"Rosenbaum," Laura corrected.

"Are you saying he was involved in Lance's theft and smuggling operation?"

"Not just involved. Lance told me he spearheaded the whole thing. It was all his idea."

Becca shook her head. "But Derek said Lance hardly gave him the time of the day. Said he was his hero, but that he wouldn't even so much as look him in the eye."

"In public, sure," Laura said. "What better way to keep their joint venture secret. But privately, Lance respected that kid like all get out. No one does research like Derek. No one knows more about ancient legends and treasures. If anyone could pinpoint the location of some secret stash of artifacts, Derek Rosenbaum is the guy to do it."

"Please," Garrett scoffed. "You're just bitter that the

network wasn't interested in your guy to be the host. You'd do anything to cast a shadow on Derek."

They argued like this for several minutes, Silas watching each of them like an overly energetic tennis match as they did so. But two things were now clear. First, they now had an excellent suspect to focus on for their investigation, and second, they weren't likely to get anymore information from these two any time soon.

It didn't take long for Becca to interrupt the argument, and remind Garrett Norris to provide her with the video files. When that was done, Silas and Becca left the conference room with the sound of a verbal Battle Royale fading as they walked away.

CHAPTER
TWENTY-FIVE

Becca Cole sat hunched over at her desk, watching the video footage she'd obtained from her laptop. She'd already fast-forwarded through four and a half hours of footage in less than two hours, and still had four more to go. Her eyes blurred, and she pressed pause to blink them back into focus. So far, nothing. Among the footage she'd watched, Kevin Aker and cameraman Gabe Williams had pretty much been fixated on the wreck, only turning toward Silas when things started going bad for him.

Her plan, of course, had been simple enough. Whoever planted the potassium inside the dive helmet would naturally be curious as to what would happen to Silas. That curiosity would subconsciously nag at them, forcing them to keep a close eye on him until he caught fire. Becca already knew that the medic, Krista Dunaway, had been fixated on Silas and the

190

dive suit. That just left Derek Drake and the underwater drone that had been remotely operated by Garrett Norris himself.

Becca pinched the bridge of her nose as she prepared to continue her vigil, and jumped when her phone buzzed. She picked up the receiver.

"Yes, Linda?"

"Chief, just wanted you to know, Tall-Dark-and-Doctorly is out here to see you," Linda White said with the slightest trace of a purr.

"Brad?" Becca sat up straight. "He's here? Now?"

Her brain raced, trying to remember if they'd had a lunch date planned for the day. She glanced at her watch, and decided that they probably didn't. It was far too early to go to lunch now.

"Okay, Linda. Just tell him to sit tight. I'll be out in a minute."

Becca queued up Krista Dunaway's footage, then pushed her laptop away with a sigh. She didn't have time for the unrequited love trope right now. Didn't have time to stroke Brad Harris' fragile ego and affirm to him that she hadn't meant to neglect him, but that things were just crazy at work at the moment. He already knew these things. Why did she always have to hold his hand? They were both extremely busy, hardworking professionals. He was a doctor, for crying out loud. Shouldn't he be even more busy than she was?

She pushed her chair out from her desk and strode over to the door of her office. She reached out to the knob, then paused, steeling herself for whatever drama the good doctor was going to bring into her world today. While she did so, she eased one of the plastic strips of the blinds she had mounted to her door's window and peeked out. She caught sight of him immediately, across the bullpen, chatting with Commander Jeremy Tanner.

Well, maybe chatting wasn't the right word. Both men looked tense as they spoke to one another. Jeremy's sleeve-covered arms were crossed over his chest, and his face was etched in a ruddy scowl. Brad held himself with similar body language. Whatever they were talking about, neither of them was happy, which was odd for Brad. He was typically such a positive person. He rarely complained about anything, and avoided unpleasant discussions as much as possible, claiming that a person's physical well-being was directly connected with their emotional one. But watching the two talking now, something seemed to definitely be upsetting both men. And given her recent suspicions of her commander, she wasn't at all comfortable with the man having such an effect on Brad Harris.

Willing herself to relax, she opened the door to her office, and stepped out into the bullpen. The moment she did, Brad shifted his gaze from Jeremy over to her, and his expression quickly changed to his typical good-natured smile. She offered a subtle wave at him, which he returned, then seemed to finish his hushed conversation with the commander, and walked over to her before planting a kiss on her lips.

"Good to see you, gorgeous!" he said, taking her hands in his and stepping back to look her up and down. "Feels like I haven't seen you in decades."

She blushed, glancing around the bullpen to see who'd witnessed the embarrassing public display of affection, but if anyone had, they weren't letting on. She squeezed his hands.

"Good to see you too." She nodded over her shoulder to her office. "Want to come in for a bit?"

He nodded, and she followed him inside, closing the door behind them.

"So what do I owe the pleasure of this surprise visit?" she asked while rounding her desk and taking a seat.

He took one of the chairs in front of her desk and shrugged. "Just wanted to see your beautiful face." He winked at her, and she smiled.

"I'm sorry I haven't been around much lately," she said, slipping directly into the role of consoling girlfriend she desperately hoped to avoid. "Skipping dates and not having enough one on one time isn't very conducive to a good relationship, is it?"

He waved her comment away. "Oh, I understand. You're police chief. The lead detective for your agency. And things *have* been a bit crazy lately."

"You got that right."

"In fact, one could say it's been insane as far as murders go," Brad continued. "Ever since your friend showed up in town."

She tensed. "My friend?"

"Silas Mot." He shook his head. "Ever since that guy came to Summer Haven, it's like this town has turned itself into the murder capital of Florida."

"You sound like Commander Tanner now."

"Guy makes some good points. Let's face it, Mot is an odd bird." He paused. "Not to mention he's totally into you."

"What?"

"Oh, come on! You can't tell me you don't see it. The way he looks at you. The way he bristles whenever I walk into the room."

She laughed at this. "Sounds to me like you're jealous." She paused, raising an eyebrow at him. "And maybe a bit paranoid."

"I'm not jealous," Brad said. "Or paranoid. Everyone else thinks so too."

"Everyone? Who's everyone?"

He waved the question away. "You know what I mean. Point is, I don't think he has your best interests at heart."

Becca tilted her head, narrowing her eyes at him. "Where's all this coming from, Brad? You never mentioned any of this before."

"Well, he's never really acted this erratic before either," he replied. "His antics at the big gala Saturday night? Him accusing Ilene Nebbles-Fielding of...well, I'm not sure what he was accusing her of, but he certainly wasn't nice about it. And humiliating Lance Avery in front of the whole town?" He shook his head. "Now, I hear he's got you going head to head against Ilene too."

"Ilene needs to stay out of police business, and stick to her community projects." Becca had to force herself to stop grinding her teeth. "She's been stonewalling me since the day Avery was murdered."

Brad leaned forward in his seat. "And you're sure he was murdered? You're sure it wasn't just an unfortunate accident?"

Becca was unable to keep her cool any longer. She stood up and glared down at him. "What's going on, Brad? Something is up and I want to know what it is."

He brushed a stray blonde hair away from his face and smiled at her. "Look, don't get mad," he said. "I'm just worried about you. About your career. Ilene came by the office today. She's one of my patients. She told me she's met with the mayor and Councilman Beaver about calling a special council meeting to discuss removing you from office. And we both know how Eric Beaver felt about your dad. It's not looking good for you." Brad shook his head. "Silas Mot is destroying your career, Bec. He'll destroy your life as well, if you let him. He needs to go."

"This is what you and Tanner were talking about a few minutes ago, wasn't it?"

"He agrees with me completely."

And he's my number one suspect in a murder investigation of a local bartender. She was smart enough not to say it aloud. *I wouldn't trust his opinion if it was the last one on earth.*

It wasn't until that very moment that she'd allowed herself to think those words. But as she did, she knew it just felt right. Somehow, Jeremy Tanner was involved with whoever had the Hand of Cain, and he'd been sent to try to kill Silas last year. When that didn't work, he'd killed Courtney Abeling, the bartender that had tried to warn Silas about the impending attack. She wasn't sure how she was going to prove it. She had no real evidence to support the theory, but she knew with absolute certainty that it was true.

"So I take it Jeremy's the 'everyone' you were talking about?" she asked.

"Bec, come on. I didn't mean it like..."

"I think you should leave." Her voice was quiet, but solid. There was little room in her words for argument of any kind.

"But..."

"Brad, if you want to continue with this relationship, you'll do as I ask, and leave. I need to think."

He stood up, and started making his way to the door. He reached for the knob and turned. "I'm sorry to have upset you. I just want what's best for you."

She held up a hand and looked down at her desk. "We'll talk later. I have work to do now."

She lowered herself into her seat, and by the time she returned her attention to the laptop screen, he was gone.

CHAPTER
TWENTY-SIX

SAND DOLLAR OASIS BAR
SUMMER HAVEN
FRIDAY, 11:37 AM

Silas Mot strode out to the tiki bar behind the Sand Dollar Oasis, and ordered a Death on a Beach. The handful of tourists who were staying at the motel gawked at his ensemble of hoodie, long black pants, sunglasses, and scarf covering his face, but he paid them no heed. At that moment, he had more pressing matters to deal with, namely the delectable strawberry and citrus-flavored rum concoction he'd come to love so well. Fortunately, after his time staying at the motel all those months, the bar staff had learned to make it expertly—although never quite as good as Courtney, the woman who'd introduced it to him just before she'd been murdered.

Taking his drink, he drifted lazily over to the beach chairs, and sat down to catch a few rays and watch the surf. For the first time since coming to the Land of the Living, however, he wasn't very comfortable. Perspiration began to soak through his clothing, and his sunglasses fogged up with each breath he took. He'd never experienced the discomfort of heat before, or cold for that matter. His ectoplasmic body had never had the capacity for such things in the past. Now, however, as he gradually and inexplicably transformed into a mortal, he was experiencing things he'd never thought possible. And it was slowly dawning on him that he didn't much care for the heat of summer at all.

Lowering his scarf just a hair, he sucked on the curly straw, pulling in a good amount of his libation, and sighed. The one positive in his ordeal, however, was that his drink seemed tastier than it ever had before. Not to mention refreshing.

"Is this seat taken?" a female voice with a thick Spanish accent asked from behind.

He craned his head to see Esperanza in an overly-revealing white bikini and wide-brimmed straw hat. He gestured to the seat next to him, and she took it.

"Want one?" He gestured to his glass. "They're delicious."

She shook her head, and leaned back in the beach chair. "Anubis came to see me yesterday after you left."

"I figured he would." He took another drink, and felt his head begin to swim. Before last Saturday night, he'd never been affected by alcohol before either. Today, the intoxication was even more intense. It was a rather pleasant sensation, he had to admit, yet disconcerting at the same time.

"He wasn't alone."

This caught Silas' attention. He raised an eyebrow over at his ex-wife.

"Tombstone was with him."

His jaw nearly dropped at the news. "Anubis and the Baron? Working together?" He laughed. "Greed certainly does make for strange bedfellows, doesn't it?"

Esperanza's face remained grim, like a piece of well-polished marble. "They're looking for something."

"Me. I think you mean they're looking for me."

She shook her head, stopped, then shrugged. "No. Well, yes. But it's not what you think."

Silas sat up. "They're looking for the Hand?"

She nodded. "And something else. They wouldn't tell me what, but they think you have it."

"As far as I know, you were the last person to see the Hand of Cain," Silas said. "You and your acolyte, Omo Sango, the Santerian Babalowa."

"And I told you. It was stolen from us."

He laughed again, this time louder. Harder. It caused the torn flesh of his jaw to wrench in pain. "Stolen from the Saint of Death? Stolen from *Los Cuernos del Diablo*? How is that even possible?"

Esperanza sighed. "I wish I knew. I've looked into it personally. None of Omo Sango's men had anything to do with it. The only thing I can think of is that it was stolen by an outsider."

"Have many outsiders visiting the lot of you at U-Store-It these days?"

She shrugged. "A few. Lawyers. The occasional doctor or two. Some mechanics for the gang's various cars and bikes. Even a few accountants from time to time."

"Accountants?"

"*Los Cuernos del Diablo* is a business, after all. It's important to keep a close eye on the books when the cartels come sniffing around. They like to know where their money is going from time to time."

Silas nodded in concession of the logic. "And this other object they're looking for?"

"Like I said, they didn't tell me. Just said that they think you've got it, and that it's a key to finding the Hand of Cain."

"Really now?" Silas said, leaning back once again in his chair and taking a long pull on his drink. "Interesting. Very interesting."

Now it was Esperanza's time to sit up in her chair. When she did, she glared down at him. "You're not taking this seriously enough, *mi esposo*." Her rich Hispanic accent was thicker than Silas had ever heard it before. "You are treating this as a game, but it is no game. You're becoming mortal. You're losing your power, and by extension, your station. Now is not the time to be so cavalier about all this. You need a strategy. You need to be prepared for what is to come."

"What I really need is another drink." Though he knew she couldn't see it under his scarf, Silas grinned, sat the glass down on the table next to his chair, and held up a finger at the bartender. He then shifted in his seat, and looked over at his ex-wife. "As to your concerns, I'm curious. When all this silly drama plays out, whose side will you be on? Are you not playing games with me, even now?"

"'Silly drama'? Ankou, look at yourself. You're in no condition to take this lightly."

"So you keep saying, but I'm still curious as to your own loyalties."

"You know me."

He nodded. "The only side Esperanza is on is her own. But if she's going to stab me in the back, she'll at least do it to my face."

"Precisely." It was her turn to smile now. "Baron Tombstone is maniacal. Insane. It does none of us any good with him on the throne, and I'll not be a party to his attempted coup."

"And the others? Do they feel the same way?"

She shrugged. "They're all pretty tight-lipped about it.

Most are not as concerned with the mortals as you or I. To many of them, mortals are only trinkets. The more souls in their collection, the happier they are. You're the only one I've ever met that has ever taken 'duty' seriously."

The bartender came over, placed a fresh glass of Death on the Beach on the table between them, and walked away. Esperanza snagged the drink and took a deep sip before Silas even had a chance.

"Mmmm. This really is quite good. I can see why you like it." She handed the half glass over to him. "Look, the majority of us are in this for the chaos and if Tombstone represents anything, it's that. Since none of us will ever get to partake in the Great Reward, they see no reason not to have a little fun while they're still allowed." She shook her head. "Point is, I think you have your work cut out for you on this."

Silas thought about that for a few long moments as he stirred his straw through the bright red coloring of his drink, then he took a deep breath. "When my murder investigation is concluded, I want a meeting."

"With who, exactly?"

He lowered his sunglasses, and cast her a wink. "All of them, of course."

TWENTY-SEVEN

SUMMER HAVEN MARINA
SUMMER HAVEN
FRIDAY 2:40 PM

E lliot Newman pulled at the lever on the side of his car
seat, slowly leaning back in the confined space of his
VW Beetle, and peered over the driver's side window
with a set of high-powered binoculars.

With him now unable to be at his master's beck and call,
lest Silas' brother Anubis track him down, Elliot had been
feeling particularly useless. Considering his entire unnatural
existence was for the purpose of being the Grim Reaper's
majordomo, his inability to carry out those duties—no matter
how revolting they made him feel about himself—had made
him restless throughout the night.

So, he'd awakened early, driven and parked a safe distance
from the Sand Dollar Oasis, and had taken up surveillance on
the film crew as they'd left the motel to carpool to the marina,
and then taken a boat out to sea for the day's filming. Having

overheard the time they planned to return, he'd now arrived in the marina's parking lot for yet another stakeout in hopes of ferreting out the killer of the show's host.

He glanced at his watch. As a matter of fact, they were due back any minute. Despite not seeing anything out of the ordinary for the morning excursion, he needed to be ready for anything upon their return. He wasn't entirely sure what his clandestine activities would ultimately help to accomplish, but it at least provided him with something to make himself useful, and that would have to do.

As his eyes fixed on the ocean's horizon, he nestled back into his seat, and watched.

After five minutes, a soft breeze blew in from one of the cracked windows, circulating through the car's interior, then dissipated. He winced at the foul stench the wind had obviously carried into his car, and fanned his face with his palm.

"Geez! What the heck is that smell?"

As his hand continued to fluctuate back and forth, the offensive odor stirred once more, nearly making Elliot gag.

"That's just not right."

His eyes were now watering from the smell, and he rolled down his windows a little bit more. He couldn't focus on the malodorous scent right now. He had to train his eyes and his mind on the ocean, and the twenty-six foot fishing boat that would be barreling into view any moment now. The returning crew, and any suspicious activity they might be exhibiting was the only thing that mattered.

He caught another whiff.

"Oh God. What is that?"

He lifted his arm, and sniffed at his clothing, causing him another fit of eye-watering wincing. The smell, it seemed, was coming from him. But he'd bathed this morning. He bathed every day in fact, but now that he thought about it, he'd been noticing a similar smell around him for the past few days. Maybe weeks.

Curious, he pulled up the sleeve of his sweater—he'd taken up wearing warm, long sleeve clothing recently as well, to keep out the strange chill that had been nagging him in recent days —and looked at the goose-fleshed skin of his arms. He stiffened at the sight.

His arms seemed to now sport a dull green hue, and were spider-webbed with darker green veins resembling jagged lightning bolts that stretched from his shoulders to his wrists. Gasping at what he was seeing, he tentatively pressed down on his arm with his index finger, and pushed it back and forth, trying to wipe away whatever was discoloring his arm the way it was. As he did so, a layer of skin began sloughing off his arm with each back and forth motion.

He yelped.

If he had an actual working heart, Elliot was certain it would be pounding in his chest right about now as his current situation was finally beginning to dawn on him.

He was starting to decompose!

SAND DOLLAR OASIS MOTEL
SUMMER HAVEN
FRIDAY, 3:32 PM

SILAS WOBBLED on unsteady feet as he trudged back toward his motel room with yet another drink in his hand. After Esperanza had left, he'd spent the last three hours soaking up the sun—despite his uncomfortably warm attire—and drinking one Death on the Beach after another. And with each drink he'd consumed, he'd become more and more inebriated... something that should have been impossible.

But here he was, three sheets to the wind, slurring the lyrics to the Eagle's song *Witchy Woman* and doing a horrible job remembering the words while trying to remain upright long enough to get to the door to his room.

Three different times during his short trek, he'd considered just lying down on the warm sand, and calling it a night. But it wasn't even four in the afternoon yet. Becca would soon be leaving the office, and would be heading over as soon as possible to fill him in on anything she'd learned since they'd last spoke. When that happened, he would need to be upright and alert...and much more sober than he was at that moment.

Some coffee and a cold shower should do the trick, I think.

It wouldn't do at all to let the police chief see him like this. It was—he wasn't sure why—essential that Silas put on a brave face in front her. He couldn't stand seeing her with pity on her face for him. Not like she had last night when she'd first seen his ghastly appearance at the mansion. His charred appearance and his ever-weakening state were bad enough, but her platitudes and attempts to console him hurt far more than his body betraying him the way it was.

Silas staggered to within a few yards of his door, when he heard the sound of a woman screaming around the northeast corner of the motel. Forgetting his intoxication, he ran toward the sound, focusing straight ahead and not on the gyrating scenery around him, and rounded the corner in record time.

He skidded to a stop when he saw the three black-clad goons in balaclavas struggling to restrain the medic, Krista Dunaway. One of the men, the largest among them, had his well-muscled arms around her waist, lifting her up while the other two flailed about, trying to grab her kicking legs. Krista's body writhed against their grip, all the while screaming at the top of her lungs.

One of her attackers gave up his attempt to gain control of her legs, and backhanded her across the mouth. "Shut up, you crazy b—"

"Hey!" Silas shouted, breaking the trio's concentration.

They turned to look at him, their eyes narrowing underneath their masks. Silas gasped when he finally caught sight of all three men, his eyes instantly landing on the sleeves of Celtic tattoo art scrawled up and down each of their arms. The same tattoos he'd seen last year when he was attacked by three balaclava-wearing goons. The same goons that had murdered Courtney Abeling, the waitress who had tried to warn him of their intentions. The same goons that worked for the one who possessed the Hand of Cain.

Of course, Silas doubted very much that they recognized him, dressed as he was in a hoodie and face-covering scarf. His odd appearance had certainly taken them aback, that was for sure, and he intended to use that surprise to his advantage.

Enraged at the sight of them, Silas leapt at the closest figure, tackling him to the sidewalk outside Krista's motel room. His fist slammed into the man's face as they struck the ground. His target recovered quickly, kicking Silas off, and rolling to his feet faster than expected. The masked man lunged, slamming into Silas, and pushing him against the motel's coquina shell wall, nearly knocking the breath from him.

"Finish him," the largest of the trio said while still grappling with the pretty young medic.

The goon continued his barrage of punches into Silas' midsection, bringing him to his knees and doubling him over. He reached behind him and withdrew a rather large revolver, and pulled back on the hammer as he pointed it at Silas.

"What's the matter, Tanner," Silas said between a fit coughing from being struck so many times in the gut. "Can't do your own dirty work? Did you have them kill Courtney Abeling as well?"

This seemed to catch the large man by surprise. He spun to look at Silas, loosening his grip on Krista. "What did you say?"

This respite seemed to be all that Krista needed. She twisted her upper body while renewing her kicks. The large man lost hold of her, and she dropped to the ground, instantly scrambling away from his and the second goon's reach, and launched herself into a full sprint around the corner of the building toward safety.

Silas looked up at the attackers, a grin stretching across his face beneath the scarf.

"The jig is up, Commander," Silas said. "I know it's you. I've pretty much known since you jumped me in the parking lot last year. More important, Becca knows as well. She might not want to believe it, but eventually, she'll figure it out."

The big guy glanced from Silas to the corner from which Krista had made her escape, struggling with the decision of which foe was more pressing. In the end, he apparently decided on Silas Mot.

"Hold up," he said to his cohort. "Don't kill him yet."

Silas, who was still on his knees, shrugged. "Not that he could," he said. "After all, who has two thumbs and is the Supreme Lord of Death?" He paused a moment, then thumbed back at himself, but let the answer hang in the air.

The large man stomped the four or five paces necessary to stand over Silas, and glared down at him. With a growl, he pulled off the balaclava, revealing the chiseled and craggy face of Commander Jeremy Tanner. Tanner's face was twisted in a grimace, his skin mottled red around the cheeks and ears.

"You think you're pretty clever, don't you, Mot?"

"It's an adjective that's been thrown my way on more than one occasion." He shrugged. "Who am I to argue?"

"Well, you've just clevered yourself into the grave." Tanner withdrew a Sig Sauer .40 caliber handgun, pulled back on the slide, and leveled it at Silas' head. "And now that I know Bec knows about me, I guess you clevered her to death as well." He pursed his lips, shaking his head. "Geez, I was hoping to avoid that. I loved her old man like a brother. Always liked her as well." He barked out half a laugh, then turned to his compatriots. "Well, what do you know? Maybe this guy really is the Grim Reaper after all. Everyone he knows is about to die."

Silas braced himself, tensing every single muscle in his body. He knew he had to stall. Krista had escaped. She would surely be calling the police, who wouldn't take very long to get here.

"If I'm about to die, there's no reason you can't tell me who your boss is then, is there?" he asked. "Who's pulling your strings, little puppet?"

Silas watched as Tanner's grip tightened on the handle of his gun. His two pals, anxiously shifting on their feet while they looked around for signs of trouble, egged their leader on. "Come on, bro. Just kill him and get it over with."

But the crooked cop ignored them as he glared down at his prey with a glint of madness reflecting from his eyes. "Oh, you won't believe me when I tell you," he laughed. "I mean, I hardly believe it myself. But I'm getting paid enough to believe anything right now."

Silas swallowed, his throat suddenly parched. "Tell me. I have to know."

Tanner stepped closer, and crouched down to meet Silas' gaze. "It's the last person you'd ever suspect, and the funny thing is, it should have been the first. You'd hate yourself for not figuring it out sooner if you weren't going to get a bullet in that crazy head of yours the moment I tell you."

"Jeremy, come on," one of his cohorts said. "The cops'll be here any minute."

Silas straightened his back and stared the cop straight in the eyes. "They're right. You better tell me before it's too..."

"Freeze!" shouted a familiar female voice to his left. "Nobody move!"

Silas and Tanner both turned to see Becca Cole standing near the corner of the building, her gun trained on the thugs. A moment of recognition flashed across her face when she saw her commander, and she only had a split second to duck for cover as the three of them opened fire on her.

"No!" Silas shouted, before tackling Tanner to the ground and knocking his gun away.

The two other goons, now thoroughly freaked out by the police chief's presence, bolted around the other side of the building without bothering to retrieve their leader. Not that the big man needed their help. In Silas' drunken—not to mention mortally weakened—state, he was no match for the veteran cop, who threw him off him as easily as a pillow, scrambled to his feet, and ran after his buddies without another word.

A moment later, breathing heavily on the ground, Silas looked up to see Becca kneeling down by his head. "Are you okay?" she asked.

He nodded, gulping in deep breaths as he did so. Then, he let his head drop to the ground with a sigh. "He was just about to tell me, Becca," he said. "He was just about to tell me who is behind it all before you showed up."

"I'm sorry for...saving your life?"

He waved it away, pulled his scarf down, and smiled up at her. "I am grateful. You just got here a lot sooner than I expected, that's all. I figured it would have taken you a few more minutes to get here after Krista Dunaway called you guys."

Becca pointed at her watch. "Got off early. I was almost here anyway when the call came out." She paused, then bent down and took a couple of sniffs. "Are you...are you drunk? Again?"

He held up his right thumb and forefinger, keeping them just a few centimeters apart. "Little bit."

She stood up and reached down to him. He took her hand, and she helped him to his unsteady feet.

"So did you see?" he asked. "Tanner?"

She nodded. "Needless to say, he's fired. I'll put out a BOLO for him as soon as I get you back to your room."

He held up a hand. "Not just yet." He looked over at Krista Dunaway's open door. "First we need to speak to our medic friend, and find out what those guys were after."

CHAPTER
TWENTY-EIGHT

SUMMER HAVEN MARINA
SUMMER HAVEN
FRIDAY, 3:30 PM

The *Mysterious Expedition* team had long since arrived at the marina, and abruptly departed back to their motel, but Elliot Newman remained in his car, examining his deteriorating flesh. His mind raced backwards, trying to remember the precise moment the signs of decomposition had begun to materialize.

There had, of course, been hints. The occasional look of disgust on the faces of people he'd walked past. A few comments about something in the air stinking like a 'pole cat' just this last week. In retrospect, even Silas had seemed to notice, making off-handed comments, then opening his mouth as if ready to elaborate, then quickly closing it again and saying nothing instead.

"Son of a..." he growled. "He knew. Silas knew this was happening to me, and hoped I just wouldn't notice."

He now had his car seat stiffly in the upright position, and for the hundredth time, examined his face in the rear view mirror. His eyes were now cloudy and gray with cataracts. Hemorrhagic red lined the whites of his eyes. The same dark green veins streaked across his cheekbones, chin, and forehead like some deranged carnival face painter art.

"Son of a..." He slammed both palms down against his steering wheel, tearing off more strips of skin with the impact.

With a string of curses, he tore the dangling bits of skin from his palms and hurled them into a rotting mess on the passenger side floorboard. He then reached for the ignition key, and prepared to start the engine, drive to Silas' motel room, and yell for all get-out to Anubis in hopes of drawing him to his master as payment for his current dilemma. But he stopped at the sound of another boat as it motored into the nearby bay.

Curious, he turned his attention in the direction of the newcomer, and whipped out his binoculars to take a closer look. Two minutes later, a speed boat—Elliot thought they were called Go-Fast boats—zoomed into view, slowed, and glided sideways to the nearest boat slip.

Elliot tightened his grip on the binoculars, trying to steady his hands enough to get a clear view of the boat's driver. He hadn't really been paying much attention when the show's crew had returned earlier, so he wasn't sure if everyone had been accounted for when they'd departed for the motel. He reasoned, of course, that there were probably plenty of other boaters out and about on the waters of such a beautiful day, and had no reason at all to think this newcomer had anything to do with the TV show or the expedition of *The Lord's Vengeance*. Yet something at the nape of his neck screamed at him to pay attention.

He watched as a sole figure, too far away to identify even

with binoculars, scrambled around the interior of the boat. At first, the person had been obscured from view by the fiberglass Bimini top that shaded the boat's console. Then, as the figure leapt onto deck to tie the vessel down, the movements were too fast and frantic to truly focus in on the face. To top it all off, they were wearing a pair of run-of-the-mill blue jeans, loose-fitting t-shirt, and a faded red baseball cap that helped conceal their face even more. making it even more difficult to identify.

Come on, dude. Let's get a look at you.

After the boat was finally secure, the figure jumped back in the boat, furtively glanced around as if looking to see if they were being observed, and picked up a large duffel bag before leaping back onto the slip again. When they did so, the bag, which had been hanging over the figure's shoulder, jostled, and something inside fell out and into the water with a splash.

The figure jerked to a stop, and even though Elliot couldn't hear anything from this far away, instinctively knew there'd been one or two expletives thrown in for good measure. It was then that Elliot could see the overall shape of the figure, and knew instantly that it was, in fact, a woman. Either that, or Elliot was feeling really really confused about how attractive a man's body was to him.

And now that he knew that the figure was that of a woman, he focused his attention to the back of the cap to see a blonde ponytail hanging behind her head.

Hmmmm. Both Laura Granger and Krista Dunaway, the two females involved in the show, have blonde hair. Elliot scratched at his temples in thought. *So that doesn't help much, does it?*

While he tried to discern the woman's identity, she crouched down at the edge of the dock, and looked into water. A moment later, she laid flat on the concrete platform, and reached her long arm into the water. Her head bobbed up and down, hurling yet another barrage of curses for a moment, then she withdrew her empty hand and clambered to her feet.

Once more, she glanced around to ensure her odd behavior hadn't been seen by anyone, placed the bag over her shoulder again, and jogged up the ramp to the parking lot.

Elliot slouched down in his car again, hoping not to be observed, but forgot the one law of stakeouts: if your target can't see you, there's more than a good chance you can't see them either. When he realized his mistake, he eased his head up just over the lip of his car door and peered out. But she was already gone.

Blowing out a frustrated breath, he sat up erect once again, and looked out the back window of his VW to see a black sports car churning up a spray of gravel, and squealing onto State Road A1A in the opposite direction his own car was facing. In other words, in the direction of the Sand Dollar Oasis Motel. To Silas and the crew of *Mysterious Expedition*.

"Swell," he muttered to himself as he opened his car door, and slid out. "Just swell, Elliot. You'd make one bang up P.I., wouldn't you?"

But he figured all was not entirely lost. He might not know the identity of this suspicious new boater...didn't even know if she was even involved in the case he was currently investigating for that matter...but he now had two options to try in order to find out.

Checking over his shoulder, he jogged down the gangplank onto the dock and crept up to the newly arrived boat. The outboard motor was now ticking as it cooled down. He pulled out a small notepad and pencil from his shirt pocket, and jotted down the boat's ID number in his scratch-like scrawl. He then looked around, much the same way the woman had been earlier, to ensure no one was spying on him, and quickly slipped on board the small twenty-foot speed boat.

His hands shaking, he quickly searched the boat's console for any clue as to who had been driving it only minutes earlier. When that proved fruitless, he searched the rest—being sure to check as many compartments as he could find—in record time. And came up completely empty.

Unperturbed, he climbed back onto the dock and moved over to where the object had fallen from the woman's bag, and peered into the water. Kelp and weeds swayed back and forth beneath the surface. A school or two of minnows raced away from a much larger fish, darting under the slip and disappearing from view. He searched for the object for nearly three minutes, until he caught a glint of sunlight reflecting up at him.

Just as the woman had discovered, although the water wasn't very deep here, the object was much too far away for his slightly longer arms to reach. He considered just jumping in and grabbing it. It would have been easy enough to do if he didn't mind getting wet, but he remembered what Silas had said about water's ability to disrupt spiritual energy and ectoplasm. He wasn't sure it would have the same effect on him. He had, after all, taken plenty of baths and showers since becoming undead. But now, considering the mangled mess his master currently was, Elliot was in no mood to tempt fate.

He stood up, ready to give up. The notion was ridiculous anyway. Yet, as Silas had pointed out, there'd been two different boats out near the *Stately Lady* on the night Avery had died...theirs and someone else. He and Silas had been to this very slip, in fact, to search for it. But there was nothing whatsoever, other than a wild hunch, to suggest that this boat had anything to do with the murder at all.

He was wasting his time.

He stretched his arms out in front of him, examining the green tinge to them.

Wasting *precious* time, apparently. He knew enough about forensic anthropology to know that once a body begins to decompose, it didn't take long to...well, it didn't take long. That's as far as he wanted to think about it.

With his shoulders slouched even worse than usual, Elliot pushed his glasses up on his nose, and began making his way toward the dock's gangplank and the parking lot above. He took his first step on the plank and stopped. Something was nagging him. Something he'd seen on the boat when he'd been searching it.

He turned around, and jogged back to the boat, jumped in, and began rummaging through the fishing equipment compartments in its deck. A moment later, he leapt out holding a fishing net with expandable handle and moved over to where he'd seen the reflection in the water. Getting down on his hands and knees, he dipped the net into the water and extended it down to the bottom with a slow swipe of his wrist. He brought the net back out, scanning its contents, and sighing with annoyance when he discovered he'd only managed to catch a few clumps of seaweed and a crab in the process.

He dumped them back into the water on the other side of the dock, then repeated the process. Three times, in fact. On the fourth—and he swore, final—time, he was successful. When he searched through the detritus he'd collected, he was rewarded with a small glass jar, sealed with a screw-on cap.

He held the jar up, squinting past the pinkish liquid inside, and his eyes widened. A few chunks of metal clinked against the glass as his hands shook. Metal that he'd recently become very familiar with. Metal that had led to the death of a world famous television show host just a few days ago.

The jar he was holding contained three good sized chunks of potassium.

CHAPTER
TWENTY-NINE

SAND DOLLAR OASIS MOTEL
ROOM 135
FRIDAY, 4:40 PM

"I told you, I don't know!" Krista Dunaway shouted. Becca and Silas, now ensconced in the medic's motel room, had been questioning her for the last half hour, asking many of the same questions over and over, and the woman was obviously getting frustrated with it. "Like I said, I found them in my room when we got back from today's shoot. They grabbed me. They kept asking about the artifact. I kept telling them I didn't know what they were talking about, but they wouldn't believe me."

Krista sat at the foot of the bed, her hands and legs shaking uncontrollably. Becca sat in the rickety old motel room chair next to the table, and Silas leaned back against the wall next to the door.

The room itself was a mess. Drawers had been pulled from

the dresser, their contents tossed and scattered across the floor. The clothes that had been in her closet had been shredded and left in a heap on the bed. Even her makeup case and toiletry bag had been upended over the bathroom sink countertop.

"So they decided they'd take me to their boss and see if he could get any answers out of me." She looked over at Silas, and gave him a slight nod. "Thank you. For coming to my rescue. I don't know how you managed to survive that explosion in your suit, but I'm certainly glad you did."

He returned the nod, self-consciously adjusting his scarf to ensure nothing of his scarred face was showing.

"And you have no idea what this artifact is that they were looking for?" Becca asked.

She shook her head. "If I did, I would tell you. I promise."

"Your team hasn't discovered anything unusual down at the shipwreck?"

"Nothing of significance. As a matter of fact, Garrett's starting to get freaked out. He never even wanted to do this shoot. Now he's pretty much ready to cut his losses and go."

Becca cleared her throat. "Krista, are you aware of the accusations against Lance? About his grave robbing? Antiquities theft and smuggling?"

The nervous woman shook her head, a look of curiosity on her face. "Grave robbing?"

"Apparently, Lance and an unknown accomplice had been using *Mysterious Expedition* as a front to steal precious artifacts from the various sites you've investigated." Becca paused. "Or at least, that's what several international police agencies are alleging. We're still looking into it, of course, and particularly looking for his partner. But is there a chance someone on your team has found something and didn't tell anyone?"

Krista shook her head with a shrug. "It's the first I'm hearing about this."

Becca's brow furrowed.

"I'm serious! I haven't heard anything about this grave robbing stuff. If I had, I guarantee I wouldn't have had anything to do with it." She paused, then held up a finger. "But if someone was involved in it with Lance, it would have been Derek."

"Derek?" Becca asked. Laura Granger had pointed them toward the new host as well. Two different people. Two different accounts. Both were pointing at Derek. "What makes you think so?"

"Derek was the real expert in antiquities," Krista said. "Yeah, he's a bit of a nerd, but he's actually the most well-traveled of us all. As the location scout—what's known in the business as Advance Producer—he had made all the connections within the countries we visited. Some of those connections weren't on the up and up, but to do what we were doing, sometimes you needed to grease a few palms from time to time. Ya know?"

Becca nodded, not wanting to interrupt.

"And I think some of the shadier types Derek dealt with were black market traders." Krista's hands were whirling around with excitement as she continued. "He said they were necessary associates to get into certain places that weren't authorized to the general public. I never really questioned it. But in hindsight, it kind of makes sense if he was involved in antiquities smuggling."

"Hmmmmm," Silas mumbled, interrupting the conversation.

Becca turned to look to find him staring up at the ceiling. He seemed distracted. She couldn't be sure, but she guessed he hadn't been paying attention to anything that was being said. "What is it?"

"The artifact Tanner was looking for," he said enigmatically.

"We've moved on from that," Becca said, annoyed with the change in subject. She was learning things about Derek Drake she hadn't known before, and the artifact her former commander had been searching for seemed somehow unimportant at the moment.

"Something that Esperanza told me today." Ignoring her protest, Silas pushed himself away from the wall, walked over to the medic, and sat down beside her. "Krista, remember that shard of stone I gave you just before my suit caught fire?"

She scrunched her nose, obviously disliking the images that sprang to mind from the incident. After a moment, her eyes widened. "Yes! I remember now."

"Shard?" Becca asked.

He nodded. "A piece, I believe, of the Hand that I found near the shipwreck. I think the artifact was damaged some time ago. Probably when Tombstone's ship sunk off the coast. I believe a fragment broke off from it."

"So the person who has the Hand of Cain doesn't have the entire artifact?"

"The Hand of *what* now?" Krista asked.

Silas began pacing the floor, then stopped, turned to Becca, and gave her a wry smile under his covering. "I've been formulating a theory since I found it. I believe this explains why whoever it is has never managed to gain complete control of it. Why his or her power isn't as precise as it should be." His head whipped over at Krista. "The shard. Where is it now?"

The woman blinked at him, then offered an uncertain shrug. "I put it in my dive bag," she said. "Then...well, then you caught fire, and everything else that day is kind of a blur. But I guess it's probably still in the bag."

"Which is?"

"On the *Stately Lady*. With the rest of the crew's dive gear." She paused. "But thinking about it now, there's something kind of weird I should tell you. When we were about to leave the yacht today, I forgot my phone in the locker. I went to get it, and found it open."

"Your locker?"

She nodded. "It looked like it had been jimmied with something, but I checked. Nothing was missing."

Becca looked at Silas. "Whoever it was probably was interrupted and had to give up a more thorough search."

"Which means they'll be back," Silas countered. "We need to get to the *Stately Lady* now."

ATLANTIC OCEAN
4 MILES SOUTHWEST OF THE *STATELY LADY*
FRIDAY, 6:05 PM

"I know this is kind of important and everything, but couldn't we have just radioed the captain and asked him to retrieve the shard and keep it safe until we could come back tomorrow morning?" Becca yelled over the sound of the wind and rain as Silas steered the Summer Haven Police Department's boat toward the spot where Ilene Nebbles-Fielding's mega-yacht was anchored.

"The captain works for Ilene!" Silas replied, steering the craft over a dangerously large swell.

They'd finished their interview with Krista an hour or so

DEAD IN THE WATER

ago, and Silas had demanded they take the police boat to the *Stately Lady* at once. Despite the fact that they had no legal right to go aboard the superyacht, she'd decided to just go with the flow for once and not argue with him. He was in no mood to listen to reason, nor was he any longer really focused on the Avery murder. To him, the only thing that mattered at that moment was the Hand of Cain.

Now, the two hunkered down underneath the Bimini fiberglass top of the police boat as a thunderstorm raged overhead, pummeling them with sheets of slanting rain and gale force winds. Lightning streaked across the darkening sky, and the vessel bobbed and yawed with each increasing wave.

"Besides," he shouted. "The longer the shard is not in my possession, the more chances Commander Tanner and his thugs have at claiming it for their master. It's a risk we can't afford to take at present."

"Well, maybe we should have at least picked up Elliot," Becca said. "He could have helped."

Elliot had called them before they left Summer Haven, excited over his day of recon at the town's marina. He'd told them about the woman he'd seen and the jar filled with chunks of potassium that had fallen into drink. From his description, he'd deduced that it was either Laura Granger or Krista Dunaway he'd seen, but since the pretty young medic had been attacked by Jeremy Tanner and his two partners at the time, it was pretty clear who the woman really was.

Lance Avery's estranged, and very aloof wife.

Silas waved her comment away as he turned the wheel to his right to avoid a rising wave, then leveled the boat off again. "The little guy gets horribly seasick. Trust me. You should be thanking me for keeping him away."

Becca cupped her hand over her ear, and leaned into him. "What was that? I can't hear you under that scarf!"

He pulled down the fabric from his mask, and repeated what he'd said, but Becca was too entranced by what she saw to pay his words much attention.

"Silas, your face!"

His eyes widened at her outburst, and she could swear his cheeks flushed with embarrassment before pulling the scarf back up over his nose.

"No, that's not what I mean," she shouted. "Your face! It's healing!"

She pulled out her cell phone, and reached up to pull down the scarf once more before snapping a quick picture. She showed it to him. Sure enough, although the majority of his face was still charred black with streaks of red, the seared gaping hole around his mouth had nearly grown over. He still held an eerie resemblance to the crispy remains of Lance Avery —no doubt a product of Silas' own subconscious manifesting itself in shaping his new body—the damage was much less severe than it had been earlier that morning.

While Silas gawked at the photo, he reached up to tentatively feel his face. He slowly began to smile at the image, and she noticed for the first time since knowing him, his hands tremble.

"Well now," he said, still smiling, "that is a bit of good news, isn't it?"

The celebration, however, was short-lived as the hulking streamlined form of the *Stately Lady* swept into view through the pouring rain. Becca put away her phone as Silas steered it carefully toward the large vessel, picked up the police radio's mic from its cradle.

"This is Chief Becca Cole to the crew of the Stately Lady," she said into it. "Asking for permission to come aboard."

There was a squawk as she released the transmit button, then silence for several moments.

"I repeat. This is Chief Becca Cole of the Summer Haven Police Department. Asking for permission to come aboard."

Another squawk, followed immediately by another. Then, "Chief Cole," came a shaky voice on the other end. "I'm so glad you're here. We need your help!" There was a brief pause, and Becca glanced over at Silas curiously. "Captain Mallory is dead!"

CHAPTER
THIRTY

"I'm so glad you're here," First Mate Tom Fletcher said to Becca after they'd scrambled up the ladder to board the *Stately Lady*. Upon seeing Silas and his hood, scarf, and sunglasses, he took a step back, but quickly recovered, and focused his attention on the chief. "We were just about to call for help."

Thunder boomed overhead as the downpour of rain raged on. The yacht itself swayed up and down, making Becca more queasy than she would have liked to admit.

Ducking under the tumult and pulling his slicker up over his head, Fletcher waved for them to follow him through the nearest door.

"So, what happened?" she asked once they were inside the vessel.

He led them into the ship's interior, down a spiral staircase below deck, and through a long hallway filled with several cabins for the yacht's crew. "The captain has been quiet all day," he said. "We got worried about him, but he wasn't answering any of the calls we put out through the intercom system. So, the men and I started searching room by room. We found him just before you radioed in. Dead. Looks like he's been shot."

The approached a T-section in the corridor and turned left. A few feet down and to the right, they came to Captain Mallory's designated cabin. Fletcher gestured to the door.

"He's in there." There were tears in the man's eyes. "I...I don't have to go in with you, do I? I don't want to see him like that again."

Becca placed a comforting hand on his shoulder and shook her head. "No, that's fine. We'll handle it from here. But I need you to go ahead and radio in to my office, and report it. I'll need some officers out here to help me, as well as the medical examiner's office."

The first mate nodded, then took off down the hall and disappeared around the corner.

"The plot thickens, it seems," Silas said, as he used his gloved hand to slide the door open.

The cabin was cramped, only about ten feet by ten feet, and complete with a bunk built into the far wall with a wardrobe constructed above it, a small writing desk and chair, and a cabinet opposite the door that bore a rich variety of liquors and spirits to make even the saltiest of sailors proud. Captain Mallory lay slumped over the mattress of his bunk with his knees on the floor, and looked entirely too big to have even made it through the narrow doorway. And yet, there he was, not breathing and laying in a pool of his own blood in the tiny space.

Becca moved into the room, being sure not to step onto any

crucial piece of evidence, and looked around. The place looked as tidy as she would expect from a disciplined boat captain. Nothing was out of place or knocked over. No obvious signs of a struggle of any kind.

She stepped over to the bunk, retrieved her flashlight from her belt, and shined it down on the body of Captain Mallory. Although he was laying cross ways over the mattress, his girth seemed to take up most of it, and she wondered how he'd ever gotten a decent night's sleep in such a tiny bed.

"Becca, look," Silas said behind her. She turned to see him pointing down at the writing desk. "There are two drinking glasses here." He lifted up a glass, which still contained a small amount of amber liquid in it, and sniffed. "Whiskey, if I'm not mistaken. The other one is completely empty though."

He picked up the second glass, and examined it more closely. "There seems to be some lipstick smudged on this one, although I can't quite make out the shade. Someone—a female someone I suppose—was drinking with the good captain before he died."

She nodded. "Put it down. You're wearing gloves, but you could still smudge any prints that might be on them. We'll leave that up to crime scene."

She turned her attention back to the dead man. There was a blood-soaked hole in his back. A ring of soot and gunpowder surrounded it, which told her that he'd been shot from behind. Probably as he was walking to his bunk.

"You trust your guys?" Silas asked, interrupting her train of thought. "I mean, you know about Tanner, but who knows who's working with him. Are you sure your people can be trusted with this investigation?"

She shrugged. "I'm going to have to," she said, crouching down beside the bunk and taking a peek underneath with her flashlight. "Until I've got evidence otherwise, Jeremy's two goons have no connection with the police department. Besides, it'll be the sheriff's office crime scene unit that sweeps this room. Should be safe."

She swiped the light back and forth until something gleamed back at her. She leaned in for a better look and smiled. "Found a shell casing. Once again, we'll have to wait until crime scene gets here to..."

"And I found something as well."

Silas' voice was quiet. Almost awed.

She turned around to see him with his nose in Captain Mallory's liquor cabinet, and she rolled her eyes. "Seriously? Now's not the time for your burgeoning bout with alcoholism."

He shook his head. "No, not the booze," he said, pointing behind one of the bottles of Jack Daniels. "This."

Proud that he hadn't just reached out and grabbed whatever had gotten his attention, she walked over, and looked at where he was indicating.

"Is that...?"

He nodded, beaming from ear to ear under his scarf, and reached up and took hold of a small glass jar containing mineral oil and three chunks of what looked like potassium metal. She let out a growling sigh that she'd given the man far too much credit for controlling his normally sticky fingers, and examined the container in the palm of his hand.

"So what's the captain doing with this, I wonder?" Silas said, holding the jar up toward the recessed lights, and peering into it. "Could he be who killed Avery? He wasn't around the day I went for my dive. Didn't see me put on the old suit. So I never saw how he reacted to it when he found out."

Becca shook her head. "What possible motive would he have for killing Lance?"

"He works for the old hag." Becca knew he was referring to Ilene, but didn't feel like scolding him for using such a pejorative term for the old bat. "We know that she wanted her dear sweet nephew to take over as host of the show. Maybe he was following orders to get Avery out of the way."

She thought about that for a moment. It made sense, but it was ignoring a major issue. "But we know Laura Granger had at least one jar of the stuff too. I'd say she had pretty good motive to kill her husband as well."

Silas laughed suddenly.

"What?"

He looked at her, his eyes twinkling from behind his sunglasses. "It's funny. Before this case, I had never seen a single piece of potassium in my entire existence—and that's saying something, by the way. And within a week's time, I can't seem to get away from it."

She joined him in a brief laugh, glad that some of his old sense of humor seemed to be returning. Then, she remembered why they'd been coming to the *Stately Lady* to begin with.

"Hey, you better go down to the locker room and look for that shard before the others get here," she told him. "If any more of my officers *are* in league with Jeremy, they don't need to see you snooping around down there."

"Good idea," he said, moving toward the door. Before he exited, he stopped and turned to her. "Are you going to be okay here?"

She gave him a scowl. "Please. I don't think the captain here's going to give me any trouble."

With a nod of understanding, he left her in the crime scene to truly begin her investigation.

"So WHEN WAS the last time you saw Captain Mallory?" Becca had gathered the remaining crew together on the bridge, and was now interviewing each of them as a group.

The storm still boiled out across the horizon, pummeling the *Lady* and sending her swaying mercilessly despite her immense size. Becca kept her gaze away from any of the windows, wanting to avoid seeing just how topsy-turvy the world outside really was to keep from losing her lunch all over the bridge's perfectly swabbed floors.

The question she just asked had been addressed to Fletcher, who seemed perfectly oblivious to the turmoil outside.

The first mate looked at the group of sailors—nine more in all. They murmured among themselves, then he turned back to Becca. "Sometime around three this afternoon, we think. He'd been out on deck to see the TV crew off. After that, we lost track of him."

"And was anyone else on board? I mean, besides the ship's crew?"

More murmuring, then one of the men raised a hand, and said something in a broken mixture of Spanish and English.

"I'm sorry. What did he say?" she asked Fletcher.

The first mate questioned the man, stopping a few times for clarification. "He says the only other person he saw on board after the show crew left was..." He stopped, questioned the Spanish-speaking man again, and continued. "He says, a blonde female. Very fancy female."

"Laura Granger?"

Fletcher nodded. "That's what it sounds like to me. Besides, I saw Ms. Dunaway leave with the crew. It couldn't have been her."

She nodded. "And did any of you hear anything unusual after they left? A loud bang or anything?"

He shook his head. "But it would actually be surprising if we did. The *Lady*'s a big boat, and the engines are loud. Unless we were near the captain's cabin, I doubt anyone could have heard anything."

"And Ms. Granger. Have you ever seen her and Captain Mallory particularly close? Did they talk frequently? Get along or argue?"

"No, no. Nothing like that," Fletcher said. "In fact, I don't think they ever said a word to each other the entire time she's been here. If there were any concerns, it was always Garrett Norris, who talked to him." He paused. "Or that other guy."

"Other guy?" she asked. "What other guy?"

"I don't really know his name. He's one of those behind the cameras guys."

"The camera man? Gabe Williams?"

Fletcher held up his hands. "No idea. Kind of a beatnik-looking guy to me. A real hippie type."

Becca riffled through her mind, sifting through her mental images of the *Mysterious Expedition* team. Gabe Williams certainly had that stoner vibe going for him. She could see him being referred to as a hippie. Derek Drake was too clean cut to be considered anything like that. Which left Kevin Aker with his shaggy dark brown hair and soul patch. He didn't really scream 'hippie' to her, but she guessed technically, his mane and facial hair might be seen as sort of beatnik. That is, if you squinted at him in the right light. But his personality and fiery temperament definitely excluded him from being mistaken for anything peace-loving or groovy.

"If I showed you images of the crew, could you point him out to me?" she asked.

"Oh, sure. No doubt."

Just then, the door to the bridge slid open, unleashing a torrent of wind and rain into the confined space, and a disheveled Silas Mot appeared. He looked at the crew, then at Becca.

"Uh, Becca?" he said. "Can I speak to you for a moment?"

The two moved away from the ship's crew, and Silas leaned into her. "I found it, but I forgot one small detail."

"What's that?"

"I can't touch it." He held up his gloved hands. "Even with these. Can't get anywhere close to touching it."

"So you need me to..."

He nodded. "And soon. I just saw the running lights of a couple of boats heading this way. I figure they're law enforcement, but just in case..."

"Got it." She turned to Fletcher. "You got some vessels approaching. Be sure to check their credentials before they come aboard. My associate has something to show me down below deck."

The first mate nodded, and Silas and Becca disappeared into the storm.

THIRTY-ONE

"You really don't trust my staff much, do you?" Becca shouted as the two ran down the short flight of steps leading to the locker rooms.

"How can I?" he said over his shoulder, leading the way. "Tanner was your dad's most trusted officer. He was your most trusted as well. How can you be sure you can trust anyone at this point?"

They entered the locker room, and Becca was instantly struck by the fetid stench of mildew and humidity that haunted all such rooms. It brought back memories of high school gym class. Her days at the police academy. Good times and bad, were associated with this very smell. But the good memories always involved friends. Friends she trusted with her deepest secrets. Friends she trusted with her very life.

She couldn't imagine going through life without trust. She couldn't allow herself to be that jaded.

"I have to believe the majority of my people are good, honest people," she responded, while following Silas over to a locker along the southeast wall. A piece of masking tape stretched near the top of the locker with the name 'DUN-AWAY' scrawled across it in Sharpie marker. The padlock lay on the ground at their feet with the key Krista had given them in it.

Silas opened it up, and gestured toward a bright green mesh bag resting on the top shelf of the locker.

"It's in the bag."

He glanced furtively over his shoulder, as if afraid Commander Tanner and his goons would burst through the door any second.

"Geez, Silas. Relax, will you?" she said, as she reached into the bag. "It's going to be okay."

She withdrew her hand and held out the irregular stone shard. "Is that a...?"

He nodded, taking off his sunglasses and pulling down his scarf. She could see that his face was continuing to heal. The blackened char-like skin was almost entirely cleared, and was now replaced with what looked like mild scar tissue.

"Yes," he said. "It's part of a knuckle and finger of the Hand, I believe. I've never seen the artifact before, but stories indicate it was carved from some arcane stone several millennia ago into the shape of a human fist."

She held it up for a closer look, and noticed as it drew closer to Silas, it seemed to glow with a strange emerald light. "Whoa! What's it doing?"

"It senses me. My power. I'm not exactly sure why it radiates like that, but I have a feeling it's not a good thing." He took a step back. "Best to keep it away from me if at all possible."

"That can be arranged, Freak." The familiar voice came from the entrance to the locker room. Silas and Becca spun around to see Jeremy Tanner and two others wielding shotguns in their direction. They were no longer wearing their balaclava masks, and despite the danger they were in, Becca couldn't help but be relieved she didn't recognize the other two men. "I'll be happy to take it off your hands."

Silas instantly moved in front of Becca, shielding her from the shotgun barrels. With a gentle hand, she nudged him aside, and stepped up next to him.

"When you guys left the motel and came straight to the marina after talking to that medic chick, I had a feeling you figured out where she hid the piece of the artifact," Jeremy said. "Easy enough to follow you out here, and give you some time to grab it. Looks like my hunch paid off."

"Jeremy, what are you doing?" Becca asked. "You were my friend. My partner. How could you do this?"

He shrugged. "Money mostly. Lots and lots of money." Then his face twisted into a nasty sneer. "Then there's the fact that you made chief over me. I was next in line. Then, the precious Rebecca Cole swooped in last minute, and snagged the gig out from under my hands." He nodded over at Silas. "But in the end, I did it 'cause I just don't like the freak very much. It's been fun to mess with his head."

"Did you find it fun to murder young Courtney Abeling in cold blood as well?" Silas asked, venom lacing his words.

"Never really thought much about it. Crazy broad overheard me talking to my employer. She was going to tell you everything, so we had to do what we had to do, ya know?"

"Jeremy, you're a cop," Becca said.

"Don't be so naïve, Chief. There are no good guys and bad guys. No white hats. No knights in shining armor with codes of honor." He laughed, and it sounded like a rake scraping corrugated metal. "Life's too short for all that. Well, it is for you two. Me and my boys? We're going to be taken care of real nice."

"Your employer?" Silas said. "Promised you immortality, did he?"

"Enough talking," Jeremy Tanner said, and turned to one of

his goons. "Get it." He nodded toward Becca. "She won't give you any trouble, will you?" He raised his shotgun up to his shoulder, and steadied his aim at both of them.

The goon stepped forward, and Becca noticed Silas' body tense.

Don't do anything stupid, Silas. We can always retrieve the shard later.

As if he'd read her mind and instantly chose to ignore it, Silas Mot stepped forward, raising his hands in the air.

"Your employer...I take it he hasn't told you who I really am?"

Jeremy let out a bellow of a laugh. "You mean the whole Grim Reaper bit? You were spouting that crap when we first arrested you last year on the beach. Didn't believe you then. Didn't believe my employer either. You're just a guy." He gestured toward him. "I mean, look at you? All scarred up. Gruesome as all get out, but you're as human as we are. Just a little more nuts, I'd say."

Becca grabbed at Silas' arm, silently warning him to stand down. She then looked over at Jeremy. "There was a murder here this afternoon. Others are on their way to investigate."

"Oh, I know. Don't worry. They were having some boat trouble back at the marina. Won't be here for a while." He then pointed to a receiver in his ear. "And if they call the sheriff's office or Coast Guard for assistance, we'll know it. We've got time. Trust me."

"You will not leave this boat alive," Silas Mot said. There was a strain to his voice Becca had never heard before. "None of you will."

This got all three of them laughing.

"In case you haven't been paying attention, Becca's gun is in her holster. You're unarmed. And the three of us? Well..." He hefted the shotgun slightly. "I think we'll be okay."

"Silas? Don't," Becca whispered.

She wasn't too concerned about Jeremy at this point, but given what Silas had been going through lately, and his weakening power, she wasn't entirely sure what would happen if he used any of his powers at this point.

Besides that, she remembered the first time she'd seen him use his powers of Death. It had been in a situation very much like this—a couple of gangbangers and devotees of his ex-wife, Santa Muerta. He'd killed them instantly just by pointing his finger at them like a gun and pulling the imaginary trigger.

But the man she knew as the Grim Reaper took duty more seriously than anything else. He loathed abusing his power. He'd brought those same gangsters back to life after he'd made his point because it hadn't been their 'Time', and Silas wasn't anything, if not a slave to the rules. Taking lives outside of their assigned Time went against everything he believed in. It was the ultimate betrayal of his sacred office. At least, in his mind anyway.

Becca wasn't sure he'd ever be able to forgive himself for betraying his office like that.

But Silas stood his ground, moving once again in front of her, his hands now clenched into fists.

"Becca, be ready to duck," he said over his shoulder. "And no matter what happens, find the Hand of Cain. At all costs, find it."

Before she could protest, Silas screamed an ear-splitting shriek of agony. He dropped to his knees as his body began to convulse on the floor. The action seemed to startle their adversaries, who stared down at him, gawking at his strange behavior. Their weapons nearly forgotten.

Then, Silas' body began to dissolve before their very eyes with columns of smoke and steam billowing up from his discarded clothing.

"What...," said one of the goons.

"The....," said another.

"Hel..." Before Jeremy Tanner could utter the word fully, a massive black cloud arose from the melted remains of Silas Mot, dousing the locker room in a shadowy haze.

Becca had seen this before as well. It was Silas' true form. The form of the Grim Reaper. No flowing cloak. No scythe. No humanoid form. Just a cloud of thick black smoke.

Somewhere in the distance, despite the thundering storm overhead, Becca heard the sound of hounds howling up into the sky. Anubis' hounds, she realized, no doubt tracking him now that he was no longer confined to a mortal body. But she didn't have time to ponder this at that moment, as Jeremy recovered from his initial surprise, and leveled his shotgun through the fog directly at her.

Remembering Silas' words to her, she dropped to the ground just as he pulled the trigger. Pellets from the gun plowed into several of the lockers where her head had just been, and he pumped the gun again for another shot.

Only this time, the black cloud was on the move.

The first goon suddenly dropped to the ground with a thud. Becca watched to see if his chest would rise and fall, but it remained steady. Unmoving. Before she had a chance to realize he was already dead, the second fell to the ground as well. His own gun clattering to the ground.

Before the cloud reached Jeremy, he fired again, not coming even close to hitting Becca this time. Then, he turned around and ran. The cloud followed him out of the locker room instantly.

Becca picked herself off the floor, and chased after them, running up the stairs to the main deck and into the raging tumult. She watched as Jeremy bolted toward the starboard side of the boat, ran past the crew of the *Stately Lady*, who were now bound with zip-ties against the gunwale, and toward the ladder that would lead down to what Becca presumed would be one of the boats Silas had seen a few minutes earlier.

Although the sun wouldn't dip fully past the horizon for another hour or so, the storm clouds above had turned the sky into night, and it was difficult to keep track of Silas' cloud in the gloom. But as Jeremy darted left and right on his way to his only escape, she could just make out the occasional dimness that made tracking her friend a bit easier.

Then, Tanner tripped over a mooring cable someone had forgotten to stow away, and sprawled clumsily across the deck. He rolled over on his elbows, looking up into the grim cloud of Silas Mot. His eyes wide with terror.

The cloud hovered over his quivering form as if waiting for something to happen. After a moment, Becca realized what Silas wanted her to do. She strode over to her former friend, confidante, and second-in-command, and peered down at him.

"Who are you working for?" she shouted over the din of thunder and wind.

His eyes never left the cloud hovering over him.

"Jeremy, it's the only way to save yourself," she said, brushing strands of wet hair from her face. "Tell us who your employer is, and he might not take your life!"

For a moment, Jeremy Tanner's eyes darted from the cloud to her. Then, they narrowed, and he laughed.

"I no longer fear Death!" he shouted back at her. "My master will soon conquer Death, and will bring me back to life!"

With that, he reached for his ankle, and pulled out a small revolver strapped under his pants, and pointed it at her. Before he could pull the trigger, the cloud descended on him. Jeremy screamed, then convulsed before going completely still on the boat's deck.

Becca stared down at the dead man, uncertain how to feel. How to react.

Then, she turned to the cloud.

"Okay," she said. "Go and find someplace to re-materialize, and I'll take care of all this when my guys show up."

But the cloud just hovered near her. It didn't move. Naturally, it didn't respond.

"Silas, come on." She waved toward the locker room. "Just go on down there and do your thing."

Still, the cloud did nothing but seem to stare back at her. Her pulse quickened.

"Don't do this to me, Mot!" she shouted, noticing for the first time that the cloud seemed a little less dense. A little smaller than it had been just a second or two earlier. "I can't do this without you!"

But the cloud continued to diminish. To dissolve.

"No! You can't go!"

For a moment, the cloud seemed to congeal once more into a semi-human shape. It raised what looked like a hand up to her.

Tears now in her eyes, she raised her own hand up.

Then, the shape evaporated entirely, and Becca stood alone on the deck of the *Stately Lady* with only the howls of Anubis' hounds to keep her company.

CHAPTER
THIRTY-TWO

Becca Cole leaned back in her chair, her feet kicked up on her desk, as she looked at the stone shard Silas had found on the ocean floor. The office was quiet, officially closed for the weekend, with only one or two of her officers coming and going while they patrolled the town on their regular duty.

Her department, as well as Summer Haven as a whole, had been rocked by the news of Jeremy Tanner's sudden, and apparently natural death, though Becca had worked hard to keep the news of his misdeeds secret. She'd convinced the *Stately Lady*'s crew to keep his involvement in the storming of their boat from the official record for now, explaining that it would hinder her ongoing investigation into his employer in the long run. Considering they were still distraught over the murder of their captain, it hadn't taken much convincing. Most

240

of them had been numb with grief throughout most of the ordeal anyway.

So now, she had two homicides, two vials of potassium connecting the captain somehow with Lance Avery's estranged wife, a broken piece of a mystically-powered artifact of Death, and the identity of the enigmatic possessor of said artifact all on her to-do list.

And still no sign of Silas Mot.

Was he gone for good? Had his last act dissipated the remaining power he had? Was he unable to recreate a new body now, or was he finally captured by his brother, the bounty hunter of the dead?

She sighed, placing the chunk of stone on her desk, and giving it one more examination.

"Okay, Becca. First things first," she said out loud. "Solve the murders. Then track down who hired Jeremy, and you'll find the Hand."

The question was, how was she going to solve the murders? Seemed to her that for every answer they discovered, they found two more questions.

"So, let's look at what we know," she muttered, pulling out a legal pad and pen. She began jotting the facts down as much in order of occurrence as possible.

First, Baron Tombstone's pirate ship, *The Lord's Vengeance*, was officially discovered some time two years ago. It had obviously been discovered previously by a person or persons unknown because by the time official archaeologists, such as Elliot Newman, got involved, the sunken ship had already been picked clean of most treasures—including the Hand of Cain, apparently. Granted, Silas had always theorized that Baron Tombstone had had the artifact taken to shore and buried somewhere along the coast, but that had never been proven.

Second, Ilene Nebbles-Fielding used her considerable clout

to sanction a reality television show hosted by her first victim, Lance Avery, to come and do a complete excavation of the ship, which would culminate in bringing its entire remains up to the surface. It just so happened that, before Lance was killed, pressure had been placed on the production team to make Ilene's very own nephew, Derek Drake, the new host of the show in light of contract issues.

Third, both Lance Avery and Derek had been implicated in a rather sophisticated antiquities ring. Despite the fact that Derek insisted he hardly knew Lance, at least two individuals Becca had spoken to had refuted that claim vehemently.

There was a buzz on her phone's intercom, ripping Becca from her thoughts. With a growl of irritation, she picked up the receiver. "This is Chief Cole. Can I help you?"

"Becca? Hey, it's me. Elliot." There was a pause. "I'm outside. Can you buzz me in?"

She took a deep breath, and did as he asked. She'd talked to Elliot last night about everything that had transpired, and he'd taken the news about Silas harder than she would have imagined. While she was worried about him probably more than anyone, she also knew Silas was resilient, if nothing else. And, it had taken him more than a day after the incident with the dive suit for him to pull himself together. She wasn't ready to count Silas out yet. But Elliot hadn't sounded as certain last night. She dreaded the conversation they were probably about to have.

A moment later, there was a tap at her office door, and Elliot entered without waiting for a response, a beaming grin on his face. With an uncharacteristic swing in his step, he sauntered over to her desk without a word, and plopped down in the chair opposite her. He leaned back, put his hands behind his head, and propped his own feet up on her desk in a near mimic of her own.

"Make yourself at home," she said, eyeing him warily.

Something was off about him today. Of course, Silas had told her about Elliot's current predicament. He had begun to decompose, and Silas hadn't been sure how long it would be before he rotted away to almost nothing. He had suspected, of course, his minion's condition was because of his own weakening power, but he hadn't been sure. Despite the number of times she'd encouraged Silas to talk to Elliot about it, he'd been reluctant to do so, claiming that the 'time just isn't right yet."

Now, as she looked at him, the green tinge she'd been seeing lately, not to mention the foul smell, seemed almost entirely gone. He seemed to have returned to his near mint condition before he'd been pulverized by the tour bus that killed him last year.

"Um, are you okay?" she asked.

He grinned at her. Seriously. His smile stretched as far across his face as she'd ever seen it. "Couldn't be better." He sat up, reached across her desk to her candy jar, and rummaged through it. A moment later, he withdrew his hand holding a Warhead, unwrapped it, and popped the sour candy in his mouth with flourish. "Haven't felt this good in..." He paused, his lips puckering as the candy dissolved in his mouth. "...well, in ever."

"Have you heard from Silas? Is he okay?"

"Who?" He then shook his head. "Oh, Silas. Nope. Not a word. But I figure he's okay. I'm still around right? Anubis hasn't sent his dogs after me yet, so I must still be under his protection." He held up his arms for her to see. "Plus, my...um... skin condition seems to have gotten better. So, guess I can't complain." He opened the candy jar again. "Got any Twizzlers in here?"

She cocked her head curiously, then shook it. "Sorry. No." She held up her notepad. "I'm just going through the facts of the case, trying to make sense of everything. I'm still nowhere close to solving Lance Avery's death. Or Captain Mallory's for that matter."

He pulled out two handfuls of candy, picking out the Warheads and tossing the rest back in the jar, and leaned back in his chair again.

"So, go ahead," he said. "Hit me. Let's figure this out together."

Her eyes narrowed, as she looked the undead archaeologist up and down. He was definitely acting very weird. Bolder. More confident, if not outright bombastic.

"Um, okay." She handed him her notepad with the first three facts she'd scribbled down and gave him a chance to read them. She then tossed him a pen, and he caught it in mid-air without the slightest fumble. It was something else that was different. Elliot was not the most graceful of men in the best of times. The man had gone through more cell phones from dropping them on pavement and tile than anyone she'd ever met. "Take notes, will ya?"

He gave her a wink and a salute. "Sure thing, boss."

"Number four..."

She then proceeded to tick off fact after fact of the case. How Lance Avery was a womanizing lout who consistently had affairs without bothering to hide it from his wife. How said wife, Laura Granger, had insisted his infidelity hadn't mattered much to her. The sound engineer, Kevin Aker, had seemed to corroborate this, implying that she had her own bit of side action quite often. Although, he'd neglected to go into any real detail on the matter.

"A lover's triangle! Spicy!" Elliot said, jotting away at the notepad.

Spicy?

She pressed on, despite her growing concern for Elliot's mental well-being, highlighting the way Lance Avery had been murdered.

"Which suggests that the killer most definitely has to be on the show," the little man said, plopping another Warhead in his mouth and wincing.

"Or on the ship's crew," Becca said. "We can't rule them out. Especially since Captain Mallory had a vial of potassium hidden in his liquor shelf."

"Then who killed *him*? And why?"

Becca shrugged. "Well, assuming that Laura Granger was the woman you saw arrive at the marina after the team—which seems to be confirmed by the *Lady*'s crew that she had indeed remained on board after they'd left—maybe she found out Mallory had killed her husband? Maybe it was revenge?"

Elliot sat up, shaking his head. "No, no. I don't think that's it. I mean, why would she bother trying to smuggle the potassium off the ship and leave the other bottle behind? It doesn't make sense."

Becca could only stare at the man now, in awe of his sudden clarity of thought. His confidence.

"Seems to me like she was trying to get the stuff off the ship to keep us, or anyone else for that matter, from finding it. Like she was covering her trail."

"Or someone else's," she agreed.

"If she wasn't trying to cover her own trail, then who?" Elliot asked. "I haven't been part of as many interviews with the crew as you and Silas, but from what I've seen, she doesn't particularly like any of them."

Becca thought about that for a moment, then a smile began to form on her face. "That's not entirely true. There's someone she *is* rather close to, and I think it's about time we had a bit of an in-depth chat with him." She stood up, pocketing the shard of the Hand of Cain. "No, I think we should have an in-depth chat with all of them. It's how Silas always enjoyed wrapping up a case."

CHAPTER
THIRTY-THREE

THE SAND DOLLAR OASIS MOTEL
SUMMER HAVEN
SATURDAY, 10:45 AM

"What is the meaning of this?" Ilene Nebbles-Fielding growled as she strode into the motel's conference room and leered at Becca. "Not only do you prohibit the crew from going out to the shipwreck, you have one of your stormtroopers drag me to this...this pigsty of an inn on a beautiful Saturday morning?"

Becca glanced over at Officer Tim Sharron and gave him a nod of thanks, silently releasing him back to his normal patrol.

"It's funny, Ilene," she said. "I've heard from a lot of people that Captain Mallory and you were very close. The man was intensely loyal to you from what everyone has told me. I thought you'd at least be remotely interested in finding out who killed him." She held up her hands. "But if you'd rather spend your day gardening or knitting..."

247

"Or drinking!" Elliot interjected. "Lots and lots of drinking, I imagine."

Becca shot him a glare.

"Or whatever you typically do on a Saturday morning, you're most definitely free to go," Becca told her. "I mean, it won't look good for you or anything, but I can't hold you here against your will."

The entire crew of *Mysterious Expedition* had already trickled around the conference table, their conversation a buzz of murmurs and questions that nearly drowned out Ilene's next words.

"Sure," she said to Becca. "Have your little fun with me now. Guess your boyfriend, who has far more sense in his head than you, didn't explain your situation well enough. But you're not going to be around much longer, Chief Cole. Mark my words on that."

Ilene Nebbles-Fielding glanced around the room, holding up her fingers like she was about to grab a clump of soggy hair out of the bathtub drain, and moved over to the table.

"Have a nice day, you old goat," Elliot said as she passed by.

"Elliot!"

He looked sheepishly at Becca, instantly covering his mouth with his hand. "I'm sorry, Becca. I don't really know what's gotten into me lately. I just keep saying stuff that pops in my head. It's weird."

"Maybe you've been eating too much candy?"

He tilted his head. "Candy? I don't eat candy. I'm diabetic." He paused. "Or I was. Before I died. Now, I don't know..." He paused, looking at his hands as they waved frantically in front of his face. "Hey! Look at that! My skin looks back to normal!"

"Uh, Elliot? Are you okay?"

He shrugged. "I think so. Why?"

"Because that was one of the first things you said to me

when you walked into my office this morning...the thing about your skin."

He looked at her funny. "I was in your office this morning?"

Okay. Now Becca was really concerned. Not only had he not been acting like himself all morning, now she needed to add amnesia to the list of ailments as well.

"Just take a seat," she told him. "Have some water or something." She gestured over to the table on the far side of the room that was filled with coffee, donuts, and a large number of water bottles. "And try to keep your mouth shut while I do this, okay?"

He nodded, and slunk over to the breakfast table in his customary slouch. With that, Becca strode over to the table, and addressed the room.

"As you probably have heard already," she began, "we had another murder last night. Captain Mallory was shot in the back at close range in his cabin sometime after the majority of you had already left for the mainland."

"So why are we here?" Garrett Norris said with a derisive sniff. "If we weren't there, then it obviously has nothing to do with any of us."

Becca smiled at this, holding up her index finger. "Good point, Mr. Norris. But remember, I said, *most* of you had already left." She began pacing around the conference table the way she imagined any classic detective might in Silas Mot's little world. "But I decided we'd start with the captain's murder first, because it is the easiest to solve, and should, hypothetically, point to Lance Avery's killer as well." She stopped, and renewed her smile at the producer. "So bear with me, please."

With that, she returned to the head of the table, and reached into a duffle bag she'd brought with her, retrieving a clear plastic baggy. It was sealed shut with evidence tape, but its contents were visible for all to see.

"A .38 caliber slug was pulled from his spine this morning by the medical examiner," she continued. "Given that I found the matching shell casing under his bunk, we can deduce it was shot by a .380 semi-automatic handgun."

Everyone seated around the table, glanced at one another curiously.

"Anyone happen to know someone who owns one, by chance?"

The room simultaneously shook their head.

Becca nodded. It was worth a try, but she hadn't really expected anyone to confess to anything at the moment. So, she pressed on.

"We also happened to find another little nugget of evidence we found interesting." She withdrew something else from the bag and held it up for all to see. "We found this among Captain Mallory's liquor bottles. It's potassium. The same substance used to start the underwater fire that killed Lance, and almost killed my partner, Silas Mot."

Her heart skipped a beat at the mention of his name. She kept waiting for the flamboyant man to burst through the conference room doors any minute, and make a complete fool of himself. And yet, for some reason, she feared it would never happen again.

"So it was the captain?" Krista Dunaway asked. "Captain Mallory killed Lance?"

"That's preposterous!" Ilene Nebbles-Fielding stood, slamming her frail hand down on the table with an electrified slap. "Brian would never do such a thing. He knew this expedition was too important to me!"

"Is it?" Becca asked. "Or was it what you could get from the expedition? Is something down there that interests you, Mrs. Fielding? A certain artifact...or a piece of artifact, maybe?"

"I...I have no idea what you're talking about," the old

woman said, taking her seat again. "You sound as crazy as that partner of yours."

The comparison stung Becca, but not for the reasons Ilene intended. It was a reminder. A reminder that she might have lost the best friend she'd ever had for good.

"But isn't that why you insisted on Derek, your nephew, replacing Lance?" Becca pressed. "After all, Lance was done with his criminal dealings and you obviously needed something from that wreck. Who better to do it than family, right?" She reached into the bag and pulled out a teletype she'd received from INTERPOL earlier that morning. "This is a document showing that Lance Avery had confessed to his crimes, and intended to help them retrieve the lost artifacts." Becca looked over at Derek. "Don't worry. He didn't give up the name of his partner. Yet. He just said he felt he needed to come clean about his own crimes, no matter what the consequence.

"It's why he wasn't sure he would even try to renegotiate his contract," Becca continued, looking over at Laura Granger as she said it. "He knew he was going to face some jail time, so why bother with contracts. He felt guilty for what he'd done and was ready to pay the price to ease his conscience." She shrugged. "I have to admit, I have a lot more respect for him now."

"These are baseless accusations," Ilene said. "I'll sue you for slander when this is over."

"Blah, blah, blah!" Elliot said, while using his hands as puppets. "It'll be hard to sue anyone when you're cooped up in the pokey." He then reached into his pants pocket, pulled out a yo-yo, and started 'Walking the Dog' with it.

Becca stared at him for a long moment, then shook her head, and turned to the door of the conference room to see the motel manager, Elroy Lincoln. She waved him forward, and he took hold of a wheeled cart that contained a television-VCR combo, and brought it over to the table.

"Thank you, Mr. Lincoln," she said. "That will be all." She then turned her attention back to the group. "As you know, my partner, Silas Mot, was injured in a diving accident a couple of days ago in much the same way as Mr. Avery. Our theory at the time was that the killer hadn't known which suit Lance would be using, so they prepared both suits. Just in case."

She pushed in a VHS tape, then pressed pause.

"When I requested the footage from that day, our belief was that the killer would be so preoccupied with Silas wearing the suit they knew would catch fire, they wouldn't be able to keep their eyes off him." She pressed play and the video started where she'd queued it. "I searched all the GoPro footage, as well as the stuff that Gabe Williams shot, and was surprised to find that no one seemed to be focused on Silas. No one, that is, except Ms. Dunaway."

"But I was just worried about the suit," Krista protested. "I didn't..."

Becca held up a hand. "I believe you, don't worry." She watched as the video footage continued to play out, then pointed to the screen. "I didn't catch this the first time I watched it. As a matter of fact, I'd pretty much decided it had been one big waste of time."

"Just like this ridiculous meeting," Garrett Norris said, leaning back in his chair and crossing his arms.

"But then I learned that Silas had found something when he was down near the wreck with you guys. Something that more than a few people have shown particular interest in. I decided to take another look." She paused the video at the proper mark, and tapped at the screen. "Now this is interesting. While no one was paying particular attention to Silas for most of the time he was down there..." She forwarded the video a few seconds, then stopped it again. "See this? This is where Silas finds something in the sand and asks Krista to grab it. When she does, there's one person among the crew that never takes his eyes off her. Not even when Silas catches fire. His eyes stay locked on Krista's every movement."

She paused the video again, and looked over at Derek.

"That person was you, Derek. You saw her place the object in her dive bag. I think you tried to get into her locker to get it, but something happened. Maybe you were interrupted. Maybe you just got cold feet. I don't know. But I think you definitely made sure your aunt knew about it." Becca turned her focus back on Ilene. "It's the only explanation for why three hired thugs broke into Krista's motel room yesterday looking for an 'artifact'."

"Oh, that's quite clever, dear Becca!" Elliot said with a clap of his hands. "Really quite clever indeed. I'd not even considered that before. Well done. Well done."

She gave him a 'will you shut up?' look, and he pantomimed locking his lips tight and throwing away the key before leaning back against the wall again.

"Pure speculation," Ilene Nebbles-Fielding protested. "You have no evidence whatsoever to back up your claims."

Becca shrugged. "Don't worry. I have time. Because I don't believe either Derek or you had anything to do with Lance Avery's death, nor the captain's." She smiled at the lot of them, then looked at Krista. "Going back to the vial of potassium in Captain Mallory's room and your original question, no. I don't believe Captain Mallory is the one who killed Lance. I think someone in this room did. I think the captain discovered the potassium hidden somewhere, confronted who he thought killed Lance about it, and was murdered himself for doing so. I think his murderer believed they had managed to grab all the evidence, but didn't know the captain had hidden some away just in case."

Becca turned to Elliot, and gestured for him to come to the table. He dutifully complied without comment. "Okay, Elliot. Tell us what you saw yesterday at the marina after the crew had already gone to the motel."

Elliot blinked back at her. "I'm sorry. What?"

"Your stakeout. Who you saw on the dock." She paused, seeing the blank stare on his face. "You know...what they did after getting off the boat?"

"How the blazes should I know?" he muttered. "I was with you the whole time yesterday."

This elicited one or two snickers from the suspects around the table.

"Elliot, you're really starting to worry me," she said to him. "We didn't see each other at all yesterday. You were keeping your distance from Silas, remember?"

"Sorry," he said, stumbling backwards while holding his head in his hands. "Got me...got me confused with someone else, I think."

"This is preposterous!" Ilene Nebbles-Fielding said. "Even her own so-called witness has lost his ever-loving mind." The old woman looked at the crew. "Let's go everyone. We don't need to hear anymore of this nonsense."

All except Krista stood and stalked out of the room, still chuckling to themselves at the odd little man who had thrown Becca's whole case out the window. When they'd all gone, the medic rushed over to Elliot's side, and helped him take a seat while taking hold of his wrist for a pulse. A moment later, her eyes widened, and she readjusted her grip on his wrist.

Becca watched, knowing full well what Krista was beginning to realize, and unsure exactly how she was going to play it off.

"This man..." Krista sputtered. "This man has no pulse."

She looked up into Elliot's eyes, who offered her a sheepish grin. "Oh, uh, it's there," he lied. "It's just really hard to find. Doctors are always having problems finding it...um, even with a stethoscope. Promise."

His ranting seemed to be the Elliot that Becca knew again. Anxious. Babbling. And definitely not good under pressure.

If Krista was convinced by his words, she didn't show it. Instead, she reached into her shirt pocket, pulled out a small pen light, and shined it in his eyes. As she did so, Becca decided to press the little man.

"Elliot, what's going on with you?" she asked. "Seriously. You've been acting weird all morning. And now, you nearly fainted. Is it because of Silas? Could that be affecting you?"

The archaeologist blinked at the bright light shining in his eyes, shaking away the blinding beam. "Silas..." He paused. "Something about Silas..." He seemed to trail off for a moment. "But I can't quite remember..."

Krista turned to Becca. "I think this man needs to go to a hospital. As soon as possible," she said. "He's not well."

Oh, you have no idea, Becca mused, although she also realized it might not be such a bad idea. While she doubted modern medicine could do much for the little guy in his current state—you know, being dead and all—she figured there was at least one person she knew who might be able to make heads or tails of what was happening to him. But it required her to bring him into the fold. It would require him to learn the truth about Silas Mot, and what was going on in their quaint little town. And most importantly, it would require him to actually believe her.

She just hoped that Dr. Brad Harris was more opened-minded than she had originally been.

CHAPTER
THIRTY-FOUR

SUMMER HAVEN URGENT CARE
SUMMER HAVEN
SATURDAY, 11:45 AM

By the time Becca pulled into the parking lot of Summer Haven Urgent Care, Elliot lay stretched out in the back seat, his head on Krista's lap, and unconscious. She'd been driving the three miles from the motel to the medical clinic that served as Summer Haven's emergency room with lights and sirens blaring, and at top speed.

"How's he doing?" she shouted over her shoulder, as she put the car in park and unfastened her seatbelt.

"I...I have no idea," Krista Dunaway said. "I've never seen anything like this before." Becca had already climbed out of the car and opened the rear passenger one. "He's got no heartbeat. No pulse. No respiration. And yet..."

"He's alive. Yeah, I know. It's weird, but you just have to trust me on this, okay?"

She reached in, and grabbed him by the arms, dragging

him out of the car with Krista's help. In tandem with one another, the two women placed Elliot's arms around their shoulders and began dragging him toward the entrance of the clinic. Before they arrived, two nurses scrambled out through the automated doors with a wheelchair. They got him seated in the chair, and he was instantly wheeled back into one of the examining rooms with Becca close behind.

"Thanks for your help," she told Krista over her shoulder as they raced away. "I'll call one of my officers to take you back to the motel ASAP, and I'll be in touch soon and let you know how he is!"

With that, she disappeared through the doors of Exam Room 3, where a nurse closed the curtains behind them. Without waiting another second, the two nurses began prepping Elliot, cutting away his shirt and pants, and hooking him up to heart monitor leads. As expected, the monitor continued to flatline.

"We need the paddles!" one of them shouted.

"We need a doctor!" the second one followed up with the first.

Becca raised a hand to get their attention, but they ignored her as a third nurse wheeled in a cart with a defibrillator and paddles.

"You won't be needing those," Becca said, still holding up a hand.

"What the...?" one of the nurses said. "Is that a Y-incision scar on his chest?"

Of course it was. Elliot had been autopsied last year, but Becca couldn't exactly tell them that.

"Don't be ridiculous," another nurse said.

"What do we have," Dr. Brad Harris asked as he strode into the examination room. He stopped when he saw Becca, a look of surprise on his face. "Becca! Are you okay?"

She nodded, then directed his attention over at Elliot.

"Doctor, he's coding," one of the nurses said. "He's got no vitals!"

He instantly leapt into action, rushing over to his patient, and doing a quick check for his pulse and pupils. "Hmmm...no pulse," he said. "But his pupils seem to be dilating just fine." He turned to look at Becca. "What happened to him?"

This time she held up both hands and everyone was now finally paying attention to her. "He's in no immediate danger," she said. "Yes, he's sick. Something is wrong. But his vitals... well, you just have to take my word that your machines aren't going to work exactly right with him."

Brad gave her a half-smile, as if waiting for the punchline, then shook his head. "That doesn't make any sense. We need to..."

"Brad!" she shouted, stopping him in his tracks. "Just listen to me. I need to talk to you. Privately."

The doctor looked shocked from her outburst, then glanced over at his nurses, then back at her.

"Uh, okay," he said, then turned to his nursing staff. "Keep an eye on him. If he starts behaving odd, come get me in my office."

With that, she motioned for Becca to follow him, and led her through a series of hallways and finally to his office. Once inside, he closed the door, and gestured toward a chair in front of his desk.

"Okay. Let's have it," he said. "Tell me what's going on."

She looked at him for an uncomfortably long moment, pinched the bridge of her nose, and sighed. Then she told him. Everything. About finding Silas Mot standing over the body of Andrea Alvarez last year and his claims of being the Grim Reaper in the flesh. Of her discovery that those claims were, indeed, true. And how Silas had resurrected a recently deceased archaeologist who'd been researching *The Lord's Vengeance* well before Ilene Nebbles-Fielding became interested in it.

And finally, she told him about the Hand of Cain, and its ability to give mortals the power over Death, and of the shard that Silas had found that was the only thing keeping the wielder of the Hand from gaining full control.

"But the Hand or the shard has nothing to do with what's happening to Elliot right now," she said. *Or is it? Could the person possessing the Hand of Cain be targeting Elliot? But why? With Silas MIA, Elliot's not exactly a threat now, right?* She brushed those thoughts aside. "Ultimately, I think it has to do with whatever happened to Silas. If he's gone for good, I think maybe his...his mojo on Elliot or whatever you want to call it might be unraveling." She shrugged. "At least, that's my best guess anyway."

Am I doing the right thing by telling Brad about all this? He's already beginning to think I've lost my mind by humoring Silas to begin with, she thought. *And now, I'm basically telling him the Boogeyman is real and there are monsters and magic and curses out there in the world that are playing havoc with people's lives. If I was him, I certainly wouldn't believe me either.*

As these, and a myriad of other thoughts raced through her mind, she became acutely aware that the office had gone uncomfortably silent. She blinked, then looked across the desk at Brad, who stared dumbfounded at her.

She inhaled a deep breath, then let it out again. "So say something. Anything. Don't leave me hanging here."

He opened his mouth to speak, then bit down on his lip, eyeing her warily the whole time. His chair squeaked as he leaned back in it, but didn't say a word.

"Come on, Brad," she said. "I know how this all sounds. But it's a hundred percent true. Every word of it."

"This shard," he said, catching her off guard. Of all the things she expected would be his first word after her explanation, that hadn't been it. "Do you have it? Is it here? Now?"

She scrunched her nose up at the question. "Huh?"

He leaned forward in his chair. "Oh, it's just that it seems that everything that has happened to your friend seemed to begin with it," he said. "Didn't you say that you had been examining it in your office and set it down on your desk just before Mr. Newman came in? And it was then that he started acting...um, odd?"

Becca hadn't considered that, but he had a point. The timing *was* rather coincidental, she had to admit.

"Uh, yeah," she said. "I've got it."

He held out his hand. "Let me take a look."

She gave an involuntary recoil at the suggestion, and he held up his hands in a 'don't worry' gesture. "I just want to examine it. Run some tests on it. If it's what you say it is, maybe it's putting out some sort of radiation or something."

"Wouldn't it be affecting me, if that was the case?"

He raised a single eyebrow at her question.

"I'm not crazy, Brad."

"Didn't say you were," he said, still holding out his hand. "But if this object is dangerous, it might..."

"I only came in possession of it yesterday...well after you accused me of acting irrationally when it came to Silas." She felt her face flush. She was getting angry, and that wouldn't do Elliot any good at all, so she took a series of deep breaths to calm herself down. "Look, Brad. I don't want to argue. I just want to make sure my friend is okay, and I don't think it has anything to do with the piece of the artifact. You have to trust me on this."

He kept his hand extended for several long seconds, then closed it, and pulled it back across his desk. Then he let out a deep sigh. "Fine," he said. "I'm not saying I believe your story entirely, but I know you well enough to give you the benefit of the doubt." He stood up from his desk. "Now, let's go check on Elliot and see..."

There was the sound of a loud crash from somewhere down the hall, and people yelling. Brad and Becca exploded from their places, threw open the office door, and dashed down the winding hallways to the examination room atrium. The curtains surrounding Elliot's room now hung, ripped from their hooks, at an odd angle. The three nurses stood, ready to move, in a semi-circle, with a crazed Elliot Newman their sole focus of attention.

He was now out of his bed, his eyes wild and hurling bed pans, tongue depressors, and anything else he could get his hands around at the bewildered women.

"Don't you hear them?" he shouted at everyone. "The hounds! They've found me!"

Everyone in the room stood perfectly still, cocking their heads almost in unison as if straining to hear what the deranged man was talking about. Becca strained as well, and after a moment, she indeed heard them. The howls were faint. Far away. But they were real nonetheless.

Judging from the looks on everyone else's faces, no one else had heard them. At least, not yet.

Becca darted over to the little guy, putting her arm around his shoulder, and she hushed him with a hiss from her lips. "It's okay. We'll get you out of here before they..."

There was a crash of shattering glass. Everyone craned their heads in the direction of the clinic's entrance where the entire plate glass window of the clinic's façade came crumbling down in front of them. The nurses all stood gawking, unable to fathom what had just happened.

"Well, what in the world caused that?" one of them asked another, taking a step toward the now crumbled glass.

Becca, however, stood perfectly still. Unable to move. Unable to hardly breathe. There, mere inches away from the clinic's interior, stood two immense canine-like creatures. Their fangs bared, saliva oozing from their curling black lips. The dogs—and she assumed that's what they were—were nearly skeletal with immense pointed ears and dark red eyes. Eyes that turned to stare at her. And Elliot.

Despite the monster dogs, the nurses still stepped toward the ruined window, as if they were oblivious to the threat.

"Stop!" she shouted at them. "Don't move. Don't take another step!"

They turned to look at her with curious expressions on their faces.

Then, she realized the horrible truth. They really hadn't heard the approaching hounds. And now, they couldn't see them either.

Becca glanced over at Brad, who stood slack jawed at the beasts for the briefest of moments, then gave his head a quick shake and turned to look at her just as the nurses had.

"Uh, why don't you want them to move, Bec?" he asked, jamming his hands in his pockets, and looking from her to the shattered glass on his floor.

Had he seen the dogs or was he just simply as bewildered by the broken window as the nurses?

She pointed at the creatures. "You...you don't see them?"

He looked in the direction she indicated. "See what?"

"They can't see them, dear Becca," Elliot said in an unnaturally smooth and calm voice. "And they're in no real danger. But we are. We must run." He took her by the hand. "Now!"

The little guy's grip was stronger than she would have imagined possible. He yanked her along with him as he took off running past Brad and down the hall leading to the various doctors' offices in the clinic.

Brad shouted after her, followed immediately by another crash and series of howls that signaled the hounds were in pursuit.

"I assume there's a back door to this establishment?" Elliot asked, not sounding at all like himself as he said it.

He sounded more like...

"Becca!" Elliot shouted. "Back door?"

His bark was the jolt she needed to jerk her back to their current dilemma. She gave him a nod, and ran ahead of him deeper into the clinic. "Follow me!"

CHAPTER
THIRTY-FIVE

Less than a minute later, Becca pushed the emergency door latch to the back exit, and they exploded into the open air before immediately slamming the door shut. Elliot rushed over to the nearby dumpster, heaving with all his might, and wheeled it against the door as a barricade.

"That won't hold them for long," he said. "Soon enough, they'll realize they can just leave the way they came, and the hunt will be on again."

He grabbed her by the wrist again, and tried to pull her away to resume their escape, but she held firm to her spot.

"Come on," he said. "We must flee. Now."

She wrenched her wrist free from him, and placed one hand on her hip defiantly.

"Not until you tell me who you are," she said, narrowing her eyes at the little man.

He shrugged. "You know who I am. Let's go."

"Not another step." She inched her hand down to her holster. "Spill."

Elliot looked at the barricaded door—it shook and rattled

as the dogs railed against it—then back at her. A moment later, he threw up his hands and sighed.

"Like I said, you know exactly who I am," he said. "Just your friendly neighborhood Grim Reaper inhabiting the body of his reanimated minion." He chuckled. "It was tough-going at first. A bit of a rocky start. Tricky figuring out the controls, as it were. But I'm back, baby! And better than..." He paused, glancing down at his portly diminutive body. "Well, not really *better* than ever, but alive. At least for now, that is."

"You jerk!" She punched him in the arm. Hard.

"Ow!"

"You big jerk!" she repeated. "I thought you were dead. Or... um, gone. Or something!"

"I actually was. For the briefest of moments. One minute, I was taking vengeance on that rascal Tanner, the next, I was... somewhere. Similar to what I experienced with the dive suit," he said, gently rubbing at his arm where she'd struck him. "Not sure how long I was there, but at some point, I remembered my connection to Elliot. Or I was reminded of Elliot. I can't entirely be sure. But long story short, I figured he wouldn't mind a roommate for a while, so grabbed my suitcases, and moved in."

"Guys," Elliot said.

"So that's why Elliot's...er, skin condition's reversed? Because you possessed his body?"

He wagged his finger at her. "'Possessed' is such an ugly phrase. I'm cohabitating with a pal. Roomies, as it were. And yes, with my remaining power, mixed with Elliot's own spirit, we were able to, at least temporarily, restrain the rot that was threatening to overtake him."

"Guys," Elliot repeated.

"Wait a minute!" Becca said. "You totally messed up my big reveal! I was just about to unmask Lance Avery's killer, and you had to do your crazy puppeteer bit and throw a monkey wrench in everything!"

"So you know who the killer is?" he asked.

"I believe so, yes."

"Guys!" Elliot shouted this time.

"Why do you keep saying 'guys'?" Becca asked.

Elliot shook his head. "Oh, that's not me. That's the minion." He paused. "What is it, Elliot?"

"Um, do you guys hear that?" Elliot asked.

They stopped, listening for a moment.

"I don't hear anything," Becca said.

"Exactly! The hounds have stopped trying to bust through the door," he said. "We need to run!"

He grabbed Becca's wrist again—although she wasn't entirely sure who it was gripping her this time—and they bolted down the alley toward the street.

"I assume your patrol car is..."

She pointed to the left, and they turned in that direction just as the hounds were scrambling out of the clinic's shattered windows. The dogs' bony legs wobbled for a second, as they caught the scent of their prey, and turned to face them.

Grabbing her keys in her pocket, she hit the alarm button, which started the mournful wail of her car's siren. The creatures whimpered at the sound, backpedaling a few steps away as Becca and Elliot/Silas leapt into the front seat and slammed their car doors shut. The electronic locks engaged, and Becca started the engine with a roar before peeling out, and away from the small medical facility.

Elliot glanced over his shoulder, his eyes widening. "They're chasing after us!"

"They may be supernatural, but they're not speed demons," Silas said through Elliot's mouth. "Keep going, Becca, and they'll tire out soon enough."

She weaved the patrol car in and out of traffic down the two lane Palm Avenue, and turned east on Coral toward A1A. The beasts remained in her rear view mirror for another three blocks before eventually disappearing behind them.

Collectively, the trio all breathed a sigh of relief and relaxed.

"So where to?" she asked, uncertain of what to do.

"Just keep driving for the moment," Silas said. "They still have our scent. The more space you put between us and them, the easier we'll be able to evade them."

She did as she was told, navigating the small town through backroads and little-used alleys, until she turned south on State Road A1A, and picked up speed.

"So who do *you* think killed Lance Avery?" Silas asked out of the blue after several minutes of absolute silence. "I'm curious."

She glanced over at him, still shaken over the fact that she'd just escaped from a pack of hellhounds. To top it all off, she was still weirded out that she might be talking to Silas, but it was Elliot in the car with her. Not an easy day to grow accustomed to.

If Silas shared her apprehension, he certainly didn't show it. Instead, he sat in the passenger's seat, legs crossed, and grinning at her with a familiar twinkle in his eye.

"Well, I have to admit, I haven't worked out all the kinks yet," she told him once she'd had a few moments to process it all. "I couldn't figure out how Laura Granger fit into all this until the murder of Captain Mallory."

He nodded, gesturing for her to continue.

"But here's what I'm thinking. Lance Avery didn't just have one business partner in his criminal enterprise. I think he had two."

Elliot raised an eyebrow at this. "Go on."

"Derek, of course. But I also think Laura was involved in the scheme too." She turned the car down an unmarked dirt road, and continued driving. "Here's the thing. I'm pretty sure Ilene Nebbles-Fielding is the one who has the Hand of Cain. I think when she realized the artifact was missing a piece—the shard you found—she realized the most likely place to find it would be near the shipwreck. She probably knew about Derek's criminal activity, and reached out to him. As executive producer, Laura would have had to sign off on bringing the show here, along with Lance as the host. With those two behind the move, despite his own misgivings, Garrett Norris had no choice but to agree."

"I have a few things to add, but I'll wait for you to finish," Silas said.

"Anyway, Ilene wanted them to find the shard for her," she continued. "But Lance had a change of heart last minute. He decided to back out of the deal, and Derek killed him because of it." She looked over at him to see his reaction, but he simply stared out the passenger window watching the jungle-like foliage go by. "So I think Captain Mallory somehow found the jars of potassium. I don't know if he started blackmailing them or wanted in on the action, but he approached Laura about it, and she had no choice but to shoot him and grab any vials from him that she could find."

"And one of those vials dropped in the water when I was staking out the marina," Elliot said excitedly.

"Okay, this is going to get old real fast with both of you sharing one mouth."

Elliot shot her an apologetic look, and she moved on.

"So anyway, that's my theory."

Silas nodded, scratching at his chin for a second. "And it's a good one," he finally said. "Excellent reasoning indeed. However, there are a few problems with it."

"Like?"

"For instance, you're wrong about Ilene," Silas said. "She doesn't have the Hand." He looked at her grinning broadly. "But she definitely knows who does."

"And how do you know that?"

He shrugged. "Two reasons, actually." He reached in Elliot's pockets and pulled out a fresh Warhead candy, plopping it in his mouth after unwrapping it. After wincing at the sour flavor, he continued. "First, Ilene Nebbles-Fielding is dying."

"Dying?"

"A few weeks. A month, tops, I'd say."

"How do you know that exactly? She doesn't look sick."

"It's the one advantage to my recent brush with my own demise," he explained. "For the briefest moment, I was returned to my natural form and once more connected with the Netherworld and all its otherworldly knowledge. I could see that the old crone had far outlived her Time, but could see the sands of the hourglass rapidly draining away for her at the same time.

"That, of course, is how I know she knows who has the Hand. He's staving off her death admirably. She should have been dead months ago. But without the shard—and its increased control of the artifact—her time is still dwindling down."

"How do you know she's not using the Hand on herself?"

"Because she can't. It doesn't work that way. From what I know about it, the Hand of Cain cannot extend life for the possessor." He glanced over at her, his expression changing quickly to one of concern. "The other reason I know she doesn't possess it is because I now know who does."

She hit the brakes hard, bringing the car to a skidding stop, and turned to give him her undivided attention.

"Who?" she asked. "Who has it?"

"You're not going to like the answer."

"Who?"

"Remember when Jeremy told me outside Krista's motel room that we'd never guess who it was?"

"Who?" She growled the word.

He eyed her up and down, as if trying how best to tell her the news. After a while, he shrugged and just said it.

"Dr. Boring."

Becca blinked at him. "Brad?"

He nodded.

"Uh, no. That can't be right. That doesn't make any sense."

He raised his hands, palms up, and nodded. "Actually, it kind of makes perfect sense." He began ticking on the reasons on his fingers. "One, he's a doctor. If there's anything doctors hate more than anything, it's feeling useless in the face of... well, me. I've known plenty of medical men driven mad by a desire to keep me in check over the millennia. Dr. Harris wouldn't be the first."

"But...but, whoever has the Hand of Cain..."

"Dr. Harris."

She scowled at him. "Whoever has the Hand of Cain is responsible for a number of deaths. How does that make sense? A doctor causing death because he wants to stop it?"

"Because the artifact itself is powered by the life force of others. Without deaths to power it, it cannot prolong another's life." He paused. "This is where I think Ilene Nebbles-Fielding comes in. I think she came to your doctor friend. I'm guessing she's a patient of his."

Becca nodded, remembering Brad's admission of that fact just yesterday.

"I'm not sure how it played out, but I imagined she offered him untold riches if only he could keep her alive. The money could go a long way toward research, facilities, medical equipment...you name it."

"But if you're right...and I'm not saying you are...how did he know about the Hand? How did he even get his hands on it?"

This elicited a renewed smile from him, and he raised a finger in the air. "Ah! That! The other day, when I was discussing the disappearance of the Hand of Cain with Esperanza, she told me that even though the *Los Cuernos del Diablo* might be a gang of thugs, they weren't savages. They were, in fact, a business, requiring the services of others such as lawyers, accountants, and...yep, you guessed it. Doctors. You need a doctor, after all, to stitch up gunshot wounds and the like, right?

"Anyway, odds are pretty good, I'd say, that your boyfriend paid U-Store-It a visit on a number of occasions over the last year and a half or so. My bet is that he learned about the artifact there, remembered Ilene's situation, and took advantage of his familiarity with the gang's hideout."

Becca sat there for a few stunned seconds in silence.

"Another reason I know it's him," Silas added. "He saw the hounds of Anubis."

"No, he didn't," she said, shaking her head. "I thought so too, but when I asked, he was just as confused as the nurses."

"I'm sorry, but that's not true. I wasn't sure myself until that moment. Dr. Harris is a good actor, I'll give him that. But he no doubt saw them." Silas sighed. "And the truth is, mortals typically cannot see such creatures."

"I saw them."

He nodded at this. "Only people who are intimately familiar with Death *can* see them. Elliot could see them naturally, because he was, in so many words, dead himself. You can see them because of your association with me. And someone

271

who has not only been in possession of the Hand, but also used it...they could no doubt see them as well."

She let his words soak into her mind, trying every way possible to discount his arguments and coming up short every time. Her mind drifted back to his office, less than an hour ago. About how she'd told him everything. About how he refused to believe her story about Silas and the Hand of Cain.

Her eyes shot up. "The shard."

"Excuse me. What?" Silas asked.

"When I told him about the shard," she said. "His eyes seemed to light up. He became very curious about it. Didn't believe—or pretended not to believe anyway—anything I told him, but when I mentioned the shard, he suddenly wanted to see it. Wanted to run tests on it."

She continued to ponder everything, and it all started making so much sense.

"Son of a..." she muttered. "He came to my office yesterday before we ran into Tanner and his thugs. Told me he'd been talking to Ilene, and tried to get me to back off from the investigation. Warned me a special meeting was being called to question my continued position as police chief." She whipped around to face Silas/Elliot again, her eyebrows furrowing. "And I caught him having a private conversation with Jeremy then too."

Silas looked at her. "I'm sorry, Becca. I truly am."

"I can't believe it. I just can't," she said. "I mean, sure. I wasn't really all that into the guy, but I thought..." She trailed off.

"You thought he was a good-hearted, decent man," Silas finished for her. "Dependable. Level-headed. And I think you were right. At least, in the beginning. But such an object as the Hand of Cain has a way of corrupting its wielder. He's not the same person you first met, I dare say." He cocked his head slightly. "Well, except for the boring part."

She didn't respond to his joke. Instead, she just sat there for the next few minutes, hands gripped tight on the steering wheel and staring out the windshield as she tried to take in deep, calming breaths. After a while, her muscles eased, and she leaned back in her car seat.

"So what do we do now?" she asked.

"Well, getting back to who killed Lance Avery. I think you're wrong about that too," he said, obviously struggling not to smile at her as he said it. "And only a woman as horrible at romance at you would have missed all the signs, I might add."

She scowled at him. "I have a gun, you know." Becca couldn't help but smile at him this time. If he was trying to cheer her up, he'd somewhat succeeded, though she wasn't quite sure where romance played in the murder of Lance Avery. "And I'm not afraid to use it."

"Good," he said. "Because you might just need it before this day is done. Now, let's go catch ourselves a couple of killers."

THIRTY-SIX

THE *STATELY LADY*
23 MILES EAST OF SUMMER HAVEN
SATURDAY, 3:05 PM

"Oh, great! You two are back," Garrett Norris said, looking up from his computer monitor as Becca and Silas/Elliot approached him at his work station on the stern of the superyacht. The screen showed the *Mysterious Expedition* team below the water's surface, surveying the shipwreck below. "Decided to disrupt us even more with your insanity, have you?"

Krista Dunaway, who'd been left behind by the crew when she'd helped take Elliot to the urgent care clinic, strode up behind them, followed by an irritated Ilene Nebbles-Fielding, having been escorted to the yacht by Officers Sharron and O'Donnell.

"Round two," Becca said with a smile. "My associate here had a bit of a medical episode earlier today. Sorry about that.

But he's better now, and it's time to wrap this case up once and for all."

"So if you'll be so kind," Elliot stepped forward, extending a slight bow to the producer. "We'd ever so appreciate you calling your crew up for a little pow-wow. Okay?" His own grin was infinitely more feral than Becca's, and not at all a smile Elliot would ever offer of his own free will.

Garrett let out a growling sigh, then looked over at Ilene for assistance. "Really? We're doing this again? Can't you do anything about this?"

The old woman, her face a wrinkled mask of disdain, shook her head. "I'm afraid not, Mr. Norris." She nodded at his radio. "Best to call them up so we can get on with it."

He did as he was told, while First Mate Fletcher and his men arranged several deck chairs in a semi-circle in preparation for the team's arrival. Elliot walked Krista over to one of the chairs, and then did the same for Ilene, keeping the two on opposite ends of the lineup.

For her part, the old woman muttered a string of curses at him as he helped ease her into the chair, but he chose to simply respond with a mischievous wink.

Several minutes later, the crew emerged from the water with irked expressions on their faces. Derek first, followed by Kevin Aker, then camera man Gabe Williams. They each looked confused as they climbed on board and stripped away the scuba gear they were wearing. None of them said a word when Becca instructed each of them to take a seat, and did as they were told.

"Now, all that's left is Ms. Granger," Silas said through Elliot. He turned to look at Garrett. "Where *is* your lovely executive producer anyway? We were told she came with the crew to the *Stately Lady*."

The producer glanced around, confused for a moment.

"Um, not sure where she is," he said. "She was here a few minutes ago, before you arrived." He reached for his radio mic, and spoke into it. "Laura, you there?"

There was a squawk of static, but nothing else.

"Laura, you're needed outside on the dive platform," Garrett said. "Copy?"

Still nothing.

Becca glanced over at Elliot, then at her two officers who were standing guard over the crew. "You two stay here. Elliot and I are going to search the ship." She turned to First Mate Fletcher. "Do we have permission to search?"

"Why are you asking him?" Ilene Nebbles-Fielding growled. "It's *my* yacht."

"And for now, I'm acting captain," the sailor told the old woman before looking back at Becca. "Yes, you have permission."

After nodding her thanks at him, Becca and Elliot moved forward along the port side walkway, making their way to the first doorway leading to the ship's cabins. When they were outside of view of the others, she withdrew her firearm, and kept it at ready as they ventured inside.

"You think you'll need that?" Silas asked her.

She squinted while her eyes adjusted to the dimmer lighting within the superyacht's interior. "Not sure," she said. "Better to be prepared though, right?"

"She's a suspected murderer of at least one person," he replied. "One quite willing to use a gun. Probably a good idea."

Elliot folded his hand into a finger gun, and pointed it forward. Shaking her head, Becca chuckled at the image...a reminder of one of her first encounters with Silas Mot. They then proceeded to search each room down the hall with no results.

At the end of the hall, they found a spiral staircase leading up. Becca, gun extended, moved up the steps first while watching for any signs of movement as her head emerged on the next level. From what she could see, they were moving up into a small ballroom with shiny tile floors and a disco ball hanging from the vaulted ceiling above. A handful of round tables circled the room, and a mahogany bar stood empty on the far side.

"Laura Granger?" she shouted as she stepped out onto the dance floor. "Are you there? This is Chief Cole!"

"And Silas Mot...er, I mean, Elliot Newman!"

Becca glared at the little man, then rolled her eyes before moving further into the ball room.

"I'm not going to jail!" a woman shouted from somewhere in the room. "Not for him! I won't do it!"

"Maybe you won't have to," Becca lied, moving the barrel of her weapon back and forth as she stalked forward. "Let's talk about it. Tell us your side of the story. Why did you kill Captain Mallory?"

Laura Granger didn't answer.

"Laura? Talk to me!"

Suddenly, a blonde head shot up from behind the bar countertop, followed by the glint of a gun. She fired at them. Three shots in rapid succession. Becca dove, upending one of the cocktail tables and using it as a pathetic means of cover. Elliot leapt behind Becca, and glanced around the room as if trying to gather his bearings.

"How much you want to bet that's a .380 she's taking pot shots with," Silas quipped.

Becca peered around the round edge of the table, her gun trained on the bar, when her radio squawked to life.

"Chief? It's Sharron," her officer said through the radio. "One of our suspects got free! He's heading your way now!"

"Roger that," she said.

"Good," Silas whispered in her ear as he hunched around her shoulder. "My plan is working splendidly."

"Really? This was your plan?" she hissed. "A crazed killer trying to shoot us and another one coming up from behind?"

He grinned with a shrug. "I admit. There are flaws. But you'll soon discover who killed Lance Avery. That's the important thing, right?"

Laura fired two more shots at them with one of the bullets crashing through the corkboard interior of the table, and whizzing past Elliot Newman's ear.

"Yowza!" He grabbed at his ear to make sure it wasn't bleeding. "Okay, so there might be more flaws than I originally thought."

"You think?" Becca said, still keeping her eyes fixed on the bar. From her vantage point, she really didn't have a clear shot. Then again, neither did Granger. "Watch the stairs. Make sure he doesn't sneak up on us."

She then turned her attention back to Laura Granger. "If you don't want to go to jail, lower your weapon now. Come out with your hands up, and we'll figure this out together," she shouted.

"He's not worth it, Laura," Silas added. "He killed your husband. I suspect you weren't aware he planned to do it. I suspect you're angry with him about it. But he killed your husband, and inadvertently implicated you by doing so. Is it worth seeing more jail time for someone like that?"

Becca glanced over at him. True to his word, he was watching the staircase while keeping his body around her back like an undead human shield. "Who?" she asked. "Who killed Lance? The suspense is killing me."

"Patience, dear Chief. Patience."

There was a crash of glass from the deck below, and Becca tried to deduce the source of the noise with no luck.

"You're right!" Laura suddenly shouted. "I had no idea he was going to kill Lance. I didn't figure it out until Mallory told me he was going to take those vials of potassium to Ilene. The man wouldn't see reason! His loyalty to the old bat couldn't be shaken. But I knew my fingerprints were on them. I'd handled them with Lance when he was trying to design his new dive gear. If you guys got hold of them, I knew I'd go down for his murder."

"So, you decided to commit another one?" Silas asked. "Not very smart of you, now is it?"

"I didn't plan for it to happen," she protested. "I just planned on scaring him with the gun. When he tried to get away from me, I accidentally shot him. It was an accident!"

"And your husband's killer?" Silas cooed. "You'd known him for years. More than a decade. Didn't you feel betrayed by him?"

Known him for years? Becca thought.

"Then again, you two *were* lovers, weren't you?" Silas pushed. "Lovers since college, I imagine. Sure, Lance won you over in the end, but Kevin Aker never gave up the torch for you, did he? And when Lance's eyes began to wander to younger, more attractive women with looser morals, he saw his chance. Wooed you, perhaps? And eventually, you resumed your romance in light of your own husband's infidelity."

There was a pause. The only sound that could be heard was from the air hissing through the air conditioning vents.

"I couldn't take it anymore. Always being sidelined for the next babe," Laura finally confessed. "We hardly ever saw each other, and even when we did, I could smell the other women on him. See their lipstick stains. Lance didn't even try to hide it. So yeah, when Kevin approached me, it was easy to fall once more into the comfort of someone familiar. Someone stable."

"Only he had far more affection for you than the other way around. Am I right?" Silas asked.

"He became obsessed! Possessive even!" Becca could hear the woman was now crying behind the bar. "Kept begging me to divorce Lance, but I couldn't."

"And not because of your contract," Silas added. "Was it? It was because you still loved your husband and you didn't love Kevin. To you, he was merely a distraction from your unrequited love of Lance Avery."

"Yes!" she shouted. "Yes! I loved Lance with every fiber of my being. I couldn't stand being away from him for another second. Couldn't imagine ever leaving him...especially for..."

"For a...consolation prize?" Silas added. He was now grinning ear to ear, but motioned for Becca to keep quiet and wait.

"I suppose," she said. "Yeah."

"Liar!" Someone shouted from just below the staircase entrance near the entrance. A second later, Kevin Aker, the team's sound engineer, rushed into view. His face was a twisted mask of rage as his eyes darted from the bar to where Becca and Silas crouched.

Something metal glinted in his hands, and Becca could just make out the shape of a fire ax in the dim light of the ball room.

"Drop the ax, Kevin!" Becca shouted over at him.

But he didn't listen. Instead, he raised the ax, and bolted straight for the bar where Laura hid.

"I'll kill you, you liar! I'll kill you!" he shouted, as he vaulted over the bar's countertop.

Becca stood, brandishing her weapon, but Elliot had already dashed away from the table's cover and ran straight for the sound engineer. A split second later, just as Kevin was bringing the ax down, Elliot tackled him, knocking the weapon from his hand.

Screaming, Laura scrambled out on all fours from behind the bar and moved straight for Becca's protection.

"You crazy freak!" Kevin shouted at Elliot, as the two stood to their feet, their arms grappling each other. "I'll kill you too!"

The killer shoved Elliot aside, and ran over to the starboard side wall where a pair of sabers hung ceremoniously as décor. He grabbed one of the swords, and lunged, bringing the blade down and barely missing Elliot's right arm.

"Ah!" Silas grinned behind Elliot's face. "Let's swash our buckles!" He retrieved his own saber from the decorative plague. "*En garde!*"

The two men thrust and parried, swinging the swords at each other in a series of clumsy attacks. It was obvious that neither had any idea how to fence, although Silas was doing his very best Errol Flynn impression as he did so.

"Avast, ye landlubber!" he shouted, leaping over a horizontal swing.

Rolling her eyes at her partner's ridiculousness, Becca grabbed Laura by the arm, and inched as close to the fracas as safely possible before clearing her throat. "Gentlemen?" She leveled her weapon at Kevin. "In case you forgot, you've brought swords to a gunfight. If you'll be so kind as to stop this nonsense."

Kevin glanced over at her, his eyes enraged, but continued swinging his blade at Elliot, who blocked with surprising ease.

"Come on, dude!" he shouted at the sound engineer. "Knock it off! This is getting embarrassing."

Still, the man pressed his attack, and Elliot continued to defend himself as best he could while backing himself into the corner of the ballroom.

"I'll kill you! I'll kill you!"

"Okay, so there it is. You're just plain psycho," Elliot said, glancing over at Becca. "Some help here please?"

She looked at Laura. "You've got nowhere to go, so don't move." She then holstered her gun, and reached for another, more appropriate weapon in her gun belt, before stalking up behind the sword-wielding psychopath. "Last chance," she told Kevin.

But the crazed man ignored her. His sword arm was now a whirlwind of rage and torment as it lashed out toward Elliot's blocking blade. Becca, for her part, counted to three, raised her taser up, and fired. Two wires, tipped with sharp prongs, exploded from the weapon and pierced Kevin's lower back and shoulder blade. A second later, the air was filled with the sound of electricity and the crisp smell of ozone.

Instantly, the saber slipped from his grasp as Kevin dropped to his knees and convulsed in painful spasms. Before Becca let up on the trigger to ease his pain, Elliot clenched a fist, and slammed it across the man's jaw, knocking him unconscious on the floor.

Becca looked at him. "Was that really necessary?"

He shrugged. "No, but it was thoroughly fascinating," he said, scooping up the sword and returning it to the wall. "Now, let's wrap this up, shall we?"

THREE HOURS LATER

BECCA AND ELLIOT watched as deputies with the St. Johns County Sheriff's Office handcuffed Laura Granger, and escorted her down to the awaiting patrol boat tied to the *Stately Lady*. Kevin Aker had already been loaded up, and taken to nearby Flagler Hospital for injuries sustained from being tased. He would be officially arrested and charged once he'd recovered and was released to avoid taxpayers paying for his treatments. Since Chief Cole had discharged her weapon—even the nonlethal form of a taser, the incident would be investigated by the county law enforcement agency.

"So, he just charged into the ballroom, waving around the ax?" Detective Jarvis of the sheriff's office major crimes unit asked.

Becca nodded. "He smashed the fire box down on the main deck corridor, and grabbed it," she said. "We think he'd originally planned to use it on us, but when he heard Granger disparaging his love, he became unglued."

"Bat guano crazy, if you asked me," added Silas through Elliot. "A cue ball short of a pool game. A syrup bottle short of a stack of flapjacks. A..."

"He gets the idea," Becca said, then turned back to the detective. She'd already briefed him on their investigations into the murders of Lance Avery and Captain Mallory, explained the motives, the evidence—pretty much everything except the scheme's connection to the Hand of Cain and Dr. Brad Harris. They'd already decided before backup arrived to take over the investigation that they would deal with Harris later. On their own and on their own schedule. "Is that all, Detective?"

"Sure," he said. "But if I have more questions..."

"You know where to find me," she said, walking away and toward the congregating *Mysterious Expedition* team near the dive platform on the stern of the yacht.

"So it was Kevin? Kevin killed Lance?" Krista Dunaway asked. Her hands shook as she brought a bottle of water to her lips.

"Looks that way," Becca said. "When it was all said and done, Kevin killed him out of simple jealousy. He saw him as the only thing that stood in his way of being with the woman he loved."

"The woman who only saw him as a way to pass a few cold nights," Silas said.

"I just can't believe it," Garrett Norris said, shaking his head. "I mean, I knew something was going on between those two, but I couldn't imagine anything like this."

"Excuse me," a grating female voice wheezed behind them. "But may I leave now?"

Becca turned to see the prune-like face of Ilene Nebbles-Fielding, her arms crossed, nose turned up, and sneer on her wrinkled lips.

"For now," Becca told her. "However, my investigation into your nephew and stolen artifacts...and whether you had any part in his operation...is still on-going. The murders might be solved, but I still have my two eyes on you right now." She paused, then smiled. "So don't do anything unbecoming in the meantime. Got it?"

With a huff, the old woman spun around, and stormed off toward her own awaiting boat that would take her back to the mainland.

After she was gone, Becca and Elliot said their goodbyes to the television crew, and headed for home.

EPILOGUE

ANKOU MOT MANOR
5 MILES SOUTH OF SUMMER HAVEN
SUNDAY, 1:32 AM

They pulled up in the winding driveway of Silas Mot's Victorian home, and sat in the car quietly for a few long moments.

"So what happens now?" Becca finally asked, staring out past the headlights into the darkness of the property beyond.

"What do you mean?"

She shrugged. "With Brad. With the Hand." Becca looked at him, moving her hand up and down as she gestured at Elliot's body. "With you and Elliot."

Silas grinned at her. "It's all part and parcel to the same thing, I imagine. Get to Brad, retrieve the Hand, and my cohabitation with my minion will no longer be necessary. Once the Hand is properly contained, its souls returned once more to their respective Reward, I regain my power as King of the

Psychopomps and can crush the Enclave once and for all. It'll just take patience."

Becca sighed. "I'm not sure I can go through with this."

Silas raised an eyebrow.

"I mean, going on with Brad, pretending not to know anything. Pretending to still be dating him. Being nice to him. All while knowing what he's done. What he's doing."

"I can imagine it'll be difficult," he said. "Uncomfortable even. But with my power nearly depleted, and not knowing who we can trust, we have to first discover where he's keeping the Hand before we can move. If he finds out we're onto him before we locate it, there's no telling what he might do with it." He paused, looking down at Becca's uniform. "You still have it? The shard?"

She patted the shirt pocket just under her badge. "Safe and sound."

"Good," he said, opening his car door, and stepping out into the night.

"Will you be okay here? By yourself?" she asked.

He nodded. "Anubis, no doubt has figured out what has happened to me," he told her. "I suspect I will see him soon, but despite his ambition and allegiances to Tombstone and the others, he will abide by the old code. I might have one foot in the grave, dear Becca, but I am not dead yet. And Elliot is still under my thrall. He is as safe as I am."

"Why isn't that a comfort?" She smiled.

He closed the car door, and waved her off.

SILAS MOT WATCHED Becca drive off into the darkness, and sighed.

"Why didn't you tell her?" Elliot asked inside his own head. "She would have insisted on coming in with us," Silas responded, walking toward the opening door of the mansion.

"She could have helped."

"Not with this," Silas replied.

He stepped across the threshold of his home, and hung a sharp right toward the elegant dining room. As they both had known before even entering the house, the immense cloaked form of Anubis sat at the foot of the dining room table, his back upright and stiff as a concrete slab. His two dogs snarled on either side of him as Elliot strode into the room.

"Welcome home, brother." Anubis' booming voice echoed throughout the house. "It has been a while."

Elliot gave a curt shrug. "Not long enough," Silas said, pulling out a small pocket calendar from Elliot's shirt. "How about we reschedule this for another time?" He thumbed through the calendar. "I think I'm free July 14, 3020 or so. How does that sound?"

The dog-like head hidden within the huge figure's black cloak lowered. His white fangs glimmered in the light of the chandelier above them.

"No more jests, brother," he said. "No more games. Your power has waned to the point where you seek refuge in the blasphemous body of this...this zombie."

Silas chuckled. "You work for Baron Tombstone! If that's not the pot calling the kettle crazy!" He was laughing so hard now, Elliot's sides hurt. "Your boss is the king of zombie riding, isn't he? At least mine maintains a mind of his own." He stopped. "Oh, wait! So did the Baron's! And his zombie trapped him in the Netherworld for nearly a thousand years. Good old Quinn Bennett. I always did like that guy."

"Enough!" Anubis' fists slammed down on the table, breaking it in two.

"Hey! That's an antique! You're going to pay for that."

"Lord Ankou, hear me now," Anubis said, standing to his full twelve foot frame, which forced him to duck his head slightly to avoid touching the ceiling. "The Enclave will convene in a month's time. I give you this warning now, as a brother. Your time is almost up. You will be stripped of your throne. Stripped of your power. Stripped of your own immortality." He paused for what Silas assumed was dramatic effect. "And then you will be put to a Rewardless death in a manner that you deserve. There is nothing you can do about it. No way to avoid it. In thirty days hence, I and my hounds will return for you, and there will be no escape from us when it happens."

His piece said, Anubis, the brother of Silas Mot and bounty hunter of the dead dissolved into a puff of smoke and disappeared. His hounds, still snarling at Elliot and Silas, melted into the floor, leaving a sulfurous stench behind them.

For a long moment, Silas just stared at the space where his brother had only seconds before been standing. Then, he blinked, turned around, and started making his way toward the kitchen.

"Well," he said, a renewed grin on Elliot's face. "Now that that unpleasantness is over, I rather fancy myself a stack of flapjacks. How about you, minion?"

"Sure," Elliot replied. "Why not? Looks like neither of us need to worry about our weight or diabetes anymore. We'll both be really really dead in a month."

Silas laughed at this, as he flicked on the lights to the kitchen. "One foot in the grave, dear minion. Also means, one foot is also on solid ground."

Then, they made one of the largest helpings of pancakes Elliot had ever seen in his life, and put their worries about Death and dying away for another day.

AFTERWORD

So I just have a few things to share with you, the readers of this book. First and foremost, thank you. You didn't have to devote the money and time you spent with this book, but you did, and I truly appreciate you for that.

Second, some of you might be scratching your head about Ankou Mot Manor. Silas has a haunted mansion? How did that happen? Was it in the first book? Short answer. No. The old Victorian makes its first appearance in a Grim Days Mystery short story that is appearing in an anthology called 'Surviving Tomorrow' which will be released later in September (2020). The anthology, which is headlined by the amazing Neil Gaiman, as well as a roster of big league authors, is donating all proceeds to a variety of COVID-19 charities. If you're curious about how Silas first discovers Ankou Mot Manor, I hope you'll pick up a copy of the anthology. Or, in six months after publication date of the anthology, the rights revert back to me and I'll be publishing it as a stand alone short story.

Speaking of questions you might have about things in this story, I thought I'd share a word or two about Baron Tombstone and *The Lord's Vengeance*. Some of you might be scratching your heads a bit, wondering if you missed something in the story. Who is Baron Tombstone? Why does there seem to be so much backstory to a character that hasn't even yet made an appearance in this series?

Well, that's because I've already introduced him elsewhere. Baron Tombstone, Quinn Bennett, and the pirate ship *The Lord's Vengeance* all had their debut in my stand-alone pirate fantasy adventure "Tombstone Voodoo", published back in 2016 when USA Today bestselling author David Wood and I conceived of a fun shared universe book franchise known as Tattered Sails. People who read it, loved the books in this series. Unfortunately, pirate fantasy adventures aren't really trendy at the moment, therefore, there were very few people who actually read them. But if you're interested in learning more about the Baron, I highly suggested you pick up a copy of "Tombstone Voodoo" today. I don't think you'll be disappointed that you did.

Now for some good news! The Grim Days Mystery series will continue with Book 3, One Foot in the Grave. It is slated for release the beginning of 2024! It will conclude the "Hand of Cain Cycle" of the series, but there will hopefully be many more mystery adventures with Silas Mot to come.

Finally, if you liked this book, I have two requests for you.

1) Tell all your friends about it. The more successful it is, the more I can justify writing Silas Mot 'til the cows come home. And I do love me some Silas Mot! So tell your friends!

2) Leave a review. It doesn't have to be a long, drawn-out dissertation on the pros and cons of the book. If you liked it, simply say that and maybe a line or two about why. If you didn't like it, feel free to share that too (but I hope you'll tell me why you didn't like it as well).

Anyway, until next time...happy reading!

9 798987 684726